Dream
Dancing

DREAM DANCING

A Novel

J. J. Lair

iUniverse, Inc.
New York Lincoln Shanghai

Dream Dancing

Copyright © 2007 by J. J. Lair

All rights reserved. No part of this book may be used or reproduced by any means, graphic, electronic, or mechanical, including photocopying, recording, taping or by any information storage retrieval system without the written permission of the publisher except in the case of brief quotations embodied in critical articles and reviews.

iUniverse books may be ordered through booksellers or by contacting:

iUniverse
2021 Pine Lake Road, Suite 100
Lincoln, NE 68512
www.iuniverse.com
1-800-Authors (1-800-288-4677)

This is a work of fiction. All of the characters, names, incidents, organizations, and dialogue in this novel are either the products of the author's imagination or are used fictitiously.

ISBN-13: 978-0-595-41208-2 (pbk)
ISBN-13: 978-0-595-85564-3 (ebk)
ISBN-10: 0-595-41208-4 (pbk)
ISBN-10: 0-595-85564-4 (ebk)

Printed in the United States of America

Chapter 1

Mark felt blind. There was a car in front of him, but it was impossible to see it with the sun in his eyes as he drove eastbound on Route 33. The visor in his box-style delivery truck had broken a year ago, and the July sun was eye level on the horizon. He feared that one of these days with the sun so bright and being tired in the morning he would fall asleep while driving. Mark normally tried to time his stops so he was indoors at this time of morning, when the sun bothered him most, but clear roads had put him ahead of schedule this morning.

His one-speaker radio played songs he liked all morning. He sang along to keep awake. He had reason to be happy, because today was his three-year anniversary as a delivery driver for Dewey's Donuts. It was a small operation, and he was the only route salesperson in the area. He had bought the rights to the route, the truck, and the stock. It had been tough to raise the initial capital, but the route had already paid for itself and turned a profit. He owned a townhouse and a car and had a substantial bank account.

His days were long, but he didn't mind. Each day started at four in the morning and ended at two in the afternoon. He serviced fifteen supermarkets and five convenience stores on his route every day.

Mark was still unmarried at thirty-four, but he had convinced himself he didn't have time for marriage anyway. His job was his life.

He parked his delivery truck on the side of Iggy's, the first convenience store on his route, and walked in with his handheld merchandise counter. It was a small device, used to track sales and the needed stock. He punched in the number of items on the shelf, and the machine did the rest. There was a printer on the truck to give him a hard copy of the calculations and a receipt for the store.

The counter person swayed to stay awake. "Morning's here," Mark yelled. "Your shift will be over soon."

As Mark entered the stock numbers, he scanned the store for her. She wasn't there yet. He went back to his truck and placed the merchandise counter in its slot on the dashboard printer. The printout took a few minutes. While it clacked out the numbers, Mark opened the back door to the truck.

Gonna be another hot one, he thought.

He yanked the printout and gathered his merchandise from the shelves and trays inside the truck. He was short enough to move around the back of the truck without hunching over, yet was tall enough to reach high displays in the stores. He didn't suffer from the backaches other drivers complained of.

Just then a truck pulled up alongside him. The driver knocked at Mark's door and yelled, "Morning."

"Hey, Smitty, how's it hanging?" Mark asked. The two of them serviced a lot of the same stores in the area.

"It's my third stop already," Smitty answered. "The supermarkets were easy. Usually that slow guy at Super Shop holds me up. He's out today, so you want to get over there before the soda guys get in and hold you up."

"This is my third stop, too," Mark said. "I really get moving when the sun comes up."

"What did they tell you about the merger, Mark?"

"I don't even know who *they* are. I have no idea what's going on. All I know is that Dewey's Donuts is up for sale."

"Yeah, that's all I know," Smitty said. "Thank God I work for the bread company. You guys who own your own routes have to be sweating. What happens if the company doesn't keep the routes going with independent drivers like you?"

"I lose my business," Mark said. He lifted a tray of doughnuts and carried them into the store.

She was behind the deli counter putting on plastic gloves. Jennifer was the deli section manager. She was twenty years old and had been working at Iggy's for two years. Mark had had a crush on her since he first saw her. He tried to talk to her every morning, but she blew him off, not even bothering to look his way.

Mark only saw the top of her raven hair, pulled up in a scrunchie, because she was about five-foot-three—the same height as the meat refrigerator in the front of the deli. Her brown eyes said she didn't want to be bothered, but that didn't stop Mark. He often told her corny jokes, which she sometimes laughed at to be nice, but she never initiated conversation.

He went to the register clerk and counted off merchandise while the clerk read from the computer printout to cross-check the stock. Mark kept one eye on Jennifer the entire time. She wore five earrings in each ear and a diamond shone from her pierced nose. She never wore makeup at work. "She's beautiful without it," Mark had once told Smitty.

Mark filled the display stand and walked to the coffeepots near the deli section, where Jennifer was organizing lettuce and condiments on her work table. Mark lifted and moved a lot of stock all day, which built up the muscles on his chest and arms. His biceps stretched the seams of the Dewey's uniforms. Even with his brawn and business success, Mark became a dork when he was around Jennifer.

"Hi Jennifer," he called to her. She didn't look up. He toyed with the lid on his twenty-ounce coffee cup. "My friend got arrested last night for stealing twenty-three cans of beer. The police had to let him go, because they couldn't make a case out of it."

She looked at him and gave an amused smile and went back to her lettuce.

"You need twenty four cans of beer to make a case," Mark explained. "I guess you don't drink." Mark cracked his knuckles as he stood there waiting for her to say something. She walked to the back without saying anything. He looked at his watch without reading it. "I have to go. Have a good day, Jennifer."

Mark picked up his empty tray and went back to his truck alone.

The residents of Marlchuck Township were the wealthiest in the county. Many corporate leaders, such as Internet company founders and health field executives owned homes there. There wasn't a car worth less than forty-five thousand dollars on Quincy Drive.

"Look at this," Carla said to her fifty-year-old husband, George, as they sat at the breakfast table. "In the want ads, they have an ad for go-go dancers. I can't believe they would put something like that in a normal paper."

George hadn't noticed. He only read the business section. Carla had been a cheerleader in high school and still liked sports, so she read the sports section, where the *Press* put ads for adult bars.

"Why are you concerned? You thinking about applying?" George mocked. "Maybe you should try out. Twenty-six isn't too old for that stuff."

Carla adjusted her flannel bathrobe and pushed her hand through her messy hair. "What's so funny?" she asked. "I work out every day. Men still turn their heads when I walk in a room."

"I know you can turn heads, but you would never do that," George said. "You'd be too scared."

"Maybe, but you don't have to make it sound like they wouldn't want to hire me. I could do it."

"No, you couldn't." George grabbed the newspaper away from her. "As your husband, I'm telling you not to even think about it."

"Don't boss me around," she said. "I might be younger than you, but I'm not a little girl."

He wrapped his hand around his coffee mug and returned to reading the newspaper, ignoring her. "You have to finish making the kids' breakfast. Your teenage daughters wouldn't want their stepmom flashing old drunks at some bar."

"You don't think I'm sexy do you?" Carla persisted.

George rolled his eyes. His daughters were coming down the hallway to the kitchen. "Cut it," he said.

Carla went to the refrigerator and pulled out cold cuts to make sandwiches. "George, you are really tempting me to do something like that. You can't just boss me around. You never bossed me around before we got married."

"The subject is closed. I said so." He closed the newspapers. "I have some associates coming over tonight. Wear something nice," he said, as he walked out of the room.

The brutal sun beat down on Mark's truck as he began another long day of deliveries. The truck didn't have air conditioning, so keeping the windows down was the only way to stay cool. He got to Iggy's at the usual time and parked next to the building, taking up four spaces, because there were no cars around, and he could use the room to work out of the back of his truck. He went through the normal routine: go inside, get the count, and go to the truck for the printout. Smitty drove into the parking spaces next to Mark.

Mark searched for Jennifer, but she wasn't at the deli section. He got his merchandise checked in by the morning manager and went to the doughnut stand to load the shelves.

"I guess she's off today," Smitty said. He could see that Mark was stalling for Jennifer.

At that moment, she trotted into the store and went to the manager to show him her hand. Mark couldn't hear what she said, but he could see a ring on her finger. He left his empty carrying trays at the stand and strolled to the coffeepots with Smitty.

Jennifer walked behind them and put her hand on Smitty's shoulder. "Look," she squealed in Smitty's ear. "My boyfriend—oops!—my fiancé gave it to me last night. We haven't set a date yet, but isn't it nice?"

Mark bit his lower lip as he eyed the ring. Smitty held her hand in his palm. "Well, it's shiny," he said. He toyed with the diamond. "How many carats is it?"

"I don't know," she giggled. "It must've cost a lot. My guy." She put her hand to her heart. "He loves me so much."

Mark stretched his fingers to stop his hands from shaking. He didn't want to make a fist. He grabbed his coffee too tightly and spilled it, causing him to jump back. Moments passed. He heard talking, but it was all muffled. He slammed his hand on the metal-topped table and grabbed his coffee again.

"I should take it off, so I don't get olive loaf stuck to the diamond," Jennifer said. Mark stomped out of the building, but she didn't seem to notice.

Mark threw his carrying trays in the back of his truck, without looking where they landed. He eyed a picture of a bikini-clad blonde that he had taped to the side wall of the truck: Miss April … another unattainable woman taunting him.

As Mark went to shut the back door of his truck, Smitty walked up behind him, startling him. "Want to talk about it?" Smitty asked.

"I have to finish my route," Mark growled. He slammed the door shut. "I can't spend all day talking about her and her engagement." He climbed in the driver's seat of the truck and started the engine. "I'm just here to get my coffee and get on my way. You don't think …" He paused but didn't wait for Smitty to answer. "If she's here, I say hi to her. That's it. I don't care if she got engaged."

Smitty backed away, his hands up like he was surrendering. Mark's anger was obvious, from the way his teeth tore at his lip. Mark slammed the shifter into gear and drove away.

When he got to the Super Shop, the slow guy held him up. Time dragged by, giving Mark more time to think about his morning. He finished his stores at three o'clock and drove to the depot to reload. His shirt was soaked in sweat; his body was tired and sore. He ignored other drivers as he tossed trays out of his truck. The truck printer jammed on his sales reports. Mark heard the paper crinkling in the feeder and put his knee to it.

"You mother …," he growled. Mark slammed his hands on the dashboard and took a deep breath. It didn't work. His arms were still tense, and his legs shook. "How could she?" he yelled at the printer. He backed away and went into the depot to get merchandise. He threw boxes on trays and loaded them into the truck without even looking to see what he had.

The air conditioner had been on all day in Mark's house. He dropped to the floor to rub the sweat off his face on the cool living room rug. He could hide in his home and stay calm; there were sodas in the refrigerator and the TV remote nearby. The mail truck pulled up, so Mark went out for the mail, even though he knew it would just be bills and advertisements.

Sue, his neighbor, stood at her mailbox, barefoot on the hot cement and hopping on one leg. Her breasts bounced under her tank top. Her drab, shoulder-length hair stuck lifelessly to her forehead and neck. She was his age and also unmarried. They had known each other since she moved into the complex over a year ago. They bonded as friends right away.

"This heat sucks," she moaned. "It was eighty-five degrees at eleven o'clock last night. I love summer and all, but this is ridiculous. I guess the mailman is taking it easy. He's usually here long before now. It's past four o'clock. Not that I blame him. I feel hot just walking over here."

"I get used to it in the truck all day," Mark answered.

"More power to you. I can't do it. Anything happens to the air in that car," she said, pointing to her Dodge Neon, "I'll sell it. I need air."

"Wanna come in for a drink?" he asked. "I've had the air on all day."

"I have to get ready to go out. Got a date tonight." She did a half turn to walk away, but stopped. "What's wrong? You're usually more talkative."

"There was this girl at a convenience store on my route. I was sort of putting moves on her, but she just got engaged." He sighed and shook his head. "What's funny is she never talked to me the entire time I hit on her, but I still did it."

"She wasn't interested. So what?" Sue shrugged. "You own a business. You're a good-looking guy. You'll find someone else. It'll be fine."

"Yeah, that's easy to say. That's what I said after my fiancée left me last year. You can find a guy easy enough, but there are no women here."

"There are women everywhere. You need to get out more," Sue insisted.

"That's easy to say."

"It's easy to do."

"No, it's not."

She nudged his sweat-covered shoulder. "Yeah it is." He opened his mouth to object, but she cut him off. "Yes it is."

"OK, fine. It's easy," he said, not believing it.

"I have to go. It'll be fine. You'll meet someone far better than her," Sue said, as she hopped back to her house.

Mark went to his house and plopped onto the couch, letting the mail fall to the floor. He turned on the television and watched glamorous women parade across the screen. It was the quiet, lonely times like this that he wished he had a girlfriend. A woman who looked like his ex-fiancée, Jessica, gave the weather report on channel five. He still regretted losing her. She wanted him to spend more time with her, but the business took twelve to fifteen hours a day. He was usually too tired to go out and was ready for bed by nine at night. She broke off the engagement because he cramped her lifestyle.

He hadn't had a relationship since then. He had dated a few women, but nothing serious. No one would say he was a dateless loser, but he couldn't get emotionally close. Work took too much time. He saw women every day at the supermarkets, but that was work time. He'd never make any money if he chased women all day. He pined for Jennifer, because as long as she was at the convenience store every day, he felt he had a chance with her.

The weather report was over, and Mark felt like he had to get out of the house. He called his friend Ed, but Ed's wife answered and said Ed wasn't home from work yet. Mark called a friend he knew from the health club, but he said he was staying in with his wife. Mark shut off the TV and decided to go out alone. He went to his closet and pulled out a button-down shirt that he wore on special occasions, a pair of jeans, and a pair of sneakers, which he wore sockless.

The heat of the sun baked him before he even got out the front door. The air conditioner in his Ford Focus came on full blast when he started the car. He took a second to wait for the coolness. Mark watched kids run around the grassy open field at the end of the row of houses. Mothers pushed strollers and talked with each other. Mr. Dumont, dressed in polyester shorts and black socks, watered his lawn.

Mark backed out of his parking space and drove to Babes Go-Go Bar, a mile from his house. He was surprised to see only three sports cars and a pickup truck in the parking lot. The place was normally full in late afternoon with businessmen stopping in for drinks and horny young guys drinking before going to the pickup bars.

The vinyl siding of the building was dirty yellow from years of neglect. Empty beer bottles, half-eaten nachos, and french fries filled the Dumpsters on the side, providing a feast for gnats and flies. Mark parked near the front. The solid black front door had a brass handle attached by one screw that Mark feared would break off when he pulled.

A black-haired dancer stood in the center of the stage, swinging her leg back and forth, not paying attention to the music. Her hair stuck to her face, and sweat glistened off her tanned skin. The men at the bar sipped beers and watched the televisions instead of her. Mark sat on a stool near the door.

The dancer spun around once in awhile and walked around the edge of the stage. Her fingers massaged up and down her body, flaunting her figure. Mark made eye contact with her and pulled out a ten-dollar bill. A young, well-endowed bartender dragged herself along the bar toward him. Denim shorts and a baggy T-shirt with the name of the club stuck to her sweaty body.

Mark yelled for a beer over the sonic boom of bass-heavy music. She took his order and walked away without saying anything. The dancer twirled around on stage just as Mark got a stack of one-dollar bills back as change. The dancer zeroed in on the bills and strutted off the stage in a straight line for Mark. She leaned over, so Mark could get a closer look at her sweat-covered breasts and would be tempted to tip her.

"Hi, Buffy," Mark said to her. He folded a dollar and tipped her. "You don't remember me, do you?" She put her hand to her ear to signal that she couldn't hear him, even though she was so close he could smell her perfume. He leaned away from her as she went back on stage.

A woman with shoulder-length brown hair was talking to the deejay. Mark noticed her face but couldn't see more of her. He motioned for the bartender and asked who the brunette was.

"I don't remember," she said, smacking her gum. "She's new, and her shift is over anyway. We only have one dancer left tonight." She pointed at Buffy. "I think that other one will be back tomorrow. You'll have to ask her."

Mark thanked the bartender, who walked off to talk to her friends at the other end of the bar. The brunette walked by. They made eye contact and sized each other up before rays of light from the strobe came between them. Buffy was in front of Mark, but he didn't turn away from the dancer who was leaving. She disappeared in another beam of light.

Mark left the bar an hour later with twenty dollars less than he came with. He had bought two beers and tipped Buffy the rest of the night in an attempt to talk to her. Each time, she said she didn't remember him from the year before. He went home and dropped onto the rug.

Why did Jennifer have to get engaged? I really wanted her to like me, Mark said to himself. *God, that sounds so high school.* He looked at his watch in the moonlight and realized he'd need to go to work soon. He rubbed his eyes, burning with sweat. *I have to work*, he thought. *I don't have time to date.*

He struggled off the couch and trudged to his bedroom. All his friends were married or had kids or both. The few women he knew were just friends. They would tell him about their boyfriends without ever thinking that he wanted to be someone's boyfriend. He could imagine that Sue was talking to her date. Smitty was in bed with his wife. Jennifer was probably with her fiancé. Mark slept alone.

Chapter 2

Mark drove into Iggy's parking lot earlier than usual the next morning. He sat in the truck, still tired from the night before, and stared at the front window of the store. Jennifer's car wasn't there. He took a deep breath and went inside. Jennifer wasn't in the deli section. He rushed to the display, counted boxes on the top shelf, and then estimated the rest so he could leave before she got there.

He sat in the truck reviewing the inventory sheets. The day was cloudy and cool, so he didn't have to rush to get out of the sun. Jennifer's car still wasn't there. The numbers in front of Mark looked jumbled and blurry, but that happened when he was tired. Just then Jennifer drove into the parking lot. She got out of her car and slouched into the store, carrying a coffee cup from a competing store. Mark turned and started the truck to avoid the sight of her ... still beautiful. There was enough stock on the shelves that he didn't have to refill them today.

After work, Mark went home and sat by a window in his bedroom. He saw Sue run into her house from her car like she had someplace to go that night.

There were no pictures on any of his dreary white walls. The dusty white blinds were raised, allowing a little light in the room. Old towels hung off the shower rod in the bathroom. He sighed as he walked away from the window and went to the closet for a wrinkled shirt. His mission was to find out who the new girl at the go-go bar was. She wasn't a regular.

The parking lot at Babes Go-Go Bar was nearly empty again, as was the bar when Mark walked in. The scent of perfume was all around. A group of men dressed like construction workers in dirty jeans and T-shirts huddled in the darkness. They spent more time talking to each other than watching the dancer. She sat on the stage, picking at her nails and talking to the male bartender instead of dancing. There were two other guys playing pool in the back of the bar. Mark sat at the center of the side bar and waited for the dancer to begin. Her distracted look reminded him of Jennifer.

The bartender was a hulking mass of muscle and sweat. Mark was shocked at just how big the bartender was. Usually this place had women bartenders, not burly men like this guy. Mark was well-muscled from all the hauling he did, but this guy was huge. The song finished its final notes, just as the bartender asked in his booming voice, "What you drinking?" Mark cracked his knuckles and ordered a beer. The dancer left the stage. Mark never did get to see her dance.

Abby was in the back locker room where she put her foot on a wooden bench to rub baby oil on her leg. She looked over her shoulder and eyed another dancer who had her head in a locker. The other dancer sniffed. Maybe she snorts coke, Abby thought, but she didn't really want to know.

A girl would have to do drugs to get through this every night, Abby said to herself. She turned to get one last look in the mirror mounted on the wall. Her five-foot six-inch voluptuous body was barely covered by her black G-string and leather bra. Her natural, full breasts were pushed up and stuck firmly into the bra, so she wouldn't fall out. Her black stilettos were worn-out enough to be comfortable and yet shiny. Once she felt satisfied with her appearance, she opened the door to enter the bar.

Her path to the stage was met by howling from the huddle of construction guys. She tossed her black satin moneybag down on the stage and surveyed the almost empty house.

Music blasted from the speakers as Abby dropped to her knees and ran her fingers along her taut stomach, making a circle around her innie belly button. She licked her finger and blew a kiss to a tanned construction guy before she got up. The two men playing pool stopped to watch her. She twirled and did splits, much to the crowd's approval. She did the same moves over and over through three songs, exciting the audience.

Abby trotted to the lockers to cool down. She couldn't wash, because it had taken her twenty minutes to fix her hair and put on her makeup, and she would need to look nice for the next three hours.

Mark never lifted his head to watch her. He stared at the foam on top of his beer and thought about Jennifer. *Why didn't I just ask her out? Why did I make small talk all those days?*

Abby poked her head out of the locker room as another dancer took the stage. The pool players and the construction guys left the bar, but some more people came in. Mark sat by himself. He stood apart from the rest. He was clean-shaven, his hair was combed, and he wore somewhat neat clothes, but he looked depressed. Abby walked along the inside of the bar that surrounded the stage area. It kept her safe from groping customers.

"I guess everyone had to go home," she yelled over the music to the sole construction worker who didn't leave. "How come you're staying?"

"I just wanna see that ass one more time," he yelled back. "Turn around."

She turned around and shook while the guy howled at her. *I miss the business men I used to meet in Vegas*, she thought. She lifted her leg on top of the bar.

"You got a great ass," he said, slipping a dollar into her garter.

"Thank you, honey." She turned away from him and rolled her eyes.

"Wait," he yelled. "Come on back."

She leaned over the bar and asked what he wanted. He reached out with another dollar for her and slipped it in her bra. She kept her eyes on his. Suddenly she felt a stinging pinch on her breast. She jumped back holding herself.

"What's wrong with you?" she screamed. "You crazy?"

The bartender rushed over and asked what had happened. The guy said nothing. Abby pointed to the red marks on her chest.

"Don't hurt the dancers here," the bartender barked. His chest muscles tightened, as he stared down the customer. "You got it?"

"I didn't do nothing," the guy whined back.

"All right then," the bartender said, as he walked away.

Abby still held her breast. "That's it?" she yelled in disbelief. "Why even come over?"

The guy pulled out another dollar. "Come on," he coaxed. "I got another dollar for ya."

"Get away," she said, and then retreated. "Jerk."

She walked around and stopped in front of Mark. His eyes were bloodshot like he was exhausted or wanted to cry. Abby put her crossed arms on the bar next to him to get his attention and asked, "Whatcha doing?"

"Just getting a drink," he muttered. He grabbed a dollar bill and put it on her arm. "How are you doing?"

"I think I'm doing a lot better than you. I just have to deal with the normal bull around here. Are you all right?"

He looked up from his beer. His face relaxed at the sight of her warm brown eyes. "I had a rough week," he said, as he leaned back and cracked his knuckles.

She nodded. "I know the feeling. I've had some rough days myself lately."

"Yeah, well," he said.

"Do you want to talk?"

Mark looked around the still-empty bar. "I think that guy wants to see you again." He pointed at the construction worker who was holding a dollar and shouting, "Who wants money?"

"I don't want to waste my time with him," Abby said. "He'll be back again, and I'll have to deal with him then. I haven't seen you before."

"I live right down the highway in the townhouse development. I don't usually come here while the sun is out. I came by because ..." He paused and looked down. "I just don't know what else to do right now. I wanted to have fun and talk, but I just started thinking about things and I'm bummed again."

"I'm stuck working days and early nights for now," she said. "I used to work nights when I lived in Vegas, but here I have to earn the spot."

"Why would you move to this little town in New Jersey from Las Vegas?" Mark asked. "Why would you work this shitty little bar?"

She ran her fingers along his forearm and smiled. "I'll tell you what. After my next set, I'll run in the back and throw something on, and we can talk."

Mark agreed. He ordered another beer, this time from a female bartender, and rubbed the goose pimples off his arm. He hadn't felt a woman's soft fingers in a long time.

Mark was attentive to everything Abby did on stage during her next set. Her body moved in time to a slow, guitar-heavy ballad that blasted through the bar. Her brown hair bounced as the ceiling lights shone through it. Her strong leg muscles tightened when she lifted her legs and shimmied. Mark thought of nothing but the stunning woman prancing in front of him.

She doesn't have tattoos or body piercing like the other dancers, he thought. *She looks incredible spinning around on the stage.*

When Abby finished, the next dancer walked out and went straight to the construction guy, where she stayed during the entire song. Abby disappeared.

"Figures," Mark said to the older guy next to him. "I can't even tip a dancer to pay attention to me." Just as he chugged the last of his beer from a frosted mug, Abby appeared at his side. She wore a one-piece orange outfit with a sheer orange cape tied around her neck.

"Hi," she greeted him. "You waited for me. I got held up trying to figure out what I was going to wear next. I know I'm going to take most of it off after one song, but I like to make a good entrance."

"You did," he answered, not knowing what else to say. He turned to her and sat with his legs open. One foot was on the floor and the other dangled off the seat. His fingers shook as he held his beer mug as a prop. She sat and crossed her legs on the seat next to him. She asked his name, and he hesitated.

Did he really want a go-go dancer to know his name? He looked at her soft, sweet face, her deep eyes, and her radiant smile. He wanted to know all about her. "My name is Mark. What's yours?"

"Baby Doll," she answered. Mark's eyes brightened and his face relaxed. The depression seemed to disappear. It made Abby relax. "My real name is Abby. I use Baby Doll as my stage name. When I lived in Las Vegas, I used Baby Breath, because I like the flower. I don't normally tell people my real name, but I think I can trust you. What did you think of the dancing?" she asked, while staring at his biceps.

"You were the only one really dancing," he said. "All the others just shake their hips and rub themselves. Hey, you want a drink?"

She pulled a bottle of water out from behind the bar. "I can handle the heat, but it's too hot to drink right now."

"Yeah," he nodded. "I don't normally drink anyway, but I was so bummed out today."

"I saw. That's why I spent so much time over here. You're not allowed to leave a go-go bar depressed. I think it's a law."

"Knowing who's in Congress, it wouldn't surprise me," he answered. She laughed. He had tried to make Jennifer laugh like that for over a year. Abby's mouth was open, her teeth showed, and her head went back. He was so excited by her reaction that he started rambling on about how he had tried to impress Jennifer, and she had the nerve to get engaged to someone else. He told Abby he had come to the bar to forget about Jennifer, but when he smelled the perfume and saw the first girl, he had thought of her again.

"Her loss," Abby said, placing her hand on his shaky hand. "I like you. I can see you're a decent guy. Forget her. You can do so much better."

"Thank you." Mark stared at her for a moment. "Are you just saying that?"

"I don't normally come out and sit with guys," she said. "I do my dance; then I go in the back and put my feet up. They don't have lap dances or champagne rooms here, so I don't have to talk to you if I don't want to." She looked at her watch. "Shit, I have to go on again. It's my last set. Look, I'll be at Babes West tomorrow. They have lap dances. Do you know where it is?"

He nodded.

"I'll be there at eight o'clock. Stop by and find me. I always use the same name, Baby Doll. OK?"

"I have to work tomorrow. I have to get up at two in the morning."

"Oh, come on," she said with a smile and a raised eyebrow. "You have to come and make me laugh again."

He agreed without another thought about his job. She put her hand on his and smiled at him. Gooses pimples went up his arms. She walked away but looked over her shoulder at him. She rubbed the goose pimples off her arms when she got to the locker room.

Chapter 3

Mark made his third stop of the day at Iggy's. He finished his inventory count earlier than usual and passed Jennifer coming in the store as he was on the way out. He held the door without saying anything.

Smitty pulled in beside Mark's truck. "Didn't see you yesterday," Smitty said.

"I was ahead of schedule," Mark replied. "I'm trying to beat the sun today if I can."

"I think it's supposed to rain tomorrow. It should break this humidity," Smitty said. "You been inside yet?"

"Yeah, I didn't sell much. I should be out of here quick," he said, gathering boxes from the back of his truck. "I have to make sure my stuff doesn't melt out here."

"There's no problem in the store?"

"Yeah, there's a problem. I'm not selling. I'll bet the ice cream guys are making a killing."

Smitty stood motionless, uncertain if he should say anything. He watched Mark gather his things and go into the store. Smitty followed and noticed Mark didn't look Jennifer's way. When Jennifer said "bye," Mark didn't appear to respond; normally he would jump at that, even if it looked like she was really talking to a customer. Today, Mark said nothing; he just walked out. He started the truck without a pause and drove off.

Mark finished the route early and was back at his townhouse by two o'clock. He was so tired that he dropped on his bed and fell asleep in his work clothes till eight at night. His uniform was wrinkled and sweaty when he awoke. His hair was a mess, and he had hard stubble on his cheek.

Abby was right, he thought, looking at his reflection in the mirror. *If Jennifer couldn't see it, why should I think about her?* He rested his face in his hands. *But today she had spoken first. I don't get women. I try to make her laugh for a year, and she ignores me. Now I don't care about her, and she wants to talk."*

He looked at his watch. *A lap dance with Abby would mean that I could get close to her. Maybe I could touch her. I never get that close to Jennifer.* He cracked his knuckles and paced around the room. *I have to get up early, I can't go out,* he thought, arguing with himself.

🍁   🍁   🍁

Abby walked on stage at Babes West dressed in a pink-leather bikini with a flowing sheer cape tied at her neck. As she twirled, she looked for Mark. A man wearing a black suit and tie, still fastened around his neck, sat with eyes focused at her chest. She dropped to her knees and ran her hands up her thighs. Her thin fingers circled her navel. The guy downed an entire bottle of beer in one gulp while watching her. Strobe lights beamed down. She blew kisses as the man gawked, but she still searched for Mark. She spun around on the brass pole at the center of the stage. A graying man with a wad of money on the bar caught her eye, and she jumped off the stage and put her breasts on the bar in front of him.

"Hi ya," she said, looking past him.

"When you're done, I want to get a lap dance with you. You're incredible," the man said to her.

He looked normal enough, or as normal as she could expect in this place. He wore a gray T-shirt, denim shorts, and dress shoes with no socks. She agreed to the lap dance.

When her set was done, Abby took the guy to the back of the club, where he paid for the dance and sat facing her on a sofa in a darkened corner. She put her right leg at his side and leaned into him. Her hips swayed to and fro with the music while his hot breath steamed her breasts. Strobe lights flashed while he pawed her backside, which was against the rules, but she was too preoccupied to notice. He left marks on her skin when he squeezed her. He slapped her backside with a stinging swat, making a loud thwack. She knocked his hands away.

"What are you doing?" she yelled. "You're not supposed to touch me. Dance over!" She backed away from the couch.

"I want a refund," he said. He smiled like he had gotten away with something.

"It's a rule here," she said. "You're not supposed to touch. Save it for your wife."

She stomped to the locker room, swung the door open, and slammed it shut with such force that it shook the mirrors. "Some guy slapped my ass," she yelled to the house mom and a dancer seated in front of a locker.

"Did they kick him out?" asked Rita, the house mom, between swigs of her scotch and soda.

"No," Abby said, rubbing her forehead. "He probably won't do it again. I should've stopped him sooner, but I was distracted."

"You seemed like you were looking for someone while you were dancing up there," Rita said.

"I met this guy yesterday," Abby said, as she sat on a bench. "He was really depressed and wanted to talk. He was kind of good looking, so I talked to him—I guess twenty minutes. All that time he looked at my eyes. He wasn't giving me tips or peeking down at the rest of me. He looked me in the eye and talked to me. No one has really talked to me since I moved here. It was kind of nice. I told him I was dancing here, but I don't know if he's going to show up."

"If he left the club in a better mood, you done your job. He probably needed someone to talk to. You cheered him up. You'll probably never see him again. It's like that. When I was a dancer, I had a couple of losers come every night just so I would talk to them. Mostly I don't think I saw the same person twice. If I did recognize someone, it embarrassed him. Twenty years ago, we didn't have all this touchy-feely stuff like now. Back then, only a real nut or a stalker would bother to come here all the time."

Abby stood up and went to her locker. "Yeah, but, he was really nice to me. I liked that."

Carla sat on a bench dressed in a pair of jeans and an oversized T-shirt and watched the glamorous dancers. She crossed her arms over her chest and rocked back and forth self-consciously. Several leggy, made-up, beautiful women wore bikinis or went topless in front of her.

"You OK?" Abby asked.

"Yeah, I'm just nervous. I signed up for an amateur night contest. I was just checking out the back, and everyone here is so thin. I work out, and I feel fat."

"When you first go out there, it's incredibly scary," Abby said, taking a seat next to Carla and removing her shoes.

"I can't be naked in front of all those people," Carla said.

"You're not naked. Look at these outfits we wear." Abby held up a piece of lingerie from her locker that didn't conceal much. She could see that it didn't make Carla feel comfortable. "I'm wearing a teddy like you probably wear in bed. Bikinis on the beach are just as revealing as what the dancers on the stage are wearing. It's not so bad."

"I'm still a little scared. I'm only doing this to show my husband. He never pays attention to me. I figured maybe if he could see me do this with all these beautiful women, he'd realize how beautiful I am. I'm almost thirty years younger than him." She watched a dancer pull a thong out of her behind. "I don't even know what to wear. I was going to run out in my panties."

"I make my own clothes. I can help you with an outfit," Abby assured her. "There was a dancer that didn't show tonight. I met her when I was working the other Babes two nights ago, but I didn't really know her. I think her name was Buffy. They're probably looking for someone new now. If you're good during amateur night, you might be able to keep this as a job. It might get him hot. I've met swingers who are into this type of thing."

Carla and Abby talked for about twenty minutes. By the time Carla had to walk through the bar to leave, she felt calm. They traded phone numbers, and Carla ran to her Lexus, so no one would see her.

Abby spent the next morning walking around the mall. She noticed the young mothers with their strollers and felt grateful she didn't have the responsibilities they had. It made her feel free that she could stay out all night if she wanted to. They were tied to those strollers. She once told Rita, the house mom, "Thank God, I don't have that problem. I got away from Penn before anything could happen. He used to spend all my money and eat all my food—or throw it out so he could put more beer in the fridge."

She walked out of the mall to her car. More mothers with kids gathered at the doors. The women, mostly dressed in sweats and sneakers or baggy shorts and T-shirts, complained that children ruined a woman's figure. One woman, dressed in heels and a dress, rushed into the mall, muttering that she would be late for work.

Abby started her car and drove by the mothers and carriages to get one more glance at them. She was convinced she saw the look of sadness and responsibility on their faces.

❧   ❧   ❧

Behind Babes Go-Go Bar, a homeless woman rummaged through the garbage pails lining the back wall. Gnats and flies going in and out of the pails didn't stop her. She reached down inside the black sock she wore on her left leg and scratched the bug bites as she went from pail to pail. Flies buzzed in and out of the Dumpster next to her in a furious swarm. She looked in.

The stooped, elderly woman used a stick to push a plastic garbage bag out of the way, because she was too short to reach very far. A hand poked out from under a plastic bag. The woman stumbled back but couldn't scream. She wobbled into the bar to find someone.

"Hey," yelled Eli, the young, muscular bartender. "You get out of here. Take your flies with you."

"There's someone in the garbage," she muttered.

"Yeah," he said, tapping the plainclothes cop seated at the bar. "Probably a friend of yours."

She turned around and walked out as they laughed at her.

"You want to go get the homeless out of our garbage pail?" Eli said to the cop, who was still drinking his coffee.

"I'm here to find out about that missing girl," the cop replied. "I don't think the girl's roommate wants to know that I'm drinking coffee and chasing homeless people out of the garbage."

"Just say you're looking for clues," Eli said. "They were supposed to empty the bins yesterday, so it shouldn't be too bad out there."

The gray-haired, beer-bellied policeman walked outside and saw the homeless woman poking around a garbage pail. He saw flies swarming around the Dumpster and went to that. He immediately saw the hand, and when he pushed garbage away, he uncovered the torso of a woman wearing a Babes T-shirt.

He ran to his cruiser and radioed for backup. Within ten minutes, two cruisers were in the parking lot around the Dumpster. As the homeless woman watched, three cops pulled the body of a young woman out of the Dumpster. Eli recognized the woman. It was Buffy.

"Good thing they didn't empty the garbage yesterday after all," the cop told Eli.

"Yeah, good thing."

Chapter 4

Abby went on stage at Babes Go-Go Bar dressed in a bright red bikini. The opening riff of her first song boomed out, and she forgot about her trip to the mall. As she twirled, a pounding bass drum sent her to her knees, where she suddenly faced Mark. He was seated at the corner of the bar, talking to another man. Mark didn't see her.

As he reached for his beer mug, he saw her. She stared at him, frozen in place. He tried to wink at her but shut both eyes at the same time. A beam of light came between them as she turned away. Synthesizer music filled the air as she toyed with her hair and shook her hips in front of some guy who she didn't even look at. She saw money thrown to the stage. Squealing guitar riffs accentuated her dance. She picked up the money off the stage, crawling and stretching her legs.

After the set, Abby walked around the bar on the side farthest from Mark, looking for tips. Another dancer took the stage. It took a song and half until Abby was next to Mark.

"Hello," she said, as if she didn't know him.

"Hi, Abby, or do I call you Baby?" he asked.

"Whatever." She looked past him at the people coming in.

"This is my friend Eddie. He lives around the block from me," Mark said. Abby showed no reaction. "How are you doing tonight?" he asked.

"Fine, I guess." She turned to the stage. "I didn't see you at Babes West last night."

"I fell asleep when I got home. I drive a truck, and it's hard work. I was just exhausted. I would do my accounting tonight, but Eddie is only allowed out one night a week." He pushed at Eddie's elbow for backup.

"Hey, my wife and I are busy most nights with the kid." Eddie could see that she wasn't listening to him. "He thought of coming here," Eddie said, pushing Mark's elbow back.

Abby leaned toward Mark. "You missed a chance at a lap dance." Mark couldn't hear most of what she said over the loud music in the bar.

"Do you want to have a drink with us when you're done walking around?" Eddie asked.

She looked to Mark for a clue as to what he wanted. She wondered why Mark was so cool to her now. He toyed with his mug handle instead of looking at her. She remembered Rita saying that men used to be embarrassed when she recognized them, but Rita had orange teeth. "I'll be back in a little while," Abby said. "I'll see if I have time." She spun on her white platform sandals and walked away.

Eddie leaned into Mark. "She wants you."

"What?"

"She wants you. Didn't you see it? She never paid attention to me."

"She's talking to another guy now." He pointed at Abby with a group of men dressed like they just left their offices. A tall guy with his tie undone leaned over the bar, but she backed away from him. "She gets paid to talk to guys."

"She's not leaning in like she was here," Eddie said. "She wants you."

Mark was confused. He watched the men around him talk to the dancers. "She's a dancer," he said. "She gets paid to be nice to people. I tried to date one last year. I was banned here because of it."

"Yeah, but this one actually wants you. Not like that other one. You used to wait for her in the parking lot. You tried to get her phone number. You called here for her schedule. You became obsessed with work after they banned you. You haven't tried to get to know a woman in a long while." Eddie sipped his beer. "What was her name again?"

"Buffy," Mark answered.

Abby collected a wad of dollars so big she couldn't close her hand around it. She walked between Mark and Eddie as she stuffed the money in her satin bag. Her left hand went on Eddie's shoulder and her right went to Mark's back. "Who's buying?" she asked.

Mark stumbled off his seat and grabbed an empty chair for Abby. Eddie yelled out for three beers. Abby lowered herself on her chair with her head high like royalty. She threw her moneybag on the bar and pointed her knees toward Mark.

Her knees brushed Mark's. He wondered if Eddie was right. Eli brought three beers for them and leaned over the bar toward Abby. "You can't get drunk, Baby Doll. You still have more sets to do."

"Yeah, yeah, Eli," she said, like she was blowing him off. "Just because he's big … can't tell me what to do. Dani is a cool bartender, but she wants to talk to guys all night."

Mark stretched his fingers and cracked his knuckles. He apologized for missing Abby the night before. He told her about his daily route. He feared it would bore her, but she seemed interested. She shook her head, leaned in, and smiled as he spoke. She seemed enraptured.

Eddie coughed from the heavy perfume smell. He didn't say anything, because there was no escaping it. His dollars were drenched from the beer-soaked bar and would reek when he left. He checked his watch through three songs and then told them he had to leave.

"I would love to stay longer, but gotta go," Mark said to Abby.

Eddie left his money at the bar and walked out. While he waited for Mark, he flapped his arms in the breeze to get the perfume smell off of him. Mark looked happy when he came out.

"What happened in there?" Eddie asked. "You look like you're skipping, which isn't something you want to do at these kinds of places."

"She told me when she's dancing again, and then she kissed me. It was half on the cheek and half on the lips."

"I told you. She wants you. All these strippers are looking for guys to screw later. It's like a supermarket for prostitutes."

"They're not prostitutes," Mark objected. "Do you think I should see her?"

"Why not? It's a dollar, and you get to feel her up. You also like to talk to her. It's not a bad deal. You have it good being single. I would've banged her by now. I'm married though. I had to get permission to go out tonight. All the good compact discs have to stay in the car, because they're too loud for the baby. I have to watch *Romance of the River* this weekend. It's a romance with no nudity. I don't want to see it." Eddie played with the door handle of Mark's car. "She wants to screw you."

"You make marriage sound so good," Mark said in total sarcasm.

"If I were single, I would be nailing that dancer now."

❦   ❦   ❦

Carla sat at the kitchen table reading a magazine while George read the newspaper. She rattled her magazine so George would look up and notice that her robe was open, exposing her breast. He responded by turning the page of his newspaper. She coughed to get his attention, but that didn't work. She threw her magazine down and stood up. The robe opened more, but she grabbed the side and tucked it in with force.

"You getting more coffee?" he asked, without looking up.

She opened her mouth to speak, but nothing came out. She stomped out of the kitchen.

Carla spent the afternoon sunning herself by the in-ground pool in the backyard. She felt comfortable wearing a one-piece, black bathing suit. The dancer clothes wouldn't be that embarrassing. Her thirteen-year-old stepdaughter, Kim, was home, so she kept the top half of the bathing suit up. Kim had the radio so loud that Carla could hear it, even though she was far from the house.

Kim was putting her good clothes away after a day trip with her summer camp when Carla appeared at the door to her room.

"Who is this?" Carla asked, with her hand to her ear.

Kim stuttered the name of the singer as she turned to Carla.

"I used to be up on these things," Carla said. "Your father doesn't listen to music, so I don't listen much." She screamed to Kim, "How do you dance to this one?"

Kim jumped up and down out of rhythm with the music till Carla stopped her. They took steps together and danced. Carla shook her hips and waved her arms like she used to when she was Kim's age. Kim tried to follow, but Carla was too fast.

Carla lowered the volume when the song ended. "Well, that was fun."

"I had fun, too," Kim said. "I have a lot of music." She pointed to a rack of about a hundred compact discs. "I like music." She watched Carla straighten her hair.

"I know. We used to do things when I dated your father. Things have changed now. You don't have to call me Mom. Whatever you decide on, I hope we're friends."

She walked out of the room and left Kim silent.

Chapter 5

Mark sped through work Saturday like he was delivering time bombs. His usual conversation with Smitty by the trucks outside Iggy's was abbreviated. They walked in together when Jennifer arrived and held the door open for her. She said hello, but Mark was talking about gas mileage on his truck and didn't notice.

The rest of the day was in fast forward. He ran down supermarket aisles to stock shelves. The truck raced around traffic, and he even ran a red light but wasn't caught. He counted his money while driving to the depot where he threw his empty trays on the loading floor without looking where they landed. Mark always did things methodically, but there was no time for that today.

He sat at a corner of the bar in Babes West, as Abby had instructed. A young, buxom bartender brought him a napkin and took his drink order. As she leaned over the shiny bar giving Mark a glimpse of her solid, round breasts, she told him her name was Dani.

"I thought you worked at the other Babes."

"Yesterday, they found that girl. I'm not going back for awhile, so I came here. It's all the same owner," she answered.

He ordered a beer and then was distracted by a red-haired Hispanic dancer wearing blue shorts and bra.

The dancer skipped around the stage to instrumental music. Her brown eyes were visible, even through fog from a machine and the strobe lights. Her long hair bounced off her shoulders in every direction as she spun around the stage. Her red toenail polish matched her hair. She knelt before Mark and blew him a kiss.

"Fire?" Mark asked, holding a dollar out to her, but she didn't answer. "I used to see you dance a year ago. Don't you remember me?"

"Of course I do. I missed you," she said even though she had no idea who he was.

Abby tried to block out the music from the stage while she paced around the locker room till it was her turn to dance. She had bought a long, blue satin dress that fell to her ankles and had a slit that went up to her hip. She thought it looked classy. She was sure Mark would remember this. She opened the door and saw Mark talking to Fire, even though Fire looked disinterested. Abby sneered and shut the door.

When her name was announced, Abby blasted through the door and stomped to the stage like she was trying to bore her stiletto heels into the tile floor. She threw her moneybag with such an angry force that it slid across the stage. Her eyes locked on Mark and Fire. Abby went through the motions of wiggling for the crowd, but all the while her eyes were on Mark.

She reached behind her neck and undid the top of the dress. She held the straps instead of letting it fall. "Suspense is the key to keep them interested," another dancer once told her. It was a mystery what was under the dress. The deejay cued a five-minute song, so Abby could tease the crowd by lowering the dress inch by inch and then pull it back up several times. One shoulder snuck out of the dress. The other shoulder popped out, and then she'd cover herself again. She blew a kiss at Mark when she lowered the dress down to her breast. The timing of the music didn't matter anymore as she performed her striptease for Mark.

Abby dropped the dress at the start of the next song. She stood at the center of the stage in a black leather bikini to applause from the other men in the bar. She extended her arms like she wanted to hug everyone as she kicked the dress to a corner of the stage.

Mark pulled out a wad of dollars for her, but she went to someone else. He thought that she would come straight to him after all the time they had spent looking eye to eye. She started toward him but turned away and went to a group of young guys who groped and grabbed at her. Then she came out from behind the bar and went to the open arms of a customer. They went to a back room for a lap dance.

Mark contemplated leaving. His beer mug was empty. She was taking too long to get around the bar. He went there for her, and she saw him but went off with someone else. That was her job. The bartender pointed to his mug to signal a refill, so Mark nodded and stayed.

Sunflower took the stage in bikini bottoms and a skin-tight T-shirt. She seemed tall but wore high platform heels anyway. The shoes were so heavy that they threw off her weight when she did a handstand against the brass pole in the center of the stage, but she was a natural athlete and could roll over and stand up in one fluid motion. All eyes were on her as she rubbed her body and wiggled around the stage, toying with the bottom of the shirt. She bent over and blew a kiss at Mark through her legs.

"Hello," Abby yelled into Mark's ear. He lit up when he faced her and grabbed an empty seat for her, but she stood.

"I came to see you," he said. "I can't stay much longer, because I've been up since three in the morning. I just wanted to see you dance again."

"Thank you," she said, like she didn't care. "It's nice to know that I have a fan club now."

"I wouldn't go that far," he said. He liked that she could joke, even though she didn't look like she was having fun with him. "I like talking to you after your sets."

She had heard this before. Still, she wanted to believe him. She even blushed a little when he spoke. She wondered why this guy spent so much time at these bars. He touched her hand, and she liked that. Fire stood at the other end of the bar staring at them. Mark nodded to her, and Fire bounced her chest in her top in response.

"Why are you ignoring me?" Abby yelled.

He froze, with one hand on her back and the other on her hand. "I'm not ignoring you."

"You're looking at her now," Abby said. "You said you came to see me. What are you doing? I'm not out here half naked to get rejected by you."

"I didn't come here to fight with you. Why are you starting with me?"

Synthesizer music blasted through the speakers, and lights flashed around them. He couldn't speak over the noise.

"Let's not fight," she said. "I don't want to ruin the night." She put her finger to his lips. "What do you do when you're not here?"

"You pick weird times to ask questions." Mark looked around at the crowd, busy with the dancers collecting tips. Abby was all his for the moment. "I drive a truck. I said that before. I stay home a lot, and sometimes have friends over. The trouble is that a lot of my friends are married or have girlfriends, and I don't. I don't feel alone when I'm here."

"I don't feel alone when I'm here either," Abby said. "I would've quit a long time ago if I were lonely." She watched Sunflower on the stage. "She's a good dancer."

Mark nodded. "I really have to leave. I've got a lot of things to do for work—the books and all that. Maybe we can talk or do something next time."

"Wanna go in the back for a dance?" she asked. She didn't wait for an answer. She held his hand and led him to a back room with empty couches.

Music swirled around them as she ran her fingers through his sweaty hair. Lights flashed around the room as she rubbed her chest against him. Her face was against his and felt warm. Her soft hands groped his solid chest. He sat frozen as she rubbed against him. The music faded, and lights flickered in their faces. Her legs shook. She kissed his cheek. The lights illuminated her hair in an aura of white. The five-minute dance seemed to pass in seconds. She braced herself on his chest and caught her breath.

"I have to get changed for my next set. Are you still going home?"

"Yeah, I probably should. I mean ... there's work and all."

She held out her hand, palm up. "I wouldn't charge you, but it's rules of the house. I can't let them know or ... you know ... think that ... you know." She slid off his legs, so he could get his money.

He gave her extra and said, "I don't know what you mean."

"Don't worry about it." She ran to the lockers and slammed the door.

She got home to her studio apartment at three AM and threw her stuff on the floor next to a paper bag full of garbage. She turned the shower on and undressed. The faces of the night became one big blur. The only faces she could recall were Mark and her old boyfriend, Penn.

Penn, you bastard. She recalled her words to him. *I can't believe you talked me into this life. I wanted a job at a casino. Brand new to Vegas, and I had to run into you.*

She could hear his voice as the cold water splashed onto her: "I don't like you up there, but we need money. It's the quickest and easiest way."

She turned off the water and laughed. *Mark—he wants to talk to me. The big truck driver has to get up in the morning but stays to talk. He's too sweet.*

She rubbed her body with the towel so hard her thighs turned red. She always felt so dirty after touching these people, but most nights she dropped into bed after work. This time she felt something when she rubbed against

Mark that she hadn't felt in years, and she had to wash that feeling off. She wrapped herself in a fluffy towel and dragged herself to bed, still scattered with her clothes from her walk to the mall.

You don't want this, Mark, she thought. *You don't know the people I know. You don't know the life I live. You don't want this with me.*

She hugged the pillow and called it "Mark" as she fell asleep.

Babes West was closed on Sunday. On Monday, Mark was there at the center of the bar watching for Abby. Dani, the bartender, flashed a hint of her chest when she leaned over to hear his drink order. The tattoo on the back of her neck turned Mark off.

The deejay called for Baby Doll, and Abby skipped to the stage in a powder-blue bodysuit. She walked around showing off her outfit and signaled to Mark as she danced around the stage. There weren't many people there, so she spent a lot of time in front of Mark. Her three songs went quickly, and she was off to the far side of the bar.

Mark reminded himself that it was her job to mingle. He watched a young guy who looked like he was in his twenties talk to Abby, while rubbing her shoulders. "Young shit, let her go," Mark muttered. The guy made her laugh, which made Mark grit his teeth.

"I love long hair," Abby said to a guy with long brown hair tied into a ponytail, even though he was bald on top. "I could spend all night playing with long hair."

"Really?" he asked. "I have long hair on my back too. I'll bet I have the longest back hair you ever saw. Wanna see?"

"No thanks," she said, with a fake smile. She wiped her hand on her outfit and walked away.

"Where's my drink?" Mark yelled, as he slid a napkin away.

"Hello lover," she whispered in his ear.

"I'm gonna guess that you have to go back on stage soon," Mark said. "You spent all your time with those guys."

"They tip really well. I'll have to empty my moneybag soon before it bursts." She saw that Mark wasn't interested. "Did you notice that I wore blue on stage?"

"I saw it," he muttered into his beer.

"I wore it for you, but I do have to change now. Are you going to wait for my next set?"

"You wore it for me," he scoffed. "You spent time with everyone here but me. What's the point if you're going to ignore me all night?"

She reached for his hand, but he kept it on the beer mug. "It's my job. I have to do it." She kissed his cheek and backed away to the locker rooms.

Mark knew dancers didn't kiss patrons like she kissed him. She was on stage again, and he thought about the kiss. She was out of time with the music. It was obvious to the crowd that Abby was focused on Mark. Most of the men left the bar or went to the pool tables. When Abby's set was done, she went to a guy in a sweat suit across from Mark and led him to the back rooms. Mark wished his neck could stretch like a cartoon character's, so he could see what was happening. Deep down, he knew what was happening. She was going to do for that guy what she had done for him two nights ago.

He felt like he had to do something. What could he do? He went to the doorway and saw Abby run her fingers through the guy's hair. He patted his lap for her to sit, so she wiggled close and sat on his left leg with her arms around his neck. He squeezed her thigh.

Mark clenched his fist while this guy grabbed his dancer. He saw other dancers do the same for their customers, so he relaxed his fist and slouched back to his seat. A petite dancer with big curly hair and bright makeup clicked past him in heels that bored into the floor. She smiled at him, but he wasn't interested. It did give him an idea.

"Wanna go in the back room?" he asked, grabbing her hand.

Abby rubbed her breasts into the man's face, so he couldn't see her yawn. She turned to grind her behind into his lap and saw Mark with another dancer. The guy ran his finger along Abby's thigh, until he was between her legs. She shook startled and faced the guy, moving his hands away, all the while watching Mark.

"Wha's your name?" the dancer screamed over the music.

"Mark. What's your name?" Mark asked, even though he wasn't interested.

"Stacy Ann."

Abby stepped away from her customer and told him the dance was over. He reached into his pocket and pulled out a wad of crumpled dollars to pay her. She waited for him to leave and sat on the couch pretending to count her money.

Stacy Ann wrapped her long legs around Mark's and sat on his lap. She mashed her soft breasts into his face. He held her small hips against him. His fingers could almost reach all the way around her.

Abby stood up and stomped to the locker room. She slammed the door and dropped on the bench in front of her locker. The music outside was distorted bass. Other dancers walked around and didn't bother her. She took off her right shoe and threw it at her locker. Her toes were red and marked. Her feet and ankles were sore. She twisted the knob of her padlock and yelled, "Fucker," when it didn't open.

"What's wrong with you?" asked Rita. She paced behind Abby with a clipboard and pen keeping track of who was scheduled for the stage.

"I did something wrong, Rita." Abby rested her head on the locker door. "Out there is a guy that I told to come here. He was supposed to have a lap dance with me, but he's out there with Stacy. She doesn't even have a real stage name," she cried.

"So?" Rita asked. "You afraid he's out of money?"

"I don't know. He said he owns his own company. I just figured he would …"

"Dance with only you? He's not just your customer. Any guy out there with money is fair game. Go find someone else with money."

Stacy skipped into the locker room. "I am cleaning up tonight," she gloated. "I don't even have to ask. They're coming to me." She said "me" with her mouth open wide showing her pretty white teeth. She was young and didn't have the struggles of some of the older dancers—or the marks of a drug user.

Abby squared off as she passed by. "That guy you were just with … back away. I invited him here, and I get to dance with him."

"Oh sure," she said. "He came to me. I didn't ask him. I didn't ask him to come either," she smirked.

Abby looked through a slit in the door and saw Mark looking around. She sat back on the bench with her head in her hands where she stayed for half an hour listening to muffled music and thinking how much she liked Mark's touch. She emerged from the locker room wearing a bright red leather bikini and red heels. She went to the stage with graceful gliding steps, walking to the brass pole. Abby spotted Mark and spun herself on the pole fast and furiously until she hung herself upside down. Her leg was wrapped around the pole to hold her up. She slithered and slid down the pole to the stage floor while flirting with the men. Mark waited for her to acknowledge him, but she wouldn't.

She went to Mark after the song was over and yelled for Dani to bring her some water.

"Hello," Mark said. She didn't answer. "We going through this again?"

She chugged the water and walked around the bar looking for a lap dance. She found a guy while Mark sat alone watching her.

"Hi ya, honey," she said to another guy, who looked about Mark's age. He even had the same color hair as Mark. "Enjoying the show?"

"We don't have shows like this where I live. This is awesome," he said, with a goofy smile.

"I'm gonna guess that you never had a lap dance," she said. Her face was inches from his. She told him to look at the back room where girls were straddling customers. "That's a lap dance." She turned to Mark to see that he was watching.

"My girlfriend doesn't do that. Do I have to buy you anything?" the guy asked.

"No," she laughed. "You have to give me money for it." She didn't have to finish explaining it to him. He was standing and ready to go.

Mark watched this guy go in the back with Abby, then another and another. He held some money for her, but she never approached him. He tipped other dancers and bought beers, while Abby was in the back. By one o'clock in the morning, he had had enough. He caught Abby before she went to her locker room.

"Are you going to see me?" he yelled.

"Why don't you dance with Stacy Ann?" she yelled back.

"I came here for you. When are we going to dance? You keep going to all those other guys."

"It's my job. I dance with whoever asks. You can dance with whoever you want."

"I want you. When is our turn?"

She hugged him. His arms were pinned at his side, but he was able to lift his wrists and get his hands on her back. She squeezed tighter when she felt his touch.

"What is going on?"

"You said you would come see me, and you …" She paused to catch her breath. "You go and dance with someone else. What is this? I'm just some dancer? Oh, fuck it. I am just a dancer." She sat on an empty bench so her feet were on a high rung of the stool and her knees were close to her chest. "I mean nothing to you. You mean nothing to me."

"No," Mark said. "You're not just a dancer. I really like being here with you. I spent a lot more money than I should have. Bills are due and I'm here." He sat next to her with his legs spread apart. "Is this what we're doing? I'm just supposed to tip you, and you're supposed to seem interested?"

"That's what's supposed to happen." She looked into his eyes. "It's not what's happening though."

"If things were different ... if I'd met you somewhere else, would we have worked out?" he asked, looking around and cracking his knuckles.

"I don't know. I don't know if you want to know."

"I do. I want to know." Mark reached for her hand.

"We can't do that here," she said. She pulled back and held her knees with her hands. "I'm off tomorrow. Want to meet at the National Diner later?"

"I'm off tomorrow. I can be there. What time?"

"Bar closes at two. I can be there twenty minutes later." When Mark agreed, she rushed to the locker room.

Mark drove to the diner and sat in a corner booth. An African-American man in baggy pants and oversized T-shirt sat at the counter drinking a soda. The guy made Mark nervous. He had seen guys dressed like that threaten truck drivers and steal things from their trucks late at night. About that time, a group of drunken white men and women walked into the diner, giggling and staggering. They were loud, but somehow Mark felt safer. No one would rob a diner with so many people.

The man in baggy clothes hollered to the cooks in the back. "I see my ride outside. I'll see you tomorrow and work those extra hours."

Mark lowered his head in shame. He realized he had trusted the drunken white people more than he did the diner's cook just because of the way he dressed. And here he was waiting for some stripper to show up. He bought a soda and moved to the counter.

Abby walked in. Her hair was matted, and the bags under her eyes were obvious without her makeup. She wore jeans with holes at the knees, a faded T-shirt, and dirty white sneakers with no socks. Mark wasn't sure it was her, until she sat next to him.

"Is anything wrong?" she asked.

"I'm not used to seeing you like that. You had glitter around your eyes the last time I saw you."

She looked down at her jeans and laughed. "That's Baby. She dresses like that. Abby doesn't like makeup and pouffy hair. Baby flirts and slides around on a slick floor. I like to sit in old jeans. I have some really nice clothes, but it's the middle of the night. I'm going for comfort now."

"So who was I talking to all those times?" he asked.

"You sat with Baby at the bar, but Abby did the talking."

"How do I know the difference?" he asked. Their kneecaps touched, and he put his hand on her knee.

She slid his hand off. "I just want to talk," she said. "I want to get to know you. It's just Mark and Abby sitting in a diner."

"How are you, Abby? It's a pleasure to meet you."

"I'm fine. The pleasure is mine."

Chapter 6

The gutters of Babes Go-Go overflowed with rain. The loose-gravel parking lot turned to mud stew. The rain made the dip at the exit more pronounced, so the fronts of cars were scraping the ground on the way in and out of the lot. Dancers' cars were lined up in the parking lot when Stacy Ann drove in. She pulled in so quickly she splashed mud on some of the other cars. Three dancers were in the locker room when she stomped in and squared herself in front of Rita's desk holding a newspaper.

"When were you going to tell us about the murder last week?" Stacy Ann demanded.

Rita stood up to face Stacy. Sunflower covered herself with a hand towel in case a fight broke out.

Rita looked at the newspaper. "You saw it."

"When did she die?" Stacy yelled, with her hands at her hips. "The newspaper said when she was found—not when she died. They found her in the garbage."

"I don't know," Rita said. "She danced here last week. I don't remember her staying late. I don't know what happened. I guess that's why she didn't show up for work at the end of the week."

"Ya think?" Stacy asked.

"We didn't close the place or say much because we didn't want to scare people. I try to keep an eye on you when you leave, just in case it was one of the customers." She could see that Stacy wasn't impressed. "The police said they were investigating."

The other dancers watched the stare-down between Rita and Stacy Ann. "If you're so scared and you have other clubs to work at, you should go there. I can find dancers," Rita said, looking only at Stacy Ann.

"She's been dead for a week," Stacy Ann said. "If it weren't for my neighbors recycling newspapers, I wouldn't know, and you wouldn't have told us. The killer could be anyone—and none of us knew."

"We have to show everyone that we're not closing down," Rita said. She watched the dancers turn away. "The owners have hired an outside security team."

"Why are we listening to you?" Sunflower asked.

"I've worked here for a lot of years," Rita said. "You can trust me and listen to me." Rita closed her scheduling book.

Stacy Ann tapped her foot and stared Rita down.

Sunflower still had her arms across her chest. She turned and went to her locker to get dressed for her set.

"There's no security here now," Fire said. She stood up and put her long red wig in a bag, exposing her spiky black hair. "I don't know about this."

"You can't leave," Rita said. "This place will be safe. Whoever did this won't come back. He knows we're looking for him. The cops have been patrolling."

Sunflower stood up. "How can we dance?" she asked, sounding anxious. "What customers will come here if there's security watching? The guys won't have a good time. We won't get tips if the guys are afraid to touch us."

"We're not going to supplement your pay you if you don't get enough tips," Rita said.

Fire slid her feet into sandals and headed for the door. "Call me when the place is safe." She walked out with all eyes upon her.

"I have to work," Sunflower said. "I'm thirty-three years old, and I have bills." She finished dressing, grabbed her moneybag, and walked out of the locker room.

Stacy Ann ran outside and caught Fire as she started her Audi. "Do you think the cops will find out who killed her?" Stacy Ann asked, tears from stressed nerves streamed down her cheeks.

"Of course they'll find out," said Fire. "I've seen cops here once in awhile. They've seen the people here."

"The cops come here to bust us for prostitution," Stacy said.

Fire stared at the Dumpster. The rain had washed the dirt and kept away the flies. The garbage glistened. "She was a good person ... Buffy."

"We could've gone to her funeral," Stacy said.

"Her family probably didn't want us."

Chapter 7

The inside of Babes West was cold and dark during the daylight hours. One stage light illuminated the whole place. Televisions were louder than the music. Customers were more drunk than horny.

Sunflower walked in and saw three half-asleep men seated at the bar, ogling a dancer who paid more attention to the televisions than to the men. She asked to see a manager.

"I'm the manager," said a gray-haired, barrel-chested old man behind the bar. "You want something?"

"I'm a dancer. The stage name is Sunflower. Rita told me that there are better schedules available, and I want to dance where the customers are."

"I got dancers," he said. He put his pudgy fingers inside a sticky plastic cup and tossed it to the garbage.

He laughed. "You're smart. You got me. Rita is the house-mom for both these bars. She has an assistant that I see more of. If the action picks up around here, I'll make you a deal." His eyes focused on her breasts, bulging under her tight T-shirt.

"What kind of deal?" she asked, leaning over the bar and flashing a hint of breast.

"You come back tonight. If there's people, you can go upstairs, and we'll talk."

🍁   🍁   🍁

Abby sat on a bench at the laundry mat squeezed in by empty baskets and folded clothes from other people. Her dancer clothes whirled around in a dryer. Dressed in dirty white sweats and a stained T-shirt, she wore no makeup and had her hair pulled up in a ponytail. She took out a pen and paper.

Dear Tiffany,

How are you, hon? It gets lonely without friends like you around, but Las Vegas was like that in the beginning, too. I haven't really made friends with anyone from the clubs, because everyone freelances and goes from club to club. There are five clubs that are twenty miles apart. I work two bars that are owned by the same corporation. Can you believe that? It's a franchise. One is a nice little place, and the second place is kind of a dump, but it gives me a chance to try new moves and costumes. You should see the cape I made for myself. It's blue sheer silk. The guys love it. I'm training another dancer. I think she's only doing this to get her husband off.

I rented a post office box, so you can write to me. I know you must be living it up with the movie coming out. I'm too scared to do a porno. You have to tell me what the filming was like. Did you get star treatment? I'll bet the clubs treat you different now.

I wish we could see each other again. I miss the times we talked and hung out with the girls at the casinos. The only person I hang out with here is a customer. I know you're thinking I'm crazy for it. I would never date a customer or anything like that, but this guy wants to talk to me. I know I turn him on, but it feels different. Now that I've written that and see the words in front of me, I see how crazy it is.

Abby bit the pen as she read through what she had written. It was wrong. She put a line through the last paragraph, except for the first sentence.

Nearby, a mother read a book to her little boy, who sat on her lap. A young couple did laundry together for what seemed to be their first time. The woman explained to her boyfriend how to separate colors and where to put the bleach and detergent. An older woman, probably in her seventies, with gray hair and an old housedress did laundry by herself.

Chapter 8

Mark drove to the depot at the end of another long day. By the time he pulled in, his merchandise counter had calculated the stock needed for tomorrow's deliveries. He eyed a huddle of managers walking through aisles of inventory racks. Other drivers watched also.

"Maybe they're checking out what's left before we're sold," one driver said. "I read in the papers that they're working on some merger. The merger would get rid of Dewey's. I don't know all the small stuff that's going on, but I don't think this is good for any of us."

Mark walked past the managers, but couldn't make out their conversation. He shrugged and went about getting his inventory.

🍁　　　🍁　　　🍁

When he got home, his townhouse was roasting in the glow of the afternoon sun. He turned up the air conditioner before the front door closed behind him. He could see four teenage boys hanging out on the street corner near the mailboxes.

Four teenage girls walked toward the boys. A boy in dirty shorts and an old T-shirt rode a mountain bike past the girls. He said something, and a barefoot girl laughed and climbed on the handlebars of the bike. She held her arms up and screamed as they rode away laughing.

Mark felt restless. He called Eddie, but the baby was crying and Eddie had to cut the conversation short. Abby's phone number was on a rolled up piece of paper next to the phone. Mark cracked his knuckles and dialed. He got the answering machine.

"Hi. It's Mark from the diner the other night. I was just calling to see what you're doing. You didn't say if you were working tonight. I don't have money to stop by the bar. I'll give you a call later or tomorrow."

He held the phone for an extra second before hanging up, just in case she was listening and rushing to the phone. The machine hung up, so Mark put the phone back in the cradle. He called her an hour later and got the machine again, so he left a similar message as before.

Abby saw the flashing message light on her machine when she walked into her apartment with plastic bags full of groceries. She guessed it was a call about a dancing gig. She placed the bags on the floor and checked the number. It was Mark's number. *He called*, she thought. *I didn't think that would happen.*

Mark toyed with the paper again at nine o'clock. He wanted to call her, even though it was getting late. He took a breath and dialed. This time she answered.

"Hi," Mark said.

"Hi."

They had a moment of silence when neither knew what to say next.

"I was just calling to see what you're doing," he said.

"I was just having something to eat. I bought a salad and a frozen vegetarian pizza while I was out. I don't dance at Babes till the day after tomorrow."

"I have off tomorrow," Mark lied. "You want to go out to a midnight movie tonight? Or actually let's say an eleven fifty-nine movie—that would still be tonight. Or we could do something else."

"Sure."

Mark rushed out of the house without shutting off the television. He got to the glass doors at the movie theater and stopped to look at himself in the reflection. His rugby shirt was wrinkled, and he wore a pair of dirty sneakers and jeans with worn-out knees. His first real date with this dancer, and he was a mess.

I can't believe I look like this, he thought. He tried to smooth the wrinkles in his shirt with his hand. *I've got a date with a dancer and I'm wearing a stained, wrinkled shirt. Geez. But I can't go home now.* He cracked his knuckles and crossed his arms over the wrinkled shirt.

Abby looked through the glass doors and spotted him. She also had rushed out of the apartment. She wore no makeup, and her hair wasn't done. Her bright blue shorts and a new, loose-fitting T-shirt were definitely not her dancer look. She found a lipstick in her purse and began applying it, using her reflection in the glass door.

"Hey, look at me," said a laughing boy, coming out the door.

Bam! The door hit Abby and bounced back at the boy, who screamed and ran when he saw her coughing and huffing on the other side of the door.

Abby hid her face in her hands, peaking through her fingers to see the people staring at her. Her lipstick fell to the ground, and she left it. *Just great*, she thought, rubbing her sore lip and smearing the lipstick onto her teeth. *I should just go home. This is a sign. This is going to be a disaster. I can't handle a real man on a real date.*

About that time she noticed Mark rubbing sweat off his palms onto his pant leg. *Oh, that is so high school. Yeah, he's going to be safe*, she thought.

Mark saw her and raised his arms like they were going to hug. Before she got to him, he put his hands in his pockets. He pulled out his hands, hooking his thumbs in his pockets and expanding his chest. "You look hot tonight," he said.

"I just threw something on. I wasn't sure of what to wear." She crossed and uncrossed her arms as she spoke. "What movie do you wanna see?"

"I don't know. What's good? I rushed out of the house without looking at movie listings or a clock to tell me that it's still before midnight."

"Oh," she said surprised at the movie listings. "Let's see if we can catch *Romance of the River, Part 2*. That sounds good."

He looked to the movie listings, hoping to find something better. Nothing sounded familiar. He searched for something to say.

"What's wrong? Don't want to see it?" she asked.

"No, it's fine," he said. "Let's go."

Mark paid for both tickets and the popcorn for a movie he knew he would hate. Eddie had told him that the first movie was boring. There seemed to be no reason for a sequel, but it made Abby happy to see it. Mark put his arm on the armrest between them. He felt her squirm in the seat next to him and took his arm down. She put her arm on the armrest and swung her legs over the seats in front of her.

"You want the armrest?" she asked.

"No, I'm fine," Mark said, with his arms crossed over his chest.

"No, you have it," she insisted.

The armrest wasn't used during the whole movie. When it ended, they were the last two people to leave.

"Some movie," she said.

"Some bad movie," Mark wanted to say, but he didn't. He nodded instead. They walked side by side as they left, not holding hands or touching.

"They say it's going to rain tomorrow," Mark said. When he saw her Mercedes, he exclaimed, "You can afford this?"

"It's used," she said. "I got it from the dealer down on Route 66. Thank God it has air conditioning. I just hate times like now, when it's about to rain. The air gets so heavy. It's just wicked brutal."

"Yeah, it's that whole humidity thing," he said. "It's what did you call it?"

"What?"

"Wicked?"

She grinned. "I guess my New England comes out when I'm comfortable. I don't think I've said that word in a long time."

Mark nodded and looked through the car windows at the leather seats. "You'll probably stick to those when it's hot out."

"Do you want to get in?"

Mark ran to the passenger door and got in. He played with the stick shift and the radio knobs. "I can't afford one of these," he said. "They're talking about some merger, and I might lose my route. I don't know what's going to happen. Why did you become a dancer?" he asked without pausing.

"Money," she said. "It was good money. I had a boyfriend living with me who was always broke, and we needed the money. He got me the job. I didn't think I would be good at it, but I guess I am."

"I don't know why a guy would want his girl to work as a dancer. I could see it if … you know … if you danced with more clothes on. I wouldn't want to share you with a bunch of guys in a bar."

"I dance," she sighed. "When I dance, my mind is somewhere else. I daydream. I try not to think about it." She slid in the car and leaned into him. "I decide who touches me and for how long. I make those rules."

He cracked his knuckles. "How did we end up here?"

"I thought you were cute, I guess. God, listen to me. I sound like I'm in high school again. You were nice to me. You wanted to talk to me."

He ran his hand along the dashboard. "I've seen dancers with tattoos and belly-piercings. Are you going to get a tattoo?"

"I don't want someone poking me with a pen. I don't want anything artificial," she added. "There are a lot of fake boobs out there."

"There sure are. We're talking about dancers, not customers, right?"

Her head dropped and her chest shook when she laughed at that comment. He stopped toying with the radio buttons and looked into her eyes.

"Why did you come here from Las Vegas? The Jersey Shore is a great place, with all the history and stuff, but you lived in Las Vegas. I wouldn't come here."

"No one knows me here. I can start all over. I'm not going to dance in bars all my life. I don't really have other plans, but I know I'm not doing this forever."

Booming thunder and lightning lit up the sky as Abby and Mark locked gazes. Each dared the other to make a move. Mark leaned in and kissed her. The bright lights of the oncoming storm shone around them.

"It's late," she said. "You've probably been up all day."

"Yeah, I've been up since three in the morning," Mark said, a little tired and out of breath. "I have to go back to my car." He opened the door and turned back to her. "See ya."

❦ ❦ ❦

Sunflower walked into Babes West and saw the exact scene she had seen earlier in the day. Five customers sat at the bar, paying more attention to their beers than to the dancer on stage, twirling around to pounding hip-hop music from a jukebox. Sunflower gritted her teeth and asked for the manager. The dancer yelled for her to go to the back.

"Is the bar always this bad?" Sunflower asked when she was surprised to see Rita. "You called me and told me to hurry in at midnight, and this is all I see. It's almost fucking closing."

"You could say, 'Hi, Rita, love your new tattoo.'" Rita held a cloth soaked with rubbing alcohol pressed to a rose on her arm. "The customers are waiting for the weekend."

"I'm losing money by not dancing, and I'm not going to make money here," Sunflower said.

"The owner of the bar got you a set on Friday night, but he wants to meet you afterward," Rita said. "Be sure to stick around after closing."

"I plan on it. Tell me what time to be here," Sunflower said.

"The manager will be very happy," Rita said with a smirk.

❦ ❦ ❦

It was a rainy day. Mark was behind schedule, and there was no way to make up lost time due to the traffic. Smitty was in Iggy's by the time Mark got there. He asked Mark why he was so obviously ignoring Jennifer.

"I don't have time to talk to her," Mark said. "I'm not rude, but I have a route to finish. She's getting married anyway."

"You knew she was dating that guy for a while," Smitty said, "and you still hit on her."

"Well, I guess it's a little more official now," Mark said, turning to the deli section. "And I've been seeing someone else anyway."

"Whoa," Smitty said. "You never said anything. How long has this been going on?"

"We're not officially dating," Mark said, as he walked with Smitty out to the trucks. "We've met each other after work a couple of times, but I don't know if I would use the word 'date.'"

"So what is it then?"

"I don't know if there is a word," Mark said. He opened the back of his truck and stepped up on the back bumper. "We're just seeing each other. Her name is Abby."

"You're better off. I've noticed you were acting different. You used to wait for Jennifer every day, and she ignored you. It was pathetic."

"Thanks, man, I needed that."

It took Mark a long time to leave Iggy's. He spent more time talking to Smitty than he wanted to. The rain beat on the top of his truck all day. Finally, he got to the depot. He calculated his sales and noticed they were down, but he didn't dwell on it. It had been a long day, and Mark just wanted to get home. As Mark reached the inventory floor, a group of drivers gathered around one of the drivers.

"Webster's wife had their baby yesterday. He's showing pictures," one of the drivers told Mark.

"Eight pounds, five ounces," Webster said. "They're coming home tomorrow. I have to get someone to take care of my route for a couple of days."

Mark didn't stop to listen. He packed his things and left the depot. The bed was calling.

🍁   🍁   🍁

Abby bounced off the stage of Babes Go-Go Bar and headed toward the men with money in front of them. A construction worker still in his orange safety vest had the largest pile of money. Abby slouched in front of him, so her breasts rested on the bar.

"You got great legs," he told her.

She swung her leg up on the bar and held the garter on her leg out. He wrapped a dollar around his finger and ran it from her ankle, over her knee, to her garter.

"Bye, sweetie," she said, as she dropped her leg from the bar. She turned and saw Mark at the door. She walked toward him, waving him to come to the bar.

"How long you been here?" she asked.

"Not long. I just got here," he yelled over the music.

"You didn't tell me you were coming. I wish I'd known."

"I didn't know I was coming either. I was just sitting around and started thinking about seeing you. Don't let me stop you."

"I have to go." She turned but stopped. "How long are you going to be here?"

"I don't know. Is something wrong?"

"No," she said. She went to the stage and twirled for the customers, always looking Mark's way. He bought a beer and watched. She went to a customer at the far end of the bar from Mark, but she could feel Mark's stare with every move she made.

"I have to talk to you," she said to him after her set. "I wish I had known you were coming."

"It was just impulse. Do I have to clear it with you?"

"I don't know. I just …" She stopped. "I don't know. How are you?"

"OK. I also wanted to know if you were free on Saturday night."

She sighed. "I have to work Saturday night. I used to do days, but they're short dancers. I'm free after the bar closes tonight."

"I have to get up at three in the morning."

"So go home and get up at one. I'll meet you at the National Diner."

Mark agreed and left. He dropped into bed but couldn't sleep because it was hot in the room. He had his work pants on, and the keys in his pockets bothered him. The alarm was set, but he was paranoid of oversleeping and standing Abby up. Just as he finally drifted off to sleep, the alarm sounded and woke him up. He put on his wrinkled uniform shirt and ran out of the house. He was late getting to the diner.

Abby was seated at a booth looking out a window. He could see that her hair was wet, and she wore no makeup. Her tight fitting red tank top was wrinkled. When Mark got inside, he saw that she wore black spandex shorts and sandals.

"I always had a thing for men in uniform," she said. "Is it always this humid here? I saw a sign that said it was eighty-five degrees. I'm used to desert heat, but the humidity makes it feel worse."

"It gets like this. There's more rain coming, which will help for a while. How was your night?"

"I can pay for anything you want," she said.

"I'm the guy. I get the check," Mark said. "That's how it works."

"Not all guys get the check. I'm used to paying. My last boyfriend never got the check." She rubbed her nose. "I really didn't think you'd be here. You still have to work."

"Then why are you here?"

"I was hoping that you would show—just didn't think you would. I like the time we spend together. I have so much bullshit to worry about, but when I'm with you, it doesn't matter." She yawned. "Whew, it's late. When do you have to leave for work?"

"No rush," he said. He grabbed her hand. "I like our time too. As hot as it is out, I'm still going to get a coffee."

"Our schedules don't exactly fit, do they?"

"We can think of something." Mark grabbed a menu and looked through it.

Abby watched Mark and smiled. He still went out of his way for her. Her last boyfriend never made any effort for her. The customers don't care, but he does. She wasn't hungry, but she wanted to stay as long as possible just to be with him.

Chapter 9

Dani arrived at Babes West on Saturday morning to open the bar. When she went to unlock the door, she found it ajar.

"Lazy night crew," she muttered, as she walked in. The only light was a flashing red light over the stage. The door to the empty deejay booth was open. She reached along the wall and flipped on the lights for the whole bar.

Bar towels were hung to dry by the sink. The glasses were put away as normal. The register draw was open and empty, which meant the money tray was in the safe. The bottles of liquor seemed to be properly capped. There was a light on in the manager's office.

"What are you doing here so early?" she asked, on her way to the office. "Usually I'm alone when I open."

The club manager had his back to her, sitting on a metal chair. He didn't move when she walked in the office.

"What are you doing here so early?" she repeated. Again, no response. "Hey, did you sleep over?" she asked, as she walked in front of him.

The manager's chest was covered in blood. His tongue hung out of his mouth and had punctures in it. His pants were undone but still up. Dollar bills stuck out of the pocket of his shirt. Dani screamed and ran out of the office. Her arms swung like windmills, knocking over barstools that had been turned over on the bar.

"Phone. I need a phone," she screamed. She jumped over the bar and fell onto the floor. She grabbed a phone near the ice chest but couldn't punch the numbers, because her hands shook too much. She crouched and looked in the mirrors to see if anyone was there. Her hands steadied, and she punched in 911.

"Hello," she screamed into the phone. "You gotta come here. There's blood and a mess, and I can't stay here."

"Ma'am, please calm down," the operator said.

"Fuck you. I'm not staying here." She dropped the phone and ran out of the bar to her car and hid.

Abby was napping at two o'clock when the phone woke her. Rita was on the line, and her voice sounded shaky and scared.

"There was a horrible accident at Babes West, and the manager is dead."

"Who?" Abby asked, still half asleep.

"The manger," Rita yelled. "He was there last night. The police told me about it. They questioned a bunch of us this morning. Buffy's killer could be a customer. I left early. I'm so messed up. Did you know Buffy?"

"I've heard of her," Abby said. She sat up and gripped the phone tightly. "I never met her. What murder?"

"Buffy was found in the garbage. Now the manager is dead."

"That's messed up. I never liked the guy. He was always trying to grab me, and he walked in the locker rooms all the time. I know other dancers hated him. He might have slept with a few of the younger girls. He tried with the rest of us." She ran her fingers through her hair and sighed.

"Slept with dancers," Rita repeated, as if she were questioning it. She laughed. "He never slept. I'll call you when the club opens again." She hung up, with Abby still on the line.

Carla walked past a floral silk blouse at a store in the mall. She saw the two hundred-dollar price tag as she held the blouse to her chest. She didn't have that much money on her, but she knew if she put it on a credit card, George would pay it. She folded it onto her arm and noticed Kim in the shoe section trying on sneakers.

"Is that what you're going to wear after school?" Carla asked.

"Yeah, they're silver. They have lights at the bottom for when I run at night."

Carla looked at the price on the box, even though she knew about what they would cost before she looked. She saw that she was right. They cost two hundred dollars. She put the blouse down and told Kim to get them.

❦   ❦   ❦

Mark dragged to the couch after work and dropped. A flashing red light on his answering machine caught his eye as he landed. He was exhausted and sweaty, but two hours later, he was on the beach with Abby.

"I thought the beach would be a nice place to relax," she explained. Mark focused on the short summer dress she wore that was tight across her chest. Her tanned legs took long strides on the boardwalk. Black-framed sunglasses hid her eyes.

He wore long pants and a T-shirt that said, "Suck 'em at Oyster Inn."

"It's cool here," he said. "It's practically deserted."

Abby seemed to be deep in thought. "People go home. Lifeguards are off duty. There's no reason to be here. I come here during the day sometimes and watch."

"You need time to relax each day before work? You're so frantic at work, dancing and walking."

"I'm another person when I'm at work," she said. "I think I'm another person each place I go. I'm not the same person I was when I used to live in Rhode Island. Las Vegas was totally different. I don't know about me sometimes."

"People can change," Mark said. "It's why you moved here, isn't it?" They walked to a pizza stand. "Two slices," Mark ordered.

"For a dollar more, you get soda with that," said the teenage girl at the register.

"Fine," Abby said. "I'll pay the dollar. What's funnel cake?'

"It's this big piece of fried dough," the register girl explained.

She shook her head. "Can't. Diet. There's no place to hide fat on stage. I'm getting on the older side of this anyway. Five years ago would've been different."

She and Mark walked away from the stand and sat at a small table. "Someone killed the manager at Babes West," she said.

"Really?" he asked. "Are they going to close the place?"

"I hope not," she answered. "I need the money. It's no big deal having no manager. I suppose I'll have to go his funeral. I don't want to."

"It's someone you worked for," Mark said.

"I work more for Babes Go-Go than Babes West. I was at Babes Go-Go last night. The whole time I was there I was thinking about the night before at the diner with you." She took a bite of pizza and wiped a splotch of grease off her lip. "I never liked the guy anyway. I don't like a lot of those people. They treat dancers like crap. They complain that we don't make enough money, but I don't see them wearing those uncomfortable shoes and dancing." She sipped her soda. "I like you, but I don't like most of the people associated with those places."

"Aren't you scared? Someone you work for was murdered."

"It isn't the first time that I've known someone who was murdered," she said. "I don't see the best people in the world where I work."

They finished their pizza and walked the boardwalk till the shops closed, and police started patrolling the boardwalk for vagrants. Abby invited Mark to come up to her place. He hesitated because he wasn't sure what her place could be like. She seemed eager to show him so he accepted. She sat on the floor and talked about Vegas. Mark sat next to her, leaning against the front of the couch.

"I'm not good at craps, but I can play blackjack," Abby said. "I don't gamble. There's more to do. Try going to Circus-Circus and watching acrobats at two in the morning."

The compact disc in the stereo stopped playing, but they didn't seem to notice. Mark kissed Abby. She lowered her back to the floor and pulled his body close to hers. His tough, callused hands gripped her waist and squeezed. His hands moved under her skirt, squeezing her thin legs.

She took her summer dress off and threw it over Mark's shoulder. He reached for her shoulder and lowered her bra strap. She held his other hand tight. They rolled over, so he could reach behind her and undo her bra with one hand. She pulled away.

"What's wrong?" Mark asked.

"Nothing. It's right," she said and kissed him. She lowered the other bra strap and took off her bra. Mark explored her body. "Touch me," she heard herself say, her thoughts betraying her.

"I am," he said.

"Touch me," she repeated. Mark took that to mean that she liked to talk during sex, so he told her every place he touched. "I'm at your stomach," he said. "I'm touching your hip."

Abby felt his hands envelop her waist. "You're touching through me. Kiss me. Just kiss me. Just … kiss me," she whispered. She was lost in the thought that he wanted to touch *her*—not Baby Doll or any dancer. She knew he wanted her—Abby.

🍁   🍁   🍁

Carla stared at George in his sleep. His arms were on his chest, his mouth was wide open, and his head was propped on two pillows. She closed his mouth with two fingers, which made him grumble and turn. The snoring didn't stop, so she threw off the thin cover and stomped to his side of the bed. Her silk nightgown reached to her ankles, so she lifted it up to her hips and spread her legs shoulder-width apart.

"George," she said with authority.

"What the hell are you doing?" he asked, startled, when he opened his eyes and saw her bare hips.

"The girls are asleep, and the summer heat is getting to me." She put one knee on the bed and positioned her hips close to his face. "I'm on fire. I want you," she said in a loud whisper.

"What time is it?" He rolled over and looked at the clock, which said it was twelve thirty. "We can't do it now."

"Then when?" she yelled. "I'm twenty-six years old. Maybe I want a child of my own—of our own. Don't you find me sexy?"

He pulled her on top of him with his eyes were still closed. "I think you're very sexy," he said, "but I don't know if I want another child. I have to work a lot now. I don't have time for that."

"Aren't we ever going to have sex again? It is part of being married."

"I know what being married means. I was married twice before. You're crushing me." He threw her off him and sat up. "I've got to go to work in the morning."

"It's Sunday. There's no work today. Just touch me."

He leaned back and fell asleep.

Mark woke when the sun burst through the white bed sheet Abby used as a window curtain. Abby's head was on his chest, and her arms were wrapped around him. He looked at his watch and saw that it was seven AM. At least there was no work on Sundays.

"Morning already?" Abby asked when she felt Mark move. "I don't want to wake up. Are you going anywhere today?"

"I was going to do laundry and watch a ball game on TV. What are your big plans for the day?" he asked.

"I was going to do laundry, too. Want to go to the Laundromat together?"

"I have a washer-dryer at my house. Why don't you come by?"

"No one has held me into the morning like this in a long time. I want to stay here," she said.

If my friends could see me now, he thought. *She's a babe and a go-go dancer. They'd shit themselves.*

"At the diner you said something about a boyfriend. Is he still around?" Mark asked.

"Nope. I came out here alone. He's in Vegas, and I hope he never finds me," she said. "He never touched me like you did. We just had sex. Fast. When he was done, he was gone. He never stayed in bed all morning. He got up and went to do his thing," she said. She pushed hair away from her face but didn't look at Mark. "I don't even have family here. They live in Providence. They don't care what I do."

"My family lives in Tinton Falls. It's not far from here. I wish they lived in Providence," Mark said. "My parents like to point out that my brother is married and has a son, while I live alone. My brother owns a house, while I have a townhouse. I like my life, but they don't. It gives them something to criticize on a regular basis."

"I wouldn't criticize you," she purred.

He ran his fingers along her back, until he got to a bump next to her spine. She felt him stop.

"It's from that old boyfriend," she explained. "No one can see it when I dance. Please don't touch it."

"I want to spend the day with you," he said, changing the subject. "It's easier to see you in the day. These nights are tough on us." He looked around her apartment. There were no pictures, no scrapbooks, no signs of other people. "I guess I'm your boyfriend," he said, half asking, half stating.

Her eyes opened. She didn't know what to say, except, "I guess so.

❦   ❦   ❦

Sue knocked at Mark's door as Abby sorted their laundry in Mark's living room. She wanted to ask Mark about parking spaces but stopped when she saw Abby. Mark saw Sue looking at Abby.

"I have one top left," Abby said. "I'm going to throw it in with your whites."

"I drive a truck," Mark replied. "It's not going to make my stuff smell all girlie, is it?"

"That would be an improvement," Abby joked. "It's a shirt, not a bottle of perfume, honey."

Sue motioned for Mark to walk outside with her. "Who's that?" Sue asked, but didn't wait for an answer. "Two weeks ago you didn't say anything about a girlfriend. You were carrying on about a young flirt in a convenience store. Now you're doing laundry with this one." Sue paced while Mark stared at the ground. "I don't know about you anymore. This is serious. You can't do laundry with someone you just met."

"I was doing laundry, and so was she," he said, oblivious to why Sue was anxious.

"You're mixing. Couples mix laundry. I don't mix laundry for at least six months, and no guy has lasted that long in a long time." She tugged at her loose-fitting top. "My clothes get next to me. *This* is touching my skin. I can't let a guy's laundry touch the things that touch me."

"This is ridiculous. It's laundry."

Sue grabbed Mark's shoulders and tried to shake him, but he didn't move. "What if she wants to wash her bras?"

"I've seen a bra before. I'm thirty-four years old. I'm not afraid of a bra," he scoffed.

"Her bras are swirling around with your underwear. I could see washing a shirt to be nice before you returned it. You're mixing, and you know you're doing it. This is serious, and you're acting like it's nothing. The next thing you know, you'll have all mixed loads. The laundry will practically be married." She gasped. "That's what you want. You want to be married. That's the rush."

"This is why you're single," Mark said. "You're insane."

Abby went to the door and could hear them on the other side. It was comforting that Mark had no problem doing a "couple" thing. She flashed back to the young couple doing laundry together for the first time at the Laundromat last week. The dryer stopped making noise. Abby stopped daydreaming because she could hear Mark coming back to the door.

"Just folding my clothes," she said, when Mark walked back in the house. "I think I should go home. My things are pretty much done. I'm sure you have things to do, and I have to dance tomorrow. I have so much to do before then."

"You don't have to go," Mark said. "I don't have to hit the sack till nine or ten tonight. I've gone to work on less sleep."

"I just think …" She stopped and put folded pants on top of a pile of clothes. "I think we should have a little space for the night. We've been together since early last night. This is one hell of a wicked long date." She bit her lip.

"Are you sure?"

"Yeah, I have things to do. I'll call you on Tuesday. We could go out after the bar closes. I had fun at the movies. We could do that." She picked up her clothes and headed for the door, which Mark held for her. She went out without kissing Mark. She passed Eddie on the way to her car, but he didn't recognize her.

"New girl?" Eddie asked. "Are we still watching the game later?'

"Yeah," Mark said. "I have to run to catch up to her for a minute."

Abby was putting her clothes in the trunk of her car when Mark caught up to her. "I'll call you Tuesday," she said.

Mark kissed her before she could say more. She went to the driver's door and said good-bye, but Mark followed her and kissed her again. She laughed while trying to untangle and hook the seatbelt. She started the car and drove away, leaving Mark standing.

Carla's backyard was the largest in her neighborhood. From the kitchen window, she could see Kim in the swimming pool. George was tossing inflated balls into the water for Kim to catch. Their elder daughter, fifteen-year-old Kendra, came down the stairs from her bedroom and said she was going to the mall with her boyfriend.

"In his car?" Carla asked. "Are you sure you should?"

"The mall is ten miles away. There's no other way, Carla." Kendra put emphasis on Carla's name like it was an insult and an annoyance to say it.

"Did your mother tell you about boys and all that stuff?"

"Sex?" Kendra asked. "My mother told me about sex. She didn't know as much as you, but she got the point across. You don't have to worry about playing mother to me."

"I'm not trying to take your mother's place."

Kendra squared off with Carla and said, "Let's see. You sleep on my mother's side of the bed. You live in my mother's house. You married my father. Doesn't it sound like you want to replace her?"

"I'm trying to be your friend."

"You're too old to be my friend," she said and walked out of the kitchen.

Carla looked out at Kim and George, so happy together. Kendra slammed the front door.

Carla went to her bedroom and found Abby's phone number. *I'm gonna go where I'm appreciated*, she thought.

❦   ❦   ❦

Jake Hersh walked around the now-empty Babes Go-Go with his cousin Eli, the bartender, before opening Monday morning. "That dancer had stab wounds all over her arms and chest," Jake said. "The newspaper said the manager had stabs in his head and chest. Whoever killed them is very strong."

"Do you think it's a guy? They sound related, like someone disliked them both. I read in a paper that police are looking into both of their backgrounds to see if they were having affairs," Eli said.

"You'll probably see a lot more rumors in the papers," Jake said. "I've been reading every article on this. I spent hours on the Internet. I know there will be more police around."

"I hope they catch him," Eli said. "The dancers don't like cops around here. They're not sure about you. I mean a security guard is a good idea, but there are all kinds of people here." Eli walked behind the bar. "We're having some big blowout on Friday. Rita doesn't want to handle all the dancer stuff without a new bar manager."

Jake sat on a stool. "Watch yourself," he said. "With all the heat on now, the police will be around looking for prostitution. You might want to tell the dancers not to get too involved with their customers."

"So you gonna do the security here?"

"I guess so," Jake replied. "When the owners hired the security company, I jumped at the chance to guard here. We'll have a chance to catch up on things, Cuz. I worked for twenty years hoping I could be involved in something better than guarding empty buildings and parking lots."

"You don't know what this place is like," Eli said.

"I've been in worse places," Jake said. "When I screwed up guarding that one bank, they sent me to all kinds of places. Strippers are no big deal."

"They're not strippers. They're erotic entertainers. The customers are worse."

Abby walked into the Babe's Go-Go Bar at two in the afternoon with Carla behind her. They weren't there to dance. They didn't have on makeup or have their hair done up. The place was empty—no dancers or customers. Eli was at the bar, so Abby asked him if Rita was around.

"She'll be in later," he said. "What do you want?"

"My friend here wants a spot on stage," Abby said. "I want to see if Rita can help."

"I don't know," Eli said. "The company has a new manager coming. The last guy got scared and quit. I don't know what he's going to do."

Abby stepped away from Carla. "This new guy can't be as bad as the one at West was. She's not the type to suck a manager off for a spot."

Eli snorted. "Well then, just like you, she'll be dancing at eleven in the morning for a drunk with no money."

"She only wants one dance. She's ignored at home," Abby explained. "Put her on stage in the middle of the afternoon on Thursday to try her out."

"Do you know how embarrassing it would be to the new manager if she comes out and gets stage fright? I think it would be funny. They're going to make her audition."

"That's why I think the afternoon is the best idea. I'll dance with her. She gets stage fright, I can cover it," Abby said.

"I'll leave a message for Rita." He looked past Abby at Carla. "I'll be looking forward to seeing her."

"Good," Abby said. She turned away and motioned for Carla to leave in front of her. "You're on," she said, when they got outside. "You sure about this? Your husband won't mind?"

"No," Carla said. "This is what we need. It's what I need. I'm not ready to be mother to two girls, one of whom is almost my age."

"I'll see you tomorrow for practice at your place." Abby watched Carla drive off before she got in her car. "She has no idea."

Abby went to Mark's place after setting up Carla's spot at Babes Go-Go. It was four o'clock, so she knew he would be home from work. Her blouse was pressed, her jeans clean, and her black boots had the shine of being new—everything in good shape. She knocked at the door.

"Yeah?" he said, opening the door in old shorts and a faded T-shirt. "Come on in," he said. "I'm gonna run to the bedroom and change clothes again because I didn't expect you. You can grab a seat on the couch." He was down the hall before he finished speaking.

She stood at the windows and stared at the cloudless blue sky. Five boys, probably sixteen or seventeen years old, huddled by some older cars to smoke cigarettes while their girlfriends played lookout.

"I've got some juice in the fridge," Mark said, when he entered the room tucking a button-down shirt in his trousers. "It's murder to drive around all day. I just sit and sweat. Those supermarkets are cool, but man, when I go back outside, it kills me. So when I got home, I threw the air conditioner on."

He went to the kitchen and got juice out of the fridge. "I thought you were busy today dancing. You left in a rush yesterday."

"Yeah, but there's no dancing till later."

Mark came back with two filled glasses. She took one and saw his answering machine.

"The message light is beeping," she said.

"It's my mother," Mark said. "She calls when I don't. I usually call every four or five days, but I hadn't called in a week. She's going to tell me how my brother always calls. If he can't call, his wife does. Then she'll tell me about my sister-in-law, Denise. Denise is trying to get pregnant. We have this conversation every few weeks. I'm going to call later and suffer through it."

"You talk to your brother a lot?"

"Once in awhile—he rubs his happy marriage in my face. I never met anyone I wanted to marry. It seems important to my mother that both of us get married and have kids. Does your mother give you the same thing?"

Abby sipped her juice. "I haven't talked to my mother in a long time. We had this big argument." She leaned back on the couch and ran her fingers through her hair. "Sometimes I wish I could talk to her again, but she doesn't want to see me."

He put his hand on her knee. "Do you have any other family?"

"I don't have anyone. I have friends in Vegas, but that's far from here. I'm exploring life here now. I feel like exploring."

"I gave you all my money at the bar." He moved a piece of hair from her eye. "It was worth it, but I'm broke tonight."

She looked around his place. There were pictures and furniture, like a coffee table, that she didn't have. "I'd rather be here. This is a nice place. I wish I had this. My place is tiny. I lived with a guy in Las Vegas, and I don't ever want to see him again. But I do miss living with someone."

"Want to move in?" Mark asked, before his brain had a chance to realize what his mouth was saying.

"Sure," she answered before she thought.

"I have to get a key," he said. He stood up, confused. His mouth was wide open, and he didn't know which way to turn. "I have to get it in the kitchen. I have spares as a safety measure."

He went to the kitchen asking himself what kind of idiot he was. He paced around trying to figure how to retract the offer, but he couldn't think of a way. She was alone on the couch, alone in every sense of the word, except when she was with him. He grabbed the key off a key holder in a drawer. The sunlight reflected off the silver metal. He took a deep breath and palmed it.

"Couldn't find a key?" she asked, like she knew he wasn't going to get one. "I understand if you don't have one today."

He showed her the key and let it drop from his hand into hers. She closed her hand around it and held it so tight that her knuckles turned white.

"Thank you," she said. "I can move most of my stuff in by the end of the week." She held up her fist with the key in it.

"Good," he said, with no enthusiasm. She looked at him trying to read his response. "Good" made her feel secure. They kissed, as his fingers raked through her hair.

"I was scared of moving too fast, but this feels so right," she said, hugging him. She saw deadbolts on the door for which she didn't have a key. "You can't use your deadbolt unless you want to keep me out."

He smiled, because he thought he should. "Of course I won't lock the deadbolt. Do you want dinner or anything?"

"I have to dance tonight, so I don't have time." She walked to the kitchen and saw that the cabinets were mostly empty, except for some canned Italian foods and Dewey's Donuts. Mark owned two pots and a frying pan. His stove was sticky with grease. "I'm going to clean this place up, too. You'll see. I don't cook much, but we'll be great roommates." She kissed him and left for work.

Mark went back to his couch and wondered what he had just done.

Abby threw boxes of clothes in the trunk of her car the next day and drove to Carla's house. She had to reread the directions when she got to Carla's street. It couldn't be right. Carla lived in a new development where each house was more elaborate than the next. One had a three-car garage. The next had a four-car garage. One had a huge front lawn and the next house had a bigger one. Statues adorned the lawns, and wide walkways and looped driveways framed the houses. Abby had driven through forty minutes of traffic and red lights to this area that she couldn't believe existed.

Carla's three-story house had a driveway that stretched for a quarter of a mile. The iron gates at the street were open. Abby parked in front of the four-car garage and climbed two flights of stairs to get to the front door.

"I see how you keep in shape," Abby huffed when she saw Carla at the doorway.

The hardwood parlor floor was so shiny that Abby saw her reflection. Carla led her to the kitchen, where paintings of the seashore done by local artists lined the walls.

"Wanna drink?" Carla asked. She walked around the ten-burner stove on an island in the middle of the floor. "You can sit at the table."

Abby sat at the breakfast table, which was big enough to seat six people. She could see the in-ground pool in the back. "It's OK. I'm ready to work."

"I have a workout room on the third floor," Carla said. "I could show you that I can do a split." Carla led Abby out of the kitchen.

Abby didn't say anything as she walked the halls lined with paintings and wall-to-wall carpet. The carpeted stairs felt like cushions under her feet. Carla had a wood dance floor set up in the workout room. There were shiny mats on the floor and bars on the mirrored walls to assist in stretching. A sit-up board, a stationary bike, and a running machine filled one side of the room. There was no dust. The room smelled like roses, not sweat. Peppy dance music from the 1990s played over the speakers attached to the ceiling.

"OK, I can show you," Carla said, emerging from the back room after changing from her shorts and tank top to spandex. She ran to the center of the room and spread her legs. Her white socks slid along the mat until her legs were fully apart. "Ta-da," she yelled. "What's the next thing I should do?"

Abby was still fascinated by the room and needed a second to think again. "Close your legs and roll up. You have to have a good smile when you do that. People know it's tough to do a split, but you have to look happy to do it."

"It's not." Carla closed her legs and rolled onto her back, where she got stuck. "I can't move," she said. Abby pushed her over.

"I need to work on that," Carla said. "Cheerleading stopped a few years ago."

"Why don't you shake your hips? They like it when you stand there and move your hips." Abby stood behind Carla and rocked Carla's hips in time with hers. "You just move slowly. It's sexier. You're really getting this," Abby said. She stepped back from Carla, who twirled and laughed.

Abby went to the stereo and shut off the music. "You've got a lot of it already. It's not like there's a lot to do, and you've got the idea."

"Well, I have time to practice. I bought some strip dance videos, and I practice with them. My younger daughter is in summer camp all day, and the older one spends her days with friends, so I'm usually alone."

"You have all of this," Abby said, pointing around the room. "I've never been in a house like this. There are gates at your driveway. Why do you want to go to a dark, beer-soaked bar and take off your clothes for a bunch of drunks?"

"I'm twenty-six, and I have two teenage daughters. I was a teenager yesterday. Don't get me wrong. I love them both. My husband loves me. We used to do things before work and stuff. Now he doesn't pay attention to me. I'm just a mother to his kids. I'm still a young woman. I want someone to look at me and think, 'Wow, is she hot!' I see you dancers on stage and the way people look at you. They pay you just to be near them. They watch every move you make. They fantasize about you. You're like goddesses or dream girls to them. I want that feeling."

"Why did you get married?"

"I love my husband. We used to spend so much time together. We used to travel. We used to talk. We used to drive far away just to make love. He still listens to me, I think. He asks my opinion on stuff. I know I'm important to him. But he doesn't reach for me in bed just to touch me." She paused and sighed. "He used to do those things."

"Why don't you get a divorce?"

Carla laughed. "I'd miss Kim. And I know one night he'll realize that he hasn't touched me in a long time, and he'll be that sweet guy again. When he does, it will be wild. Don't you love it when he remembers that he forgot you? The guilt gets to him, and he goes crazy trying to make it up to you."

"I wouldn't know," Abby said. "I never met anyone who gave a shit. Maybe one."

"You never married?"

Abby laughed. "I never saw any point in it. The whole ceremony, reception, and dress thing just aren't me. I can't understand married people. My parents are still married, and they seem bored. I really can't figure out why a married woman, who has all this wants a part of my life. You've got the life. There are some married dancers, but most of them are there for fucked-up reasons."

Carla sat on the floor with her legs crossed in front of her. "What kind of reasons?"

"Husband has no money. Married a guy who got turned on by erotic dancing. Likes swingers. Some just marry guys who don't give a shit."

"This is different," Carla said. "What do I wear on stage?"

"Go to the lingerie store and get yourself a teddy and a garter. A lot of guys like go-go boots, but just as many like pumps."

"Where do I get those capes you wear?"

Abby shook her head. "I make the capes for me. That's my trademark. Don't get crazy about this. You might get up there and get stage fright. Let's just take this one night at a time."

"Yeah," she said with a smile. "This might only be for one night."

"You know a lot of women dance for the tips. They need the money. You don't."

"I'm doing it for fun," Carla said.

Abby knew there was no way she was going to understand Carla's motivation, so she said it was time for her to go. Abby passed statues and paintings by the stairs. Shiny door handles were on the doors. The grass was perfect. Every blade was the same height.

Abby couldn't drive her car fast enough out of there. She went to her place and packed things to take to Mark's. By the time she was ready to go, her car was loaded with plastic bags and boxes of clothes. She got to Mark's door and stared at the entrance before taking a deep breath and putting the key into the lock. It fit.

This place is too neat, she thought when she got inside. The bed was made. The rug was vacuumed. The dishes were put away. She was never that clean.

At the end of the day, Mark drove to the depot for more stock. He was exhausted and had a difficult time staying awake. As he walked around the inventory docks half asleep, a couple of drivers asked him if something was wrong.

"I'm getting a roommate," Mark told them. "She'd freak if the place looked like it normally does. I stayed up late to clean. I'm trying to be on my best behavior."

"What's the big deal about a roommate?" one driver asked. Then he realized what Mark had said. "How did you get a woman roommate?"

"I'm not talking about it," Mark said. "She's my girlfriend. My girlfriend is moving in."

Chapter 10

Mark opened the door to his house at five PM. There were plastic bags next to the television and new cups in his sink. Clothes on hangers draped across the couch. He tripped over a paper bag full of socks in the hallway. He picked it up and brought it to the bedroom. He had cleaned out a drawer for Abby's things, so he dumped the socks in there.

Then he noticed a note taped to the side of the television.

> Mark,
>
> I had to go to work early tonight. I don't know if I'll see you when I get back later.
>
> Abby

A knock at the door startled him. It was Sue, ready to go out for the night. Her hair was done, and her face was made up. Her high heels clicked on the sidewalk when she shifted from foot to foot.

"What's with the garbage bags?" she asked. "I can see them behind you."

"It's Abby's stuff," Mark answered. "She's moving in. I had to work today so I couldn't help."

Sue looked beyond Mark at the full scope of bags in the room. "She's moving in. Isn't this quick? All those bags ain't 'moving in'—she's in. She's moved in. What kind of game is she playing with you? How can you not see that this is quick?"

"We hit it off," he said. "I invited her."

"Mark. You hit it off. Is your dick doing the thinking for you?"

"Is my dick doing the thinking," he repeated in shock. "What kind of question is that? I really like her."

"You like her? That's all you can say? Isn't this a big step for someone you like? Don't you think you should move in together when it's more permanent?"

"This is permanent."

"It's a few weeks."

Mark gritted his teeth. "This is permanent. This is the most permanent relationship I've had since the engagement. I haven't had a lot of women since then. She's really into me. I like her."

Sue pointed at him like she was going to say "gotcha." "You said 'like' again. Do you love her?"

"I don't know." Mark shrugged. "I don't know what love is."

"What does that mean?"

"I don't use that word. I drive a truck. Men who drive trucks don't use the word 'love.'"

"Oh brother," she said, rolling her eyes. "That is ridiculous. Being a truck driver has nothing to do with it. You don't love her. You were pushed into this."

"Sue," he said. He was annoyed, because maybe she was right. But he wasn't going to tell her that. "She's moving in. This can work out."

"I have to go. I was going to see if you wanted to go out, too, but it looks like you'll be busy trying to find out what love is."

"Thank you for the sarcasm, Sue," he yelled, as she walked away from the door.

As the night progressed, Mark brought bags into the bedroom. When he went to bed, he tried to stay on one side so Abby would be comfortable when she got home. The three AM alarm buzzed, and he rolled over to see the other side of the bed empty. He called out for Abby, until he saw her asleep on the couch. "Abby," he whispered, as he cradled her and carried her to bed. She was light in his arms, which wrapped almost around her. The heavy stench of stale perfume made his eyes water as he carried her down the hallway. He put her on the covers and went to the bathroom to put on his uniform. Her travel bag was open by the front door. It was tempting to see what she carried around at night, but he went past it.

The parking lot at Iggy's was empty when Mark got there. The store was ransacked. Magazines were on the floor. Soda cans rolled around his feet when he walked.

"Anyone around?" Mark yelled.

The register was open, but there was no cashier. The doughnut stand was on the floor. Mark bent over to pick up the stand and saw dirty sneakers in front of him. There was a sudden sharp pain to his head. He fell to the floor and saw more sneakers. Mark rolled out of the way and swung his arms. He connected with one guy's leg and sent him to the floor. Two other guys tried to grab him, but Mark swung until everything went blurry. The guys held him and hit him until he didn't move.

"Hey, Mark," Smitty yelled when he entered the store. "What the hell?"

The manager stumbled from the back room covered in blood. "Dude," Smitty yelled. "What happened?"

"These guys came in and trashed the place. They wanted me to open the safe. I don't know the combination. Only the day manager knows it. I tried to tell them. They hit me again and again. The Dewey's guy came. I thought they would leave, but they jumped him. They rammed my face into the front of the safe."

"Where's the Dewey's guy?" Smitty saw a pile of boxes on the floor and legs near them. There was Mark. He was slumped in an aisle, like he had tried to crawl away. Smitty yelled for the manager to call the police. "Mark, wake up," Smitty hollered.

🍁   🍁   🍁

Abby felt the sunlight on her face at eight AM. She sat up, looked around the room, and noticed her bags at the foot of the bed. She looked around the room to find her socks in a dresser drawer, and she noticed that Mark had cleared out part of his closet for her. She lifted a bag of shirts and dumped them into an open drawer. As she pulled a pair of pants from another bag, the phone rang.

"Where the hell is the phone? Keep ringing," she said aloud, as she ran circles around the room trying to follow the sound. She pushed a bag away from the door and tripped over another bag but still couldn't find the phone. It was on the floor next to the bed.

She listened to the guy at the other end of the line for a minute. "I don't know any 'Smitty,'" she interrupted.

"Mark gave me this number," Smitty said. "He told me to call you. They just took Mark to the hospital."

"The hospital," she screeched. "What for?"

"It's just better you go. They're taking him to Shore Care on Route Nine. Do you know where it is?"

"No."

There was silence. Abby bit her lip waiting for the guy to say something.

"I don't know where you live, so I can't give you directions," he finally said. "You could call the hospital."

Abby called and got the directions. It was luck that there was light traffic on the main roads. She sped to the hospital parking lot and ran for the building. People in wheelchairs and a woman on crutches got in her way, but she maneuvered around them. When she got to the nurse's station, a nurse asked Mark's last name. Abby drew a blank.

"I know it." She slapped her forehead. "I'm just nervous. I had to call for directions. I don't know where I am. I know he told me what it is. I know it."

"Abby?" Mark called, wobbling out into the hallway with a bandage wrapped around the top of his head. He also had a black eye and a bandage over his nose.

"You're all right," she said, rushing to hug him.

"No, don't," Mark yelled. "I'm in pain. But I'm really calm after those pills the doctor gave me," he added with a smile.

"You together?" the nurse asked.

"Yeah, she's my roommate," Mark wheezed. "My ribs really hurt when I talk."

"She couldn't remember your name, Mr. Winston," the nurse told him.

"I knew it," Abby said.

"How did you know?" Mark asked.

"You told me."

"No, not my name. How did you know I was here?"

"Some guy named Smitty called. He told me to get here. That's all he knew."

"I told Smitty to call? It was such a blur. I went to Iggy's at my normal time. I guess it was being robbed. I could've got 'em, but they sneak attacked me."

"How many were there?" Abby asked.

"Loads. They jumped me from behind so I couldn't identify them. They're lucky."

"Will you be all right?"

"I better be. I have to drive tomorrow. The company has managers who will help out the independent people like me when we can't drive, so they're getting me through today. I have to go back to work tomorrow."

"You're whole head is bandaged. You can't work. I'm taking you home, and you're staying still. I'll take care of you tonight."

"You have to stay in bed with me to stop me from leaving," he joked. The nurse behind them rolled her eyes, and then helped Mark complete the paperwork for his release. He declined a wheelchair, and instead walked out of the hospital leaning on Abby.

When they got to Abby's car, he leaned on the side of the car while she unlocked the doors. The inside of the car was clean and empty—no fast food bags, nothing hanging from the mirror; it was like no one ever used it.

"How come you didn't sleep in the bed last night?" Mark asked after they got in the car.

"I was scared," Abby answered. "A few days ago I was just Abby. I went to work and came home alone. I left a bad relationship not that long ago, and now I'm living with a guy. We're mixing laundry."

"Is that a woman thing?"

"I heard your neighbor. We're not exactly young kids rushing into something. We're adults. We know how to take things slowly, but we're not. It hit me yesterday how fast things were moving. I need to get to know you better." She started the car. "I moved out of my place, so I'm staying at your house, but I need to slow it down."

Mark closed the door to the car but couldn't get the seatbelt around his chest. He held it across his lap in case any police drove by. Once they got in the house, Mark fell to the couch and turned on the television. Abby asked if he wanted anything from the kitchen, but Mark said he was fine.

"Shouldn't you sleep or something?" Abby asked.

"I can't," he answered. "There has to be something on TV."

She grabbed the remote control from him and told him that TV was off-limits. He should sleep.

"I'm wide awake. The pills are wearing off and I can't close my eyes. I should've got those guys."

Abby sat by his side. "I know. You're pretty strong. I have no doubt you would've hurt them." She continued to talk while Mark faded in and out without her noticing. She moved onto the floor in front of the couch talking about her favorite color, her childhood toys, and seasons in Rhode Island.

"I love the movie *The Gold Rush*. It's an old Charlie Chaplin movie," she said. "It's a silent film, but it's easy to follow his actions and expressions. It's like a class on body movement. In my work, body movement means a lot."

"Never saw it," Mark said.

The phone rang, and Abby answered. She didn't say who the caller was, but just said "yes" and "maybe" until she hung up.

"It was a manager from Dewey's," she told him. "They're having a mandatory meeting tomorrow, but you can't go like this."

"I'm fine," Mark insisted. "It takes more than a few guys to keep me down. I have to know what's going on with the merger."

"You can't drive," she scolded. "Your head is bandaged. You can't see to the side. Not to mention the pain killers they gave you."

He thought for a second and looked Abby up and down. "You drive," he said. "The truck's an automatic. I'll do the lifting and stuff, and you drive the truck. It could be a team effort."

"Can't we just take a car?" she asked.

"There are hundreds of boxes to take to stores."

She was nervous about the idea but agreed. Mark fell asleep at eight o'clock aided by the medications. Abby stayed awake till midnight after staring at him for hours. She never had to nurse someone, so she was nervous about forgetting something or neglecting something. The alarm went off at three in the morning, which woke them both. She fought to stay in bed, but Mark nudged her. He gave her one of his Dewey's caps to wear. They figured she could get away with a pair of jeans and a top since she wasn't actually handling the merchandise.

He gave directions to the depot while she drove the car. The truck was already loaded by the driver the day before so they just had to go. She got behind the wheel of the truck at the depot. It took her a while to get used to driving a truck. She ran over a curb going out of the parking lot and jumped another curb making a right turn. Several times she crossed the centerline.

Mark jumped out of the truck at the first stop and yelled, "Thank God, we're alive. Ab, I'm going inside. You want to follow me in?"

"No, I'm going to pout, because you don't like my driving."
"I was kidding. It's fine. Speaking of fine, that cap looks good on you."
"Thank you. And 'Ab' is not a nickname."
"Should I call you Baby?'
"No," she yelled, offended.
"Why the yelling?" He grabbed an empty tray from the back of the truck.
"That's a dancer name. I'm not dancing."
"Who's this?" asked a balding, overweight receiver at the supermarket loading dock.
"My little elf. Keep your eyes off," Mark snarled. He grabbed Abby's hand as they walked to the supermarket floor. "That guy is going to get fired one of these days for the way he watches the women here and the things he says on that loading dock. Gotta be tough with him." He looked at the dates on doughnut boxes and threw two boxes on the empty tray. "You don't have a shortened name?"
"Abby is short for Abigail. How much shorter does it need to be?"
"I don't know. It sounded long."
"It's two syllables."
"Two wha?"
"Exactly. You need to broaden your horizons. Abby is just fine," she said.
They finished the supermarket before a rush of other drivers crowded in. By the time they'd made two more stops, Abby was maneuvering the truck with ease, and Mark was able to work the stock computer. At each stop, he carried stock in and out of stores without feeling lightheaded. Iggy's was cleaned up when they got there. No signs of yesterday's robbery were obvious. Smitty was there. He was surprised to see Mark working, until Mark explained the mandatory meeting later and told him Abby was helping.
"I was the person you talked to yesterday," she said, offering her dirty hand to Smitty. "How'd I get so dirty?"
"It's the truck," Mark explained. "There's parking lot dust and depot dirt … at least your hands are still soft."
"Not like us," Smitty added.
Jennifer drove in with her coffee cup from another store and her wrinkled uniform. She ignored everyone and went straight to her deli section. There was a different register person this morning. Smitty heard rumors about the register person during the robbery needing therapy, both physical and mental. Jennifer could hear Smitty and Mark, but she stayed silent as Mark talked about the hospital. Mark took his inventory count and went out to the truck.

Abby went to the coffeepots near the deli section. As Abby poured coffee, she and Jennifer made eye contact. Abby wasn't sure if that was the girl Mark had pined for, but she felt uneasy.

"Were you here yesterday?" Abby asked her. "When that robbery happened?"

"No." Jennifer turned and got a box of lettuce. "They told me about it. Is he OK?" she nodded at the doughnut stand.

"He's fine … or … he will be," Abby said. "He told me a lot about this place. Do you know Jennifer?"

Jennifer stopped moving. "That's me. Why?"

"Oh, nothing," Abby said. She poured milk in her coffee and stirred. "Mark told me he used to talk to you all the time. Where are my manners?" She put her coffee stirrer down and offered her hand. "I'm Abby. Mark and I … well, you know."

Jennifer raised her hands to show her plastic gloves. "I can't. It's nice to meet you, though. I really have to get busy making these sandwiches for the coolers."

Abby turned and went outside where Mark was putting stale products on a rack inside the truck. "Is that the Jennifer you told me about when we first met at the bar?" Abby asked.

"Yeah." Mark stopped. "That was the girl, but that's long over. She's getting married."

"She's cute." Abby straightened her back and looked back at the store. "She's not friendly. I would've thought that someone you spent so much time hitting on would've cared more about the robbery. Maybe even wanted see the new woman in your life. Nothing."

"I guess she just didn't want to talk." He put a box on a rack and stopped. "That's not why you agreed to help is it?"

Abby pointed her finger inches from his nose and yelled at him. "I'm helping you, because you mean a lot to me. I don't care about some girl in a convenience store." She went to the driver's seat and exhaled. "I'm helping you because I love you."

"You love me?" he repeated, surprised. "I love you, too," he said. After the words were out, he realized what he said and how big that announcement was. "I'm sorry for giving you shit."

She rubbed her nose. "Don't worry about it. How do you feel?"

"I'm not dizzy or anything."

It took longer than normal to finish the route, but they got back to the depot in time for the meeting. He went into the meeting, and she went to her car to wait. Mark saw a short man in a suit standing at the front of the tired and restless drivers.

"I'm the vice president of Dewey's Donuts," the man said. "Every one of you knows that negotiations are going on for a merger. When the merger goes through, all of you will still have routes to do and products to deliver. You might even have more products to deliver. That means more money to you. Isn't that what we all want? More money?"

The drivers clapped and looked relieved. That was the important part, Mark thought, so he headed out to his car. When he and Abby got home, they took separate showers. Abby saw a message light on his answering machine when she got out of the shower, but Mark said he'd already listened to it while she was in the shower.

"It was my mother. I hadn't called in three days. She felt the need to remind me of that. I didn't call her back because I don't want to tell her about the robbery and the hospital. She'd only complain about the route and the terrible areas I deliver to. She would tell me to be careful, and I'm sure I'd never hear the end of it. My brother wouldn't be so stupid as to go into a destroyed store like that, she'd say. My brother would've stopped the robbery, she'd tell me."

"I have a feeling you're tougher on yourself than she is. No one can be like that."

"Why don't we talk about your mother?" Mark asked.

Abby stared at herself in the mirror. People said she had her mother's eyes. "It's not a happy story," she began. "My mother wants nothing to do with me. When I was sixteen, I was never popular or anything. I usually sat in class and got passable grades. I just kept quiet, waiting to get out of there. This guy and I went out a few times. I didn't know anything about birth control. A month into the relationship, I got pregnant."

Abby frowned. She noticed how her lip drooped like her father's. "You know what happens in those cases. I was labeled a slut, someone who sleeps around. He was the first guy I ever did it with." She waited for Mark to say something, but Mark was quiet. He got out of the shower and sat on the bed. "He had a scholarship waiting for him. Everyone told him to dump the just-turned-sixteen-year-old slut. What did my mother do? She called me a slut, too, and threw me out. I was four months pregnant.

"So, I did what any normal, troubled sixteen-year-old with no money would do. I got stoned. I walked on the ledge at the George M. Cohan Park and fell off. I ruptured something and lost the baby." She turned from the mirror and went to the closet, still wrapped in a towel. "I can't ever have another. It crushed everything involved with reproduction. My uterus is torn and all kinds of stuff."

She stopped when she felt Mark touch her shoulder from behind. "I went back to my mother and told her I wasn't pregnant. She slammed the door on me. My father was afraid of my mother, so he didn't do anything. My little brother was twelve at the time. When he got into high school, the kids in school still talked about his slutty sister. Even though I moved out of Rhode Island, they still talked about me. I was in a long line of girls that piece of shit had sex with, but somehow I was the slut. I was stupid enough to get pregnant. Just me. I was the stupid one."

She dropped her towel and put on shorts and a loose T-shirt. Mark stood behind her, not saying anything. She smiled at him, but there was sorrow in her eyes. "I don't need them," she said. "I mean, I might have wanted a baby, but there's nothing I can do about it." She sighed and walked past Mark to get something to tie her hair with. "That's why I got so nervous when something happened to you. You're all I've got."

Mark watched her rub her eyes. He looked at her bags still on the floor. "You're all I've got, too. I have friends, but no one else would've driven for me today." She sat on the bed exhausted. He could see boys on bicycles with their girlfriends outside his window. "Do you want to get married?" he asked.

"What?"

"I mean, we know a lot about each other," Mark said. "I know it's only been about three weeks, but we had nothing before. We have each other now. It only takes a few dollars at town hall and waiting a week. We can make it official."

"OK," she said, practically in a trance.

Chapter 11

Carla's head was in the oven to check on a pot roast when she heard Kim walk in the front door. She knew it was Kim from the sounds of the door slamming and the backpack hitting the floor near the stairs. Kendra never used a backpack.

"Carla, I want to go back to school," Kim said. "We rode horses today in summer camp, and my butt hurts. I hate horses."

"It can't be that bad," Carla said. "I never rode a horse till I met your father. I wish I had ridden horses when I was your age."

"What did you do when you were my age?"

"Nothing really. We used to go to movies or arcades or watch television. I didn't have an exciting life until high school. After that, I did a year of college and worked a lot."

"What's so boring about that?"

Carla leaned against a counter. "Nothing. Every once in awhile I think I missed out on things, but not all the time."

"What things did you miss?" Kim asked. She took a cookie from a jar and sat on a stool at the kitchen counter.

"Well my friends did a lot of things that I'll tell you about when you're older. I missed taking chances."

Kim put down the cookie. "Do you want to be married?"

Carla froze. "Of course, I want to be married." She waved her hand at Kim. "Silly. There are all new chances and things. When I say I missed things, I mean I *missed out*, but I don't *miss* them. Do you follow?"

Kim shook her head.

Carla wondered how this child had figured out her feelings, but she couldn't let on. "You'll understand when you're older."

"Adults always say that," Kim moaned. She got off the stool and went to her backpack. Carla was relieved to get out of that.

At six o'clock, Carla pulled four dishes out of the cabinet and saw George's car pulling close to the house. She trembled at the thought of having to tell George she wouldn't be home tomorrow. He'd want specifics on where she was going and what she was doing. Kendra was in the car with George and was following him into the house. She would only add to the tension.

Carla and George sat at different ends of the table with Kendra and Kim at the sides. Kendra sat closer to her father, while Kim sat closer to Carla.

"I'm going out with my friend Abby tomorrow afternoon," Carla announced. "I'm going to help her move some things."

"Our mother was always home," Kendra snarled, as she stabbed into a pile of string beans with her fork.

"I'm home nearly every day," Carla said. "My friend wants to see me. I really don't have to explain that to you."

"Calm down," George interjected. "It's fine if you're going to be late. I understand. Kendra, it's OK."

Kendra dropped her fork on her plate and left the table. Carla put her fork down and crossed her arms.

"I don't know what to do with her," Carla said. "I'm trying. You can see that."

"She's not used to you being part of the family," George said. "She's known you for two years. She's known her mother her whole life. She just needs time." George scooped up mashed potatoes as if everything were normal.

"She wants to knock me for everything I do," Carla persisted. "I can't win with her. I don't care if she doesn't want to be friends. For God's sake, can't she be civil?"

"That was civil," George replied. "She's a teenager. Weren't you a little rough with your parents at that age?"

"Not like that," Carla said through gritted teeth. She turned and saw Kim sitting with her head down and her arms at her side. It looked like she wanted to disappear from the scene. "It's fine, Kim. The argument is over." Carla watched George continue eating.

❦ ❦ ❦

Carla stepped out of the bathroom in an oversized T-shirt. "George," she said in a singsong voice, "the girls are asleep. Remember that night in Atlantic City. We haven't had sex in a long time. Look," she said, as she took off the T-shirt. She covered her breasts with her forearms. "Do you want to kiss one? Don't you want to squeeze me?" She shuffled across the room to the edge of the bed. "Come on, touch me," she whispered.

George sat up in bed and froze. "I think I hear the girls. The kids are awake. In two weeks they're going to stay with their mother. We can be alone all over the house."

"I'm tired of waiting." She opened her arms and leaned over George, putting her erect nipples inches from his face. He reached around and grabbed her. She lowered herself so they were eye-to-eye. His eyes wandered to the door.

"I think I hear them," he sighed. "Two weeks. The girls will be gone."

She stood up and grabbed her T-shirt. His rejection made her so furious that she got her head stuck in a sleeve and had to wrestle the shirt over her head. "This is bullshit. The walls are so thick, they wouldn't hear a thing." She walked out of the room and slammed the door behind her.

Kim's door was wide open, and her light was on. Kim was in bed with her face buried in her pillows. Carla crept in to pull a cover up, but Kim was still awake.

"You have day camp tomorrow. You have to go to sleep," Carla said, as she pulled a pillow from under Kim's head and fluffed it. "Why is this wet?"

"I, uh, drool at night," she lied. Her eyes were bloodshot, like she had been crying.

"I'm going to flip this over so your face doesn't stay wet. If you had a problem sleeping, you would tell me, right?" She ran her hand over the girl's face.

"Yes," she said, with a sniffle. "Are you my friend?"

"I hope so. Why do you ask?"

"I just want to understand what's going on. Everyone yells at dinner. Kendra and you fight. I don't want to lose another mom."

"You're not going to lose me. Now go to sleep."

She left Kim's room and walked past Kendra's. Her snoring could be heard from the hallway. When Carla got back to her room, George was sitting up in bed.

"They were awake. You were right. They're in bed now. Kim is face down in the pillows." She dropped on the bed and crossed her arms over her chest for a moment. "They won't hear us." She grabbed his hand. "I want you to touch me. I need you to remind me that you love me."

He pulled his hand back. "I have to work tomorrow. I told you before—two weeks."

"Don't you want me? Don't you desire me?" She straddled his legs. "I need you to touch me. I don't need you to work. Tell me that I'm the hottest woman on the planet. Show me how much you need me. I'll even stay home tomorrow."

"What's wrong with you?" he asked, annoyed. "Is sex the only way to tell you how I feel about you?"

She bowed her head, feeling a little ashamed, but stopped. "Yes. You need to fuck me. I need you to take me now. Let's go."

"The girls will wake up. I told you—two weeks. I'll leave you some money in the morning. Buy yourself something while you're out. Buy something tight that shows you off. You'll like that."

She got off him and fell on the bed. Kim's voice echoed inside her head: "I don't want to lose another mom." Carla closed her eyes and didn't move. She could feel George slide under the covers and try to sleep.

❦   ❦   ❦

Abby drove through the parking lot at Babes Go-Go the next day and saw Carla sitting in a Mercedes wearing sunglasses.

"New car?" Abby asked.

"No, it's one of George's." Carla made it sound like it was natural to have more than one car.

"Afraid to go in?" Abby asked. "I can see that you have your makeup on." She ran her finger over Carla's cheek, removing a streak of heavy makeup. "You think you can do it?"

"I'm a little afraid," Carla replied, "but I can do it." She got out of the car, grabbed her wheeled suitcase crammed with clothes, and walked with Abby to the door. She took a deep breath and followed Abby inside.

"We're ready today." Abby slapped the bar to get Eli's attention. Abby saw Rita and went to talk to her. Carla waited near the door for Abby to call her over. Rita pointed at Carla and laughed, but Abby pulled her hand down. Abby laughed and walked to Carla.

"Follow me," Abby said. "Things are tense here, with the murder and all, but business is business, and this place needs dancers. We're going to the locker room. We're lucky because there are only five people here. You can still back out."

Abby opened a wide locker in the back and told Carla, "See if you can get that big thing in a little thin locker. You have to keep your stuff locked. Sometimes dancers aren't the best people. A lot of them do this for drug money. They'll steal stuff right out of your hands." She took off her top and looked to Carla. "Did you buy an outfit?"

"Yeah," Carla answered. "It's bright pink. I think it will show up nice in the lights. I have this spandex skirt to walk out with. During the second song, I'll take it off, and I have this tiny stringy thing under it." She held up three orange strings tied together with a patch of cloth in front.

"That is very revealing. Are you sure?"

Carla laughed. "No. I don't know what's going to happen when I'm out there."

Rita stormed the locker room as Abby changed her bra and Carla lowered her denim pants. She looked over Carla's body like she was looking at a new car. She circled her and nodded. Carla didn't want to say anything. Once Carla's pants were pulled down, Rita inched closer to her.

"If you're going to work here, I have to make sure you're worth it," Rita said. "I manage the dancers. If you fuck up and fall off stage, I have to drive you to the hospital. If you slide down the pole and crack your pretty head on the floor, I have to drive you to the hospital." She twirled a piece of Carla's hair in her fingers. "Don't piss me off. I want to check out my dancers. Those guys don't like fat women. Raise your leg up to your head."

"I can't do that yet, but I can get my knee high."

"That doesn't tease 'em with the good stuff. Learn to do a standing split."

Abby stepped between them when Rita let go of Carla's hair. "Leave her alone. I'm here to watch her."

"Do you have a name?" Rita asked Carla.

"Carla."

"That's not much of a stage name."

"Do I need one?"

"You don't want these people to know your real name. You need something to get attention. Carla, huh?" She rubbed her arms and paced. "How about Cookie? What the hell, it's good for today." Rita wrote "Cookie" on a palm-sized notebook as she walked out of the locker room.

"She's pretty tough. I never met a woman with tattoos covering her arms," Carla said. Her toes curled in her shoes out of nervousness.

"Don't worry about her," Sunflower said from the back of the locker room. "She tried that crap on me, too. I've been dancing for years. You see people like her all the time. She's actually terrified of the owners, so she takes it out on us. What the hell—we need the money. What are we going to do?"

"What are you doing here during the day?" Abby asked.

"I went to West and it stunk. Rita told me that I had to re-earn my space." Sunflower looked at Carla's large, natural breasts. "Don't think you're coming here and taking my spot." She shrugged and left the locker room.

Outside the door, Sunflower said, "Hi, Rita. Seen the manager lately?"

Rita's hand shook. "Did you?"

"My song is on. I have to dance. You have a nice day," she said, with a smirk.

Abby put on her one-piece teddy with a sheer blue cape and sat on a bench to watch Carla struggle to fit a small bra on her heavy breasts. "You remember everything we did? You go through the first song on stage without taking tips, just teasing everyone."

"Then second song," Carla cut in, "I lift my skirt up to my hips and do a split. Then the skirt comes off. I spin a little, spank myself in front of some guy, give a few winks, and get my tips."

"Don't let them touch you for too long. Just go over, let him have a feel, and get out of there," Abby said. "Don't ask about lap dances. They don't do that here." Abby stared at the empty locker where Buffy used to keep her clothes. "You sure about this? You have two daughters and a husband."

"Yes, I want to do this. I told you. I need this." Carla took off her wedding ring and stuffed it in a small pocket on the side of her travel bag. She heard one of the songs she had picked out with Abby start. "I guess it's time." She smiled and relaxed her shoulders, but her eyes revealed her nervousness.

They opened the door and were greeted with a face full of beer scent. The stage was surrounded by men. Beers were lined up on the bar. Carla remembered the smell of stale beer and cigarettes from when she used to go clubbing with her friends. No one here drank Sex on the Beach or Long Island Iced Teas. Beer was sold in plastic cups or bottles.

Carla took baby steps to the bar with Abby behind her. She went to the brass pole and swung around, lowering herself to the stage. Men watched her spread her tanned legs to show off the triangular patch of cloth between her legs. She crawled and wiggled to the edge of the stage. The stale smells disappeared. She went to the brass pole again and flirted with some of the men. They all looked the same from where she stood. She giggled like this was fun for her.

George wasn't there bossing her around. Kendra wasn't yelling at her. The stage was littered with rolled up dollar bills. Fingers tapped wads of money on the bar. These people wanted to touch her, if only for a moment.

She forgot the routine and pranced and skipped around the stage. Abby tried to grab her and slow her down, but Carla was moving too fast. She lowered a bra strap and held her arms to her nipples, flirting with a balding man with a comb-over. She swayed her hips in circular motions and toyed with her bra.

"Just lean toward me," Abby said, as she grabbed Carla's head. "Guys go crazy when they think we're hot and kissing each other. How are you doing?"

"This is fun."

Abby let her go as soon as the second song began. Carla ran her fingers through her shiny dark hair to tease it out. Abby untied her cape and went to a man leaning over the bar.

"Hiya boys," Abby said to a man in a Harley-Davidson T-shirt and leather vest. She thrust her breasts at him and watched his pudgy fingers roll up a dollar. He toyed with it while Abby gyrated like she was having sex with the bar. He dropped the dollar into her cleavage and kept his hand there feeling the fullness of her breast.

Carla watched this as she let her skirt drop to her ankles. She twirled it on the floor with her foot and kicked it to the end of the stage. Her outfit was only strings and a little piece of cloth. She laughed out of nervousness. Abby could see men look past her to Carla, who was nearly naked.

An unshaven guy in a torn flannel shirt with a bandanna on his head and beer in his hands stood alone at the bar. Carla stepped off the stage and presented her breasts to him.

"Hi," she purred. "Have a good day?"

"It's all right. Nothing much."

She licked her lips without realizing it and squeezed her breasts together. "You been here long?"

"Just got here. I'm done with the roadwork on Route 66. That sun was brutal today. 'Bout you?"

"This isn't work. This is fun. Wanna see more?"

"Sure."

She twirled around, showing her behind to this total stranger. This wasn't someone she would ever date. She had chased money and flashy guys her whole life, but now she wanted this working man's approval. Her husband wasn't as important as this man's touch. It was so wrong to let him touch her, but his touch felt so strong.

"Sweet," he said rubbing a worn dollar on her chest. His fingers left a smudge of dirt on her soft skin. She grabbed his hand, not to move it away, but to hold it in hers.

Abby came between them and told her that the song was over, and they had to leave. Carla held his hand for a moment before she smiled and ran off to the back.

Abby hugged her in the locker room. "Good job. All those guys were focused on you. You didn't get scared. It went good."

"Did you see that guy in flannel? He was all dirty. I would never let a guy like him in my house, but I let him tip me. All those guys wanted me, and I chose him. He must feel great that he was singled out."

"The attention is something." Abby took off her shoes and rubbed her toes. "They'll trade a dollar for a second of our time. It does make you feel beautiful."

"I want to do it again." Carla took her top off and stood in the center of the locker room unafraid of her nudity. "Could you get me another chance?"

Abby's eyes widened. "I can see about that, but are you sure? What about your family?"

"They won't know. I want to do this again." She pulled her bag out of her locker. She was still topless when she put her hair up in a scrunchie. "I think I can do it alone, too—if that's OK with you."

"Yeah," Abby said. She finished changing and watched Carla procrastinate about getting dressed. Abby buttoned her blouse, while Carla sat on the bench massaging her breasts. Abby left the locker room and ran into Rita outside the door. Abby sighed and explained that Carla wanted another set sometime.

"With those big tits?" Rita asked. She seemed happy to hear the news. "If she keeps wearing that little string thing, I'll let her on. The commission I can make off her can get me another car." She took singles from Abby. "She's lucky the old manager at West is dead. He would've loved the ass on her."

"She's married."

"So what? He played with the married dancers. Do you think you can get her here Monday night three weeks from now?"

"I'll see. I don't know if she can do nights." Abby went into the locker room and found Carla talking to Sunflower. Both of them had their tops off.

"Your set is over. You can put your top on," Abby said. She stood between them looking at Carla like a parent would. "Rita wants you on Monday night in three weeks."

"I'll do it," Carla blurted.

"We have to go set it up," Abby said.

Carla dressed like a raid was coming. Her bra twisted when she put it on, but she didn't even straighten it until after her top was on. She let out a big sigh that she was ready to leave the locker room.

Sunflower stopped Abby. "I work Mondays, and I don't want to lose my time," she told her.

Abby shook her head and snorted. "You won't lose your spot."

Carla opened the windows to her car to get rid of the perfume smell. She searched the radio dial until she happened upon a song from her set. Passing drivers gave her nasty looks, because she had the radio up so loud. A red van pulled next to her when she was stopped at a red light. She blew the driver a kiss and laughed. He rolled up his window. She drove around town for an hour, just having a good time.

"She's finally home," Kendra said, when Carla got home about eight-thirty that night.

"Hello, everyone." Carla burst into the house, almost running. "Whew, what a long day," she said, passing Kendra and heading upstairs to her bedroom with her suitcase. She took off her clothes and stuffed them in the hamper, so George wouldn't notice. Carla grabbed a perfumed soap from the vanity under the sink and used it in the shower, as she danced and sang in the spray.

When her shower was over, she heard tapping at the door. She opened the door wrapped in a towel and saw Kim. "What's the matter, honey?"

"We didn't talk today."

"Oh, I know," Carla said, with real regret in her voice. "I really miss that, but it's getting late. How about you go to bed, and we'll talk twice as long tomorrow?"

Kim agreed. She stopped and asked Carla how come she had a suitcase with her.

"We did't have enough cardboard boxes for the stuff we were moving."

Kim accepted the answer and went to her room.

Carla sat on the bed and removed the towel. She grabbed her wedding ring out of her bag and put it on. There was a bottle of lotion on the nightstand next to the lamp. Carla grabbed the lotion and rubbed it on her arms. She couldn't hear anyone in the hallway, so she leaned back on the bed and let her hands glide over her body.

She could see the guy in flannel reaching out to touch her. His tar-caked fingers were long and solid. The back of his hand was course. His palm was callused. He was missing teeth, but it didn't matter. He was a solid man.

"Those stiff fingers," she moaned.

The heat of his hands went through her body. Her right leg curled on the bed while the left stretched out. She imagined his hands leaving mud and tar from the road on her clean body as he squeezed her.

I want to hold you close, she imagined him saying.

"Touch me again," she said aloud. She stretched her arm over to George's side of the bed. "Touch anything you want." The diamonds in her ring reflected light the way the club's strobe did. Her legs stretched out and curled. She slapped the bed trying to control her body. Her head turned and rolled while she imagined another's fingers on her.

"I'm alive," she moaned. "I'm alive."

The fingers went along her toes and up her legs. The room was silent except for her heartbeat. "George, touch me." She grabbed his pillow and bit the corner. "Your fingers," she screamed into it. "Your fingers make me alive." She hugged the pillow with every muscle in her arm before she relaxed.

"Your fingers," she huffed. Everything was silent. Her eyes were closed, and she was nervous about opening them and seeing George. The room was empty. She ran to the door and heard George downstairs with Kendra.

Carla wrapped the towel around herself and kissed the pillow.

Chapter 12

Abby brought Rita to Town Hall as a witness to the signing of her marriage license. Mark brought Smitty. The clerk responsible for the licenses said he'd never seen a sight like them in his thirty years on the job. Mark and Smitty were dusty and disheveled, still in uniforms reeking of gas and baked goods. Stray hairs poked out from Smitty's beard. Mark's two-day-old stubble was dark and grimy. Smitty had worn a hat all day, so his hair was matted down, and Mark's was windblown messy.

Rita wore faded, stretched slacks, a Babes West T-shirt, and sandals. Her toes were uneven and dirty, especially her big toe, which had a long, orange toenail. Her pinky toe looked like a stale corn chip. Her face had seen too many years of hard living, and her makeup didn't erase that.

Abby wore a sundress and shoes. She had on just the right touch of makeup, and her hair was perfect.

"So you're the guy?" Rita croaked when she saw Mark. Her shoulders were raised like she wanted to give him a "hello" punch on the arm. "You look familiar," she continued. "I've seen you before. Does Abby know all about you?"

"She knows a lot about me," he answered. Mark kept back from her and her fist.

"No, I've seen you before. Maybe with my dancers. I'm not sure." She turned away and read the marriage papers. "It looks legal," she told the clerk.

"What the hell was that about?" Smitty whispered to Mark.

"I don't know," Mark answered.

He and Abby signed the papers. They all left the building together but got into their separate cars. Rita watched Mark drive off. She read his license plate. She didn't want to tell Abby, but something didn't feel right.

❦   ❦   ❦

"I talked to Town Hall," Abby said three days later when Mark walked in the door after work on Friday. "They said we could be married by the middle of next week. I told them I would call them back to schedule it. I wanted you to know first."

"So call and tell them we'll be there whatever the time." He leaned against a wall near an air conditioner register. "I'm ready when you are."

"I'll call first thing Monday." She bounced off the couch and wrapped her arms around his sweaty chest and hugged him from behind. "Are you nervous?"

"Sometimes. I'm not nervous about you—I mean marriage. I've lived alone for so long now, and soon I'll have a wife. I'll be making plans with you instead of doing things spur of the moment. It's going to be a big change."

She moved around, still hugging him. Abby rested her head on his chest. "I've been helping this woman dance," she said. "She's twenty-six years old and bored with being married. Somehow dancing naked in front of strangers will make her fulfilled."

"And why are you helping?"

"If I didn't, someone else would. Rita would have her buck naked in some dive. The manager at Babes West would have slept with her—if he weren't dead. I had to help her. I thought she would back out of it."

Mark tried to see her face, but she looked down. "Did the manager ever try anything with you?" he asked.

Abby laughed. "He tried. I've done this before. I have a card from Vegas. Dancers have to be licensed out there. I'm purely business. That's why I wanted to talk her out of it. I thought she'd get embarrassed and run out." Abby sighed. "She likes it." She squeezed Mark tight till Mark had to separate her hands to stop her from re-injuring his ribs. "Even though her husband neglects her, Carla has someone. So many of these dancers look for someone to care about them, and they never find it. She called me this morning still talking about this guy in flannel who tipped her."

"Is she getting a divorce?"

"I thought it was just a phase. I don't know." Abby put her hands down at her sides. "I once asked Penn why I had to keep dancing. I thought he would get jealous or something. He said I had to bring in the money. He said that he couldn't find a job. Can you imagine that? Las Vegas. The whole place is jobs." She sighed. "I knew he threw my money around town. I let him do it."

She took a deep breath and stepped back. "I have to go to work. I'm getting out at one tonight. It's kind of nice that I'm getting out before closing on a Friday night. When I dance till close, I have to wait until all the registers are done and the bar is clean and the parking lot is empty. They say it's because of the killer out there."

She went to the hallway and turned around. "Mark, when I said that I let Penn throw my money away ... I won't let that happen again."

Mark walked to her, but stayed back. "I wouldn't waste anything—not your money or ours. I know we're not married yet and ... I just think that woman who's married ... maybe she shouldn't be dancing like that. I think she should only dance for her husband."

"You'd like that," she said. She turned for the bedroom with a smile on her face. "You liked that lap dance I bet." She grabbed her bag of outfits and shoes off the bed. She smiled at him because he was still standing in the same spot. His arms were straight down at his side. There was no attempt to stop her as she walked out the door. She saw him watch her from the windows and blew him a kiss.

"They're worried about the killer," he said. "They should be."

Sunflower was in the locker room fixing her bright pink leather bikini. She said hello to Abby, but didn't look her way. "I saw your friend last week. She's a pretty good dancer."

"Thanks," Abby said, as she put her bag on the bench. "I trained her myself. I thought she would get stage fright, but she pulled it off. I mean that literally too."

"She's married?" Sunflower waited for a response, but Abby had none. "She's getting another spot, too. I was almost married." She sighed. "It didn't work out. We had a boy, but the state took him away. It was this big drug thing that's nobody's business here." She waited for Abby to say something, but Abby was preoccupied with her clothes. "So what's your story?"

Abby told her about Penn. "We broke up, and now I'm engaged to this guy who owns his own business."

"That guy you were so excited to dance for?"

"Yeah. He wants me to stop dancing. I'm willing to do it. What's the future in this anyway? I'll get old and work afternoons. I could dance at a nicer place and make more money. Then I'd get old and work afternoons in a nice place." Abby placed her clothes on the bench. "I have a friend who made a porno, just so she could get better dancing gigs."

"Did it work?"

"I don't know. There's an adult bookstore around here. I'll have to see if they ever heard of her."

Sunflower heard her music play outside. "I have to work. If you leave, I can take your spot. I just don't want to lose my spot here."

Abby woke at nine o'clock Saturday morning. Mark was gone, but she couldn't bring herself to roll over to his side of the bed. The sun was too bright over there, anyway. She got up and went to the window to watch the people walking around the parking lot and the kids riding bikes. It looked cool out, so she threw on her running shorts and a T-shirt. She left the front door of the townhouse unlocked as she put on her sneakers sitting on the front sidewalk. The streets were clear when she stretched and jogged across to the parking lot.

Monty Dumont looked out his front window and watched this young brunette with a tanned face and tight, blue spandex shorts jog by. Her breasts, though held in a sports bra, bounced up and down in her oversized T-shirt. Her ponytail wagged like a young girl he once knew.

"What are you looking at, Monty?' Leslie Dumont asked.

"We have a new neighbor. I think she came out of that guy's house."

"She's young enough to be your granddaughter," Leslie laughed. "Stop staring before she gives you a heart attack—watching her bounce like that."

"I'm not watching her bounce," he scoffed. "I'm only sixty-four, so I can't be old enough to be her grandfather. You're the same age."

"You don't see me staring at the young boys here, do you?" she asked as she walked into the kitchen for coffee, scuffing her flip-flops along the tiled floor.

"Maybe she's his sister," Monty said. "I never see any women around his house."

Abby got to the end of the street and turned. She saw three preteen boys stop their bicycles to ogle her. She smiled at one boy, who blushed. The boys followed her on their bikes, but kept a distance. She saw them hide behind cars so they weren't obvious. They circled around each other and pretended they were talking when they were really watching her spread her legs and touch the ground as she stretched.

"Look at her," one boy said.

"She's got long legs."

"When did she move here?"

"She's going into that guy's house," Monty yelled to Leslie, who walked to the living room with her coffee. "I guess it is his sister or something."

"I don't care what others do, Monty," she said, as she dropped on the couch with a tabloid newspaper.

"Yes you do. You and the rest of the cackling hens are going to gossip about this later. I hear about all the times that Sue brings men to her house."

"That's Margie," Leslie protested. "She's the gossip. I don't gossip. I don't care what people do in their spare time." She turned a page.

As her husband had predicted, a group of women gathered with Leslie in her home that afternoon. They all had questions about the new woman.

"I think it's probably his sister," one gray-haired woman said.

"That's what Monty thinks," Leslie answered. She looked out her front window. "I haven't seen anyone else go in that place."

"She was bouncing all over the parking lot this morning," a woman said.

"She has a lot to bounce."

"I used to bounce like that," another added. Everyone was quiet for a moment, and then the whole room laughed.

Mark got home as Abby left for work. It was another brutally hot day, and Mark was exhausted. He sat on the bed watching television until he fell asleep. The hours of time passed in a blur. Next thing he knew, Abby was nudging him as she climbed into bed, reeking of bar smells. He had no idea how late it was, and it bothered him that he had missed the whole night. The bar smell was so overpowering that he got out of bed to go to the kitchen and get away.

"Can't sleep?" Abby asked, rubbing her eyes. "It must be those hours driving early in the morning."

"Maybe." He grabbed a cola from the refrigerator and sat down. "I just slept through the whole night. This," he said, holding up the cola, "is dinner."

She sat on his lap before he could drink.

"Married in a few more days," he said. She nodded, and the smell of the bar intensified. "I still smell the bar on you," Mark remarked.

"It'll come out when I take a shower," Abby said. "I'll use the dryer for my hair, and the smell will be gone just in time to go to work again."

"What do you think about dancing?" Mark asked.

"I meet a lot of people. Some are nice, and some are lonely. It's a strange job." She tightened her shirt around her chest. "Some guy will pay me to see my nipple. Did you ever notice? My nipple looks like anyone else's. I have that big red part and that little bump in the middle—like everyone else. The thing is, it's my nipple, and that's what someone wants to see."

"How long will you keep doing this?"

"I don't know."

He bit his lip. "I was just thinking …" He paused. "I was thinking that you should give this up. I have my own business. They're talking about some merger, but they aren't going to buy out all the drivers. We'll have money. I think you should look for another job. We're not rich enough for you to stay home and not work at all."

"I'll quit," she said, cutting him off. "Fine by me. I'll get a job at the mall. You have enough malls here. You have malls like Vegas has casinos."

"OK," he said, surprised. She kissed him and took a swig of his cola.

"Do you want to go jogging some morning?"

"Jogging?" he repeated. "Not really," he muttered. He felt her body slouch. "I'd love to. Jogging?"

Abby saw Sunflower, Fire and other dancer she didn't remember the names of at Babes Go-Go on Monday night. Sunflower was adjusting herself into an outfit. Abby threw her bag on the floor just missing Sunflower's heel.

"I'm quitting dancing," Abby announced as she stepped up on a bench for everyone to see her. "My fiancé and I talked about it, and I'm quitting."

"What's the wedding going to be like?" another dancer asked. "Are you having a big wedding?"

"We're going to Town Hall," Abby answered. "After the wedding, we're going home."

"Did he get you a ring?"

"No," Abby said. She looked at her fingers.

"Are you sure you've thought this out?" Sunflower asked.

Abby paused when Stacy Ann walked in the locker room. She wore a red bikini that showed her tight stomach muscle cuts, her tanned thin legs, and her solid ass.

"I heard someone say they're getting married. Is it you?" she asked Abby. "Is he nice?"

"Yeah. He's great. He owns and drives a truck."

"That Mark guy?" Stacy Ann asked. Her mood changed to solemn. "I remember you said he was your customer. He's cute. I don't blame you. Mark used to come here all the time. We all know him—Kimberly, Fire, and Portia. Buffy said he used to hit on her."

Rita walked in with an open notebook. "Why are all of you in here?" She slammed down her book. "Someone get your ass out there."

"Abby's going to marry that Mark guy who comes here," Fire said. She walked out of the locker room. Abby could hear her laugh on the other side of the door.

"It sounds like everyone knows him," Abby said.

Chapter 13

Abby dreamed about Penn pushing her into a door. He took her purse and threw the contents on the floor in another dream. He pocketed fifty dollars and left Abby crying on the floor in her last dream.

She bounced up in bed, wide awake. Mark was at work. The room was silent. She had had dreams like this for the past two nights. Her thoughts were scattered. She tried to focus on her upcoming marriage. The beige dress from a formal-wear store in the mall she ordered was ready. She made an appointment for her hair for later that morning. Carla called to talk about dancing. Carla's complaining of her marriage became a normal part of the morning for Abby. Abby tried to cut the conversation short but couldn't.

As far as she knew, Mark had done nothing to prepare for the wedding. He came home from work and fell asleep on the couch. They hadn't had sex since living together. He said the attack at work was still causing headaches, or he was tired from a long day. Some nights Abby had to work.

Today's the wedding, she thought, looking at herself in the mirror. She felt disappointed Mark hadn't taken the day off.

Her hair was flat, her cheeks pale, and bags formed half circles under her eyes. She sighed and rubbed her nose like she always did when she was nervous. There was no protocol given on how she should arrive to pick up her dress. She threw on shorts, a tank top, and dirty white sneakers and set out for the mall.

The dress was at Nora Daniels, the highest-priced clothing store in the mall. They had a shoe section, where Abby tried on some two-inch heels. They had small handbags and costume jewelry. She tried everything on.

"They look nice on you," the saleswoman said, watching Abby stumble around in shoes too small for her feet.

Abby could hear strains of the wedding march in her head. She spied a pair of gloves and tried to turn in mid-step to see them closer. She fell over into a shoe rack.

"I don't like these shoes."

🍁   🍁   🍁

Mark was counting inventory at Iggy's when Jennifer came in. She put on her apron and tightened it around her waist. Mark lost count of what he was doing.

"How's the girlfriend?" Smitty asked, patting Mark on the back.

"I have to get things done quickly to be ready in time," Mark said, loud enough for Jennifer to hear. She ignored him. Smitty kept talking, but Mark kept his eyes on Jennifer. Even out in his truck, he watched the inside of the store. Jennifer was busy setting up the deli section for the day.

Mark's hands shook as he gathered his stock. He checked in and stocked the shelves so quick that Smitty couldn't keep up with him. Mark went and stood at the customer side of the counter where Jennifer was working. "They say animals in the wild play games when they're young," Mark said. "Leopards can't play hide-and-seek, because they always get spotted."

She looked up and shook her head but didn't say anything.

"Leopards have spots," Mark said. She didn't respond, throwing a torpedo roll into a bin and grabbing another. He lowered his head and walked out, shrugging his shoulders. This was Jennifer's last chance, and she didn't try to stop him. He stomped back to the truck and threw his empty carrying trays in the back.

"Mother," he yelled, when he caught his finger in the door. He smeared the dirt from the truck deep into his pores as he rubbed away the pain. Jennifer's car was three spaces away. He sighed looking at it. "Oh shit, I forgot," he said as he wiggled feeling back into his fingers. He ran to the front of the truck and started it.

🍁   🍁   🍁

"I'm getting married later today," Abby told the hairstylist washing her hair.

"That's great. This is for your wedding?" she asked. Her lips were pursed. "How do you want your hair done? I can do anything you want. I wish you'd brought your veil."

"I don't have one," Abby said. "I can't think straight."

"How long did you have this planned? We could've talked this through." She put her hands on her hips for a second. "Look at me getting angry at you." She then hugged Abby. "You should've told us when you made the appointment. Where's the ring?"

Abby's eyes widened. "The engagement ring? I left it home so nothing would happen to it," she lied.

"I've never heard of that. Every woman wears it everywhere." She paused and picked up a brush. "It's your life. Do you want something different with your hair? I can do a curl." She grabbed long scissors. "Or I can cut it real short."

"I just got it to grow back," Abby said. "I had it real short when I first moved out here. I need long hair for my job … but I'm quitting."

"I don't think a job can fire you for having short hair," the woman said. Her face crinkled like she was puzzled by what Abby meant.

Abby ignored her. "Should I go short? No, I like it long."

"Brides usually have stacks of magazines when they come in," the stylist persisted. "You have to have some idea."

"Well, I've had a lot of stuff to do," Abby said, as the stylist yanked her head back.

"Leave that stuff for the bridesmaids."

"Don't have any."

"Are you sure you're getting married?" the stylist asked, even more confused.

The stylist took an hour going over ideas for changing Abby's hair, just to leave it the same but curlier. Abby went back to the dress shop and another hour after that window shopping. She returned to the townhouse with her arms full of bags. She saw the message light blinking on the answering machine and dropped the bags to check the message. It couldn't be for work tonight, she hoped.

"Mark, it's your mother," said a scratchy voice on the machine. "Why haven't you called this week? I talked to your brother, and he has some news to tell. You didn't call your brother either. Your brother told me during his weekly call that you don't call anymore. What's wrong with you?"

He hadn't told his parents about her.

She scooped up the bags and dropped them in front of the mirror in the bedroom. Her hair was curly now. Her face was tanned, and her eyes were alive. She took off her top and admired the reflection of her svelte figure. She got ready for Town Hall quicker than planned. The one piece beige dress was snug at her chest and hips, yet not form fitting. She had dark nail polish on her fingers. Her new shoes were more comfortable with every step. She called Mark's cell phone. There was no answer. She drove to Town Hall at two thirty and called him again. Still no answer.

She guessed maybe he'd clean up at the depot and meet her at three. That's when they were supposed to get married. *He won't be late*, she told herself, trying to stay calm. *He said not to worry.* People passed by her in the hallways and stared.

Two forty-five. Where is he?

She went from sitting up to crouching over with her face in her hands.

Two fifty-five. Where is he?

Her flowers fell from her hands to the chair.

Three o'clock. Maybe all those people were right, she thought. *Maybe we rushed into this. Where is he?*

"We can only hold your appointment for five more minutes," a clerk told her.

"Where is he?" she asked, even though the clerk didn't know. Her legs were crossed and her shoe hung off her big toe. She rested her chin in her hands.

"We'll be right in," a voice said. It was Mark, dressed in a black suit with an undone tie and hair still wet from a shower. He was huffing, bent over holding his side. His shoes were so shiny she could see her reflection in them.

He sat next to her and ran his still-grimy hand over her cheek. "I'm sorry I took so long," he said, as he reached into his pocket. He pulled out a small box and took Abby's hand. "I ordered this last week and had to pick it up today. He put a diamond ring on her finger and kissed her cheek. "You got your hair done?"

She laughed. "Yeah, I had a busy morning. Is my makeup running? I got nervous."

"You look beautiful. You don't need makeup anyway." He leaned back for the full effect. "You wore light brown?"

"It's beige," she said. "I wasn't going to wear white. Let's not kid ourselves. I just wanted to look nice. I didn't want sexy or glamorous or young virgin white."

He looked at the people in the office watching them. "I guess it's time."

"I don't have a ring for you," she said, when they got to the justice of the peace's desk.

The justice looked up, puzzled, and went back to reviewing their file. "Where are your witnesses?"

"Who?" Abby asked.

The justice sighed. "You need witnesses to a marriage. You don't have witnesses. What else did you forget? This isn't something I do lightly. I expect that you have thought this out."

A tear rolled down Abby's cheek as the justice scolded them. Mark threw up his hands and walked out of the office, slamming the door behind him. The justice apologized to Abby when Mark burst back in the office with two women and a man.

"Our witnesses. I can't wear a ring because of my job. I lift and carry things all day so she's giving me …"

Abby took out her loop earring and showed it to the justice. "This. It's round. I think that's everything."

The justice stared at her with a blank look and laughed as he shook his head.

"Love you," Abby said, leaning into Mark.

"Love you, too," Mark answered.

The wedding took ten minutes including paperwork. Abby threw her flowers over her head and knocked the clock off the wall before a woman in the office could catch them. Mark picked Abby up and carried her to the door. She was taller than he realized, and he banged her ankles into the door frame on the way out. He dropped her leg when she squirmed, and they almost fell over each other.

"I can walk out," Abby said.

"But you want romance." He stepped forward and held the door for her as she hopped out of the office.

"What a mess. We'll see them for the annulment in a few weeks," the justice said to the clerk.

They had lobster dinners at a restaurant near the boardwalk in Belmar and went home. Abby ran in the house while Mark parked the car.

"You OK?" Mark asked. He could hear Abby in the bathroom. The sounds of bottles being knocked over went through the door.

"Just wait."

He took off his suit jacket and pulled out the earring. It had snapped in his pocket. He hid it in a dresser drawer when he heard Abby turn the door handle. She appeared in a black tube dress with black high heels and no stockings. There were no panty lines either. She swiveled her hips as she walked to the radio and turned on a blues song with loud harmonicas and electric guitars. It wasn't her normal dance music, but she improvised. She ran her fingers through her hair and swayed to Mark in time to the music until their faces were inches apart.

He stood frozen as she continued to dance against him. They both could feel the warm body heat generated. She held his hand and danced him to the bed where she dropped down with him on top of her. Their faces meshed in kisses. He cupped her breasts instead of pinching her, like the men in the bars did. He could smell her perfumed hair without the stench of bar.

Penn never tried to make her comfortable during foreplay. He pounced. Men at the bar tipped her and then looked the other way. Mark faced her. Mark held her till his arms were tense and shaky. They moved in synch. Mark slid his hands under her dress and felt her. She undid his pants with ease. The light was on, but they didn't notice. The music became feedback. They held each other and rolled. Nothing broke them apart. Clothes flew off any which way. She swayed. He rocked. Her toes curled and she screamed out. Mark moved around and in. She released and felt drained. Mark caught up to her a moment later. They grunted in ecstasy at the same time.

She smiled till she fell asleep in his arms.

"I don't think we can spend the whole day in bed," Mark said, when he woke up the next morning. The morning sun blinded him. Her leg was on his chest. "We got twisted here."

"I think we're a perfect fit," she purred.

They stayed in bed all day. They talked and laughed. The clothes stayed on the floor until they had to call for food. Dinner came from Vinny's Pizza, and they ate on the bed. They weren't going anywhere, so they didn't bother getting dressed in anything but nightwear.

"It's a shame we have to get back to the real world tomorrow," Abby said. "I wish we never had to work again."

"I'll be home at four," Mark assured her. "We have the whole night. We have the rest of our lives. There's plenty of time."

"Not really. I have to work again," she said. Abby felt sudden tension when Mark stopped separating pizza slices. "I just couldn't quit. I had to finish out the schedule. I filled out an application at a clothes store yesterday." She paused because she didn't fill out an application and didn't like having to lie about it now. "I'm quitting dancing, but I'm on the schedule, and I just have to finish one night." She held his hand. "They're having a hard time getting dancers, and I could use the extra money till the next job starts."

"We have money," he said. "I thought you said you were going to stop."

"Just one night—I promise." She stopped and sat quiet for a moment. "I don't have a savings account. I'll put this money in a savings account."

Mark was deflated. His shoulders sagged. He toyed with the cheese on a pizza slice. "How did you get a car without any savings?"

"I paid cash. I get paid cash for everything, so I spend cash," she explained. "I don't like having extra money that people can steal."

"We could get a joint account," he suggested. "The checking account could use a few more dollars. I spent a lot on your ring."

She twirled it around her finger. "I don't want to work, but I have to."

Mark sighed. "I understand. I don't like it. You might as well take more pizza before it stains the bed."

"I can wash the sheets. I'm the wife." She waited for a response or a chuckle from Mark. "Don't get used to hearing me say that."

Abby went to the mall jewelry store the next day.

"I need a wedding band," she told an older woman behind the counter. "I don't know his ring size, but he has big fingers."

"Ma'am, that doesn't help us," the woman responded. She lowered her reading glasses and crinkled her nose. "There are several 'big finger' sizes."

"Well, he's kind of like this," she said, as she made a ring around one of her fingers. "Can I buy something and have it sized later?"

The woman showed her rings, but Abby's mind drifted. Penn had rings. He stole them from gamblers and kept them in a bag. She had found them and told Penn she didn't like it. He gave her the scar on her shoulder for being nosy. She shook the memory out of her head and thought about Mark. A plain, round, gold ring would work since he would never wear it. She put down cash on installment and went to Nora Daniels to fill out an application.

Leslie Dumont was at Abby's front door when she returned home. Leslie said she was head of the homeowner's association and wanted to meet her new neighbor. Abby introduced herself using her maiden name.

"Oops, I made a mistake," Abby said. She grabbed Leslie's forearm and laughed. "I'm changing my name. I'm not getting an alias or anything like that. We just got married, so my name is Abby Winston."

"I live right down …," Leslie said, but then paused. "He's straight?"

"Straight what?"

"He's over thirty, and I've never seen women there. I just thought that … maybe I shouldn't say anything." Leslie took a step away and turned. "Married? Really?"

"Yes," Abby said. It took her a moment to realize what Leslie was implying. "Wait. He's definitely straight. He's an incredible lover. We did it all day yesterday."

Leslie covered her ears and picked up her pace leaning, which made Abby laugh. Mark wasn't home, so Abby set up a bath for herself and dozed off in the tub. The once-warm-now-cold water woke her up. She jumped out of the tub and looked at herself in the mirror. Her skin was shriveled, and her eyes were bloodshot from sleeping. She checked the clock and realized it was already four o'clock. She dressed in jeans and a top, grabbed her work clothes, which were already in her bag, and left just before Mark got home.

He dropped onto the couch without changing out of his uniform. As Mark flipped channels in an effort to stay awake, someone knocked on the door. He didn't want to get the door because his legs were tired, but he could hear that it was Eddie.

"Is it true?" Eddie asked. He burst through the door before Mark had it fully open. "Are you married?"

"How did you find out so soon?"

"My wife told me," Eddie replied. "Your wife met Leslie Dumont. Need I say more?"

"I never talk to Leslie Dumont. I guess if Abby met her already, the whole development is talking about us by now, isn't it?"

"Of course. When did this happen?"

The parking lot was empty except for three cars when Abby arrived at Babes Go-Go. She parked her car at the side of the bar near the back door. Eli was alone inside at the bar.

"What's going on?" Abby asked him. "The place is empty."

"I don't know. There's no dancing tonight," Eli answered.

"Why?"

"Rita got a letter with a small knife in it. The knife had blood on it," Eli told her. "You know how that manager was killed? He was stabbed." He rubbed his arms even though it wasn't cold in the building. "We had to call the police. They took the knife and the letter for fingerprints. Everyone's freaked out. No dancing. It's going to destroy the night's tips. I won't get tips for bartending. No dancing. I don't know why anyone would come here if there's no dancing. I don't know who sent that letter, but if it was intended to close us down, it worked."

Abby stayed with Eli while he vented about the lack of customers. A telephone rang and Eli had to answer it. It gave Abby a chance to run back to the car and head home to Mark. When she got there, Mark was playing five-card poker in the kitchen with Eddie.

"I don't have to work tonight," she told them. "It was a lucky break. It was lucky for me anyway. Rita's got this problem, but it's not my problem." She laughed leaving the kitchen.

"She looks familiar," Eddie said. "I don't know why."

Mark dealt the cards and told Eddie that he had met her at Babes Go-Go.

"*You married a go-go dancer!*" Eddie blurted out.

"Would you calm down," Mark said, with a wave of his hand. "She used to dance. She's going to work at a clothes store soon."

"Well, that's ironic—a stripper who sells clothes," Eddie said with a laugh.

"Get the fuck out," Mark said, as he collected the cards. "I told you that she stopped doing that. She's my wife, and I don't want anyone calling her a stripper. She never stripped anyway. She danced in very few clothes, but the clothes stayed on."

"OK, I'm sorry. Calm down. I won't do it again," Eddie said. "You tried to date all those dancers for so long. I thought you could handle a joke about it."

The next morning, the security guard, Jacob Hersh stormed out of the locker room at Babes Go-Go. He picked up a bar stool and threw it on top of a pool table.

"A whole night's business lost to a threat," he said. "This didn't go over well with the bar owners, and it didn't go well with the security bosses. I'm supposed to be on guard, and all this is happening. It turned out to be a joke, too. The knife was covered in ketchup. I'm in so much trouble." He rubbed his temples. "If I have to, I'll investigate every woman, man, customer, vendor, or whoever else comes around here. This has to stop. They hired me so this wouldn't happen, and now look."

"Calm down," Eli said. "I'm sure it was a customer being funny."

Behind the bar, an alley ran from the parking lot to the back of the local cable company office building. Many cable technicians walked through the alley to get to the bar at the end of their shifts. While Jacob was throwing things around the bar, a technician was walking up the alley.

The technician saw a woman on the ground. "Hey, what are you doing?" he asked. He figured it was a homeless person hiding out. The woman didn't respond, so he unclipped his flashlight from his belt and flashed it at the person to startle her. There was still no movement. He held the flashlight like a club and stepped near the person.

"Hey, lady," he yelled. The woman was thin, with long red hair, a small waist, and breasts as large as her head. "You pass out here?" He tapped her shoulder with his foot. She didn't move. Flies and gnats circled around them. The technician crouched down and saw blood on her side. He put on a work glove and flipped her over. Her shirt and pants were covered in blood.

"Oh, God," he yelled. He fell to his knees. Then he noticed the bar lights on, so he ran for the bar. "Hey," he yelled when he got inside.

"What?" Jake yelled. "We're not open yet."

The technician leaned against the wall to catch his breath. He pointed behind him. "I think I just found a dancer outside. She's bleeding. It's really fucking gross, man."

"What? Show me," Jake yelled.

"Fuck that. I ain't going back in that alley. I shouldn't have moved her. I probably ruined the scene. I saw that on TV. You're not supposed to alter the crime scene. I was just trying to get her to wake up. I figured passed out. Right? She's covered in blood. I saw that on TV too, but that is fucked up in real life."

Jake ran out to the alley and saw the dancer. He had never seen a dead body before, and it made him feel sick. The technician came up behind him and scared him.

"See. Look at her eyes. Their still open," the technician said. He looked at Jake. "I wanted to make sure you found her. I've seen this stuff in the movies, but it's not like this."

"This is messed up." Jake grabbed her cold arm. "She's been dead for awhile. Her arm is all stiff. We have to call the cops."

"They cut part of her head off," the tech said between gags and coughs.

"It's a wig," Jake said. "She really has black hair not red."

They ran back to the bar where Eli was waiting.

"What happened? I can't leave the bar. What happened?"
"There's another dead dancer," Jake answered.

Chapter 14

The Lexus was George's birthday present to Carla last year. She knew he searched around and comparison-shopped before he bought it. The car had every convenience she could want. There was cruise control, power windows, power locks, a stereo system with compact disc player, station preset, and satellite radio.

Carla drove it to Babes Go-Go. She got out of the car and walked by the blinking neon lights that lit up the parking lot. The gravel was littered with gum and cigarette wrappers. She tugged down her leather miniskirt, which kept riding up as she shimmied across the lot. She saw her reflection in the darkened windows. Her hair was teased. The reflection didn't show the heavy blue eye shadow with hints of glitter. She hadn't even worn this much makeup when she went out clubbing with her friends. The perfume from inside was prevalent out by the door. She puckered her lips before she grabbed the upside-down door handle held on with one screw. The inside was darkness with blurs of people and neon. The crowd was an obstacle to the lockers, but she moved quick and straight for the locker room door. No one noticed her because of the dancer on stage.

"I saw you dance last time," Sunflower said to her in the locker room. "You were good. Baby taught you well."

"She did," Carla said with a smile. "I probably would've stumbled all over the place if she hadn't helped me. She called me and said she was retiring." Carla dropped her bag on the wooden seat in front of the lockers. "She got married the other day. She said there are married dancers, but she didn't want to be one of them."

"Follow her advice," Sunflower said. "You show too much, and we'll all get in trouble. The police are all over the place looking for that killer. If you do something for a tip that gets us closed down for prostitution, it'll piss everyone off."

"I'm not going to sleep with anyone," Carla proclaimed. "How could anyone call what we do prostitution?"

"When the mayor wants a headline, he'll call it whatever he wants. You have a great slot tonight, so don't screw it up—literally." Sunflower walked out past Rita while fixing her thong. She had to give Rita attitude before starting her dance just because she liked to. "I heard the new manager here quit after he heard about the manager at West. He didn't even get the chance to fuck the dancers, like the dead guy did." She waited for Rita to respond. "You must not have had the time to line a girl up for him before he quit. Since I hear that you pimp out dancers to the managers."

Rita stood up off her stool and grabbed Sunflower by the hair. "You're still dancing tonight. If you don't want to, I can arrange that." Sunflower was taller than her, but Rita held on tight. "I'm not a pimp. All managers ask the dancers to stay after closing. What the dancers agree to do is up to them." She let go of Sunflower's hair. "You're lucky that you weren't killed along with him."

"So are you," Sunflower said. She sashayed to the stage like nothing was wrong and danced. Rita watched her, hoping that Sunflower would fall off the stage.

Carla walked out of the locker room wearing a stretch skirt and bra top. Her bare legs wobbled in her new high heels. "When do I dance? You said I was up soon."

"Get back in there," Rita yelled. "I'll tell you when to come out."

"Am I still Cookie?" Carla asked. Rita nodded. Carla frowned. She went back to the locker room and waited for her turn. The time dragged so she tried to think of a better name for herself. She sat on the bench with crossed legs and played with her long hair. Dancers walked in, toweled off, and went back out. Carla watched a pencil-thin dancer with breasts so big that she could hardly hold herself up straight pull money out of her G-string. The thin dancer opened a plastic bag from her locker and took a pill. Another dancer snuck a cigarette by the window.

Carla heard her stage name and jumped up. She ran to the stage and twirled around in silence. The deejay stared at her with his hands up.

"Did you pick out music?" Sunflower yelled. The group of guys surrounding her laughed.

Carla turned to the deejay and yelled, "Play anything. I'll dance to it."

"Bitches want my rocks," were the first words to some hip-hop song that blasted out. She tapped her foot for timing, but the words were so offensive she couldn't concentrate—even though she was almost naked in a bar. She undid the zipper on her skirt after the first song and took a deep breath. The next song began with the sounds of gunshots. She cupped her ears and let the skirt fall, but it got caught on her G-string. She fumbled with the strings, moving toward any light she could find. She yanked the skirt and almost took her bottom off with it.

"Did I just see hair?" Sunflower asked her customer.

"I think you did."

"That wasn't hair," Rita said from her bench.

"Man she flashed us," one guy said to another.

"She's a natural brunette," another said between laughs.

"Gotsta ride the city," the song continued. Carla almost fell, trying to fix her outfit.

"Is it over?" she asked, when the music came to a sudden stop. A bass drum pounded and shook the bar. She ignored the music and danced with the hope it would look coordinated. The guy with the flannel shirt wasn't there. A group of older businessmen huddled together on the side of the bar where the man in flannel sat last time.

"Business attire. That's more my kind of man," she mumbled. She went to the stairs and walked down, not even trying to look sexy. Her head was high and her back was straight, because these were her kind of men. "How's your night?" she asked, twirling her hair.

The eldest of the group was bald except for a few long gray strands of hair. "Nice tits," he said. He held out a dollar like she meant nothing. This offended her. She knew her husband could buy and sell these guys. All this guy can say is "nice tits?" she thought. She took the dollar before he could grope her.

"Hey what's this?" he yelled. "You don't just get money for walking over here. Get back here, and let's try it again." He held out another dollar. "Not so quick," he said, when she tried to grab the money. "Play like the other dancers do." He pinched her breast as he stuffed a dollar down her cleavage. Another man turned to her with a folded up dollar. He wouldn't let her leave till he handled her breast, squeezing it and cupping it while his dollar soaked sweat from her sternum. All the men waved dollars to get a chance to do the same.

"Spin around," said a younger guy, with his tie still tied and his suit still closed. She was eager to get away, until she realized how much money she'd collected. "Thank you guys," she said with a smile. She bobbed along to the music. Back on stage, she danced with more excitement than before. After the song, she went back to the group of men.

"Spin around."

"Shake it."

"Nice rack."

She didn't pay attention to what they said. She continued to see dollars—more money in her hands after three songs than she got from George in weeks of allowance. She almost ran to the locker rooms, but she was fearful of falling in her heels. Her toes crunched in her shoes as she walked at a quick yet calm pace. The money was locked up as soon as she got to her locker.

Dancers smoked cigarettes or popped pills while rubbing their feet. One dancer was on her cell phone giving instructions to a babysitter.

Rita stormed in. "That was the most unprofessional bit I ever saw. Back when I danced, I never would've looked like that. Don't you know how to dance?"

Carla froze in fear. "I don't know how to dance to that stuff. I didn't know about picking out the music."

"Now you know," Rita said. "Get out there and tell the deejay what to play."

Carla went to the deejay, scuffling in her shoes and falling out of her tiny outfit. It was embarrassing to face the deejay so clueless. Her face was red and her arms trembled. The deejay's room was wall-to-wall compact discs and computer screens.

"Didn't anyone tell you about the music policy?" he asked.

"No," she said. "The person who showed me how to dance must have done the music for me. This is my first time by myself." She read the magic marker scribbling on the jewel case of a compact disc. "I think I know some of these songs."

He took the disc and noticed how her knees shook and how she fidgeted with her fingers. She was so innocent, so unsure, so naïve about this business. "They didn't tell you about the deejay tips?" he asked. He sighed when she shook her head. "I'm sorry I didn't explain this to you sooner. I get 40 percent of the money you make while dancing. It's how I get paid. Your manager's probably getting another 10 percent or so."

"Rita said she gets almost 20 percent," Carla said. "You get 40 percent before I even get to the bartenders."

"How much did you make during the songs out there?" the deejay asked.

"Forty dollars," she lied. It was much more.

"That's pathetic," he told her. "You have to work it more. Figure this—after me and Rita, you're taking home sixteen dollars. If you're not stingy with the bartenders, you made ten bucks for three songs. That's not bad. How many jobs pay like that on a bad night? You'll probably get four more sets, so you can make a lot more money. Dancers walk out of here with hundreds of dollars, because I play the songs for them. They tip me well. You need to pick a lot of music."

It took her twenty minutes to pick out enough songs for the night. The deejay said he was OK with her picks. Before she could leave, he opened his arms to her.

"Welcome to the family," he said. His hairy arms were glistening with sweat. She dragged herself to him and wrapped her arms around him. His fingernails went down to the small of her back and up to her shoulders. He smelled like uncooked beef. His chest was flabby and moist.

Sunflower saw them embrace. The deejay smiled as he sniffed Carla's hair.

"I have to get ready for my next set," Carla said. She ran to the locker room with her arms crossed in front of her chest. There was a towel in her locker that she used to wipe the deejay's sweat off her.

She was called to the stage a minute later. The group of businessmen faced her with folded bills in hand. She could see them watching her. Carla got on the stage and dropped to her knees at the first note of her first song. She ran her fingertips over her body while leaning back. Her hand went into her bottom where she simulated rubbing herself. She crawled across the stage, raising her hips and swaying to the much calmer music. Carla rolled to the edge of the stage and jumped off. The eldest businessman had a dollar ready for her. She rubbed his hand as he reached for her.

"This is gentle," she thought.

He pinched her. She kept calm as she stepped back, shaking her hips and bouncing her breasts. The next guy kept the money between two fingers and ran his hand down her stomach to her bottom half. She'd seen other dancers let guys do this, so she let him get lower. She stared at the mirrors on the walls instead of at the guy. His finger went very low, and she thought she felt the guy try to reach inside her. She pulled away, crouched over, and ran for the stage.

Two guys that looked about her age sat on the other side of the bar. She shook, swayed, and bent over for them. They didn't pay attention to her. She did a split and didn't see a reaction. She licked her fingers and puckered her lips like she tasted the last guy's sweat on her. Her hand lowered inside the bottom of her costume. No reaction from the men. She slithered off the stage to the two guys and squeezed her breasts, but they continued talking.

"Hi," she yelled.

"You can just take the dollar," one of the guys said. "That was good." He didn't bother to look at her. He turned to the other guy and said, "So the Boston deal isn't going to work."

The other guy held out a dollar for Carla but didn't look at her either. "Yeah, the people up there aren't sure about it."

Her fake smile disappeared. When the set was done, Carla went back in the locker room and sat on the bench.

"Good job," Rita said. "That wasn't so bad." She put her cold hand on Carla's leg as she talked.

Carla wasn't listening. Rita calmed down and even smiled at her. The music still blared outside. Rita wrote on her clipboard as she followed another dancer leaving the locker room. Carla banged her head on the locker and sighed.

"It goes away," Sunflower said. "I imagine your feet hurt."

"I'm sore all over," Carla said. "I strutted half naked to two guys who ignored me. I showed them more than I showed a lot of old boyfriends and they ignored me."

"You're halfway done. The place will be empty by the last set anyway. You won't have to do much. It looks like Rita is treating you better. Did she say anything about seeing the managers after hours?"

"No," Carla answered. "She never said anything about managers." She looked down at the wad of money in her hand and realized more than half of it was going to someone else.

"Did the bar owners put the moves on you?" Sunflower asked.

"No, but the deejay did. I think everyone else realized that I'm married."

Sunflower shook her head and stomped out of the locker room. She shuffled to the stage and did a split in front of the businessmen. Rita watched by the locker room door as Sunflower pointed her finger at her, pulled it back, and blew on it, like she had a Wild West revolver. The men smiled and yelled, "Yee haw."

Carla watched Sunflower from the locker room door. Sunflower was able to take money before anyone touched her. She swayed her hips like Carla did, but everyone liked her. They didn't complain about what Sunflower did. She ran her fingers through her hair and teased men by toying with her bra straps. Sunflower had a wad of cash so big she couldn't close her hand around it when she was done.

Carla heard her stage name and bounced to the stage like she did on her first set. She twirled around the pole and wrapped her leg around it as she slid to the floor. She danced in front of someone who didn't pay attention to her. This time, she went to him, took the tip, and walked away, not caring if he ignored her. She used someone's dollar to wipe her sweat and then stuffed it between her breasts. As the guys grabbed at her, she wondered how much longer she had to do this. The songs had long guitar solos or drum solos that seemed to last longer then Carla remembered. The set lasted a very long time, but did finally end. She ran for the locker room and changed into a pair of sweat pants and a baggy blouse.

"Rita, I'm not coming back," she said, as she slung her bag over her shoulder and handed Rita a wad of singles. "This is your commission."

"You can't just quit like this," Rita said. "What's wrong? Didn't you make enough money?"

"The money is good, but I can't do this."

"Next Thursday is the Go-Go-Rama," Rita yelled. "We get sixty dancers in here, so there are always four or five dancers on stage. This place is packed, and everyone makes a lot of money. I could use a dancer, since your friend Baby quit. The place will be so packed you won't have to spend a lot of time with any guy."

"I just don't want to."

"It's not like we're going to advertise that the CEO of Doro-Tech's wife is dancing here."

"What?" Carla asked, shocked.

"We have security cameras all over now. You're on tape, and I did a little research. I just found out after your second set."

"No," Carla said, shivering. "Don't." She held out the rest of the money to Rita. "Here, take it all. Don't say anything about this."

"I don't need that. I need dancers," Rita said, with a smile. Her blackened teeth swallowed the lights flashing from the ceiling like a black hole. "Just one last time. I help you, and you help me."

Carla froze. "The first time was fun, but this was not what I thought." She could see tired dancers walk out of the locker room have to dance again. "This wasn't glamorous and sexy." She knew George would be furious, not turned on. He would be embarrassed if he found out. "Sure," she said, almost in tears about the thought of doing this again, but it was better than being found out. "What time?"

Rita told her what time to be there as the deejay walked out of his booth. A dancer was on stage dancing to a long song which gave the deejay time to walk around. He opened his arms for Carla, but she walked past him into his booth where she threw money on his mixing board.

"This is 40 percent of what I made tonight. Thank you for playing the songs."

"You're welcome." His arms were still open. She sighed and relented. He wrapped his hairy arms around her, holding her close to smell her hair. "I can't wait to do this again."

She backed away and straightened. "Go-Go-Rama is the last time. Don't hug me like that again."

His face went pale. "You're feisty and fun. I like you." She turned away, but he grabbed her arm and kissed her full on the lips. She pushed off him and went for the door.

"That one leaving had huge tits," she heard someone say.

"I'd fuck her."

"I wouldn't fuck any of these skanks. You don't know what drugs they're on. I'm going home," one guy said.

Carla stopped at the door and turned. It was the businessmen talking about her. She ran to her car and sped out of sight. She got home and stomped up to the front door, which was locked. She got out her key and entered the security code in the alarm box before she sneaked to her bedroom, where George was sitting up asleep. She went to the shower, turned it on full blast, and threw her clothes in a pile on the floor. Her hands didn't stop moving as she rubbed soap all over her body. She cupped water from the shower and threw it on herself when the downpour didn't feel strong enough.

I feel so dirty. I can't feel clean anymore, she thought. She rubbed the soap so hard that it melted down to nothing. *Those people. What kinds of people do these things? We could buy and sell all those people. How dare they treat me like that.*

A man with a buzz cut haircut, a dirty white T-shirt, and jeans with holes in the knees walked into a go-go bar in North Jersey. A small stage was set behind a bar against a mirror-covered wall. The only light was from a neon beer sign. A pre-programmed MP3 player provided music.

The dancer, clad in black leather, had her nose, navel, and ears pierced. Tattoos covered her tanned, flabby legs. Her greasy hair was dyed blonde. Her skin was dried and sun-burned.

The man took a seat and ordered a beer while he watched the dancer. "Hey, you know this dancer?" he grunted to the woman bartender. He held a picture of Abby.

"No," the woman replied.

The dancer came to him for a tip but kept back because of his body odor. "What's that?" she asked, when she saw the picture.

"She's a good friend," he said. "She ran away from Nevada. I have to find her."

"Wow," she said. "You came here from Nevada. That's a couple of states away. What's her name?"

"It's more like a couple of thousand miles away," he said, taking out a cigarette. The dancer put her hand on his hand so he continued. "In Nevada they called her Baby. I don't know if she changed her name out here. It's why I have her picture with me. Can I have my hand back to light my cigarette?"

"There's no smoking in the bars in New Jersey," the dancer said. "Baby is a common name. You'll need to say more if you want to find her."

"No smoking." He laughed. "Are you serious?" When she nodded, he threw the cigarette across the bar to the stage. "Fucking stupid rules. Is there a way to find out where the go-go bars are in this state? Do they have guides or magazines or something like that?"

"There are magazines in the newspaper stores. Some have bar guides. This bar don't have nothing like that. There's a newspaper store a mile down the road." She held her breasts out to him.

"A mile away?" He picked up his dollar and held it out to her. "You really helped me out." He folded the dollar like it was for her but then stuffed it back in his pocket and laughed as he left the bar.

Chapter 15

George woke up at six the next morning and found Carla asleep in a fetal position at the foot of the bed. "Carla," he said, as he pushed the covers away and walked to her repeating her name. She didn't wake up. He shook her shoulder so fast that he rocked her whole body. "Carla," he yelled. "You scared me. I had no idea where you were. Why were you sleeping like that?"

She opened her eyes but didn't say anything.

"You have to make breakfast for the girls. I'll be in the shower." He walked into the bathroom, scratching his armpit.

"Make breakfast. Doesn't even know what time I came home," she mumbled. She slid her feet with her orange painted toenails into slippers and dragged herself to Kendra's door to yell for her to wake up.

"Go away," Kendra answered.

Kim was already in the bathroom when Carla walked to her room. She is such a good kid, Carla thought.

It wasn't easy making breakfast because she was so exhausted, but Carla fumbled around the cabinets to find cereal. Lunch had to be made, and Carla needed coffee.

"You look like hell," Kendra said, when she saw Carla.

"You're not supposed to talk like that. I know what I look like, anyway. I came down here to cook for you. I didn't feel up to it, but I'm still doing it for you." Carla held herself against the counter to keep her balance.

"I don't want anything," Kendra said. She grabbed an apple and left.

"You bitch," Carla cursed under her breath.

"Morning Carla," Kim said, as she pulled out a chair for herself. "I was watching television yesterday, and they had this show about dogs."

Carla hid a yawn and fought to stay awake the entire half-hour that Kim sat in the kitchen talking about television, her bike, and the new song that she heard on the radio.

"Bye, Dad," Kim said to George, when he came in the kitchen. "Debbie's mother is giving me a ride today."

"That's great," George said. Carla sat at the table across from George as he flipped through the business section of the paper.

"What is it?" Carla asked. "I hear you grumbling." Her eyes were closed, and her head was on the table.

"It's nothing," he answered. "You wouldn't understand. I'm got these meetings and seminars going on. I'll be out of town most of next week. I have meetings lined up for Thursday. The whole thing is a mess."

Carla's head bounced up. "I have to go somewhere Thursday. Can we drop the kids off at their mother's for the night?"

"You're their mother now. Can't you be home one night for them?"

She slammed her hand down on the table causing George's coffee to splash. "I'm home every single night with them. I talk with Kim about her day camp. I get cursed out by Kendra every night. I need one night to go out with my friends. I'm twenty-six years old, in case you forgot. People my age go out at night."

"Not the ones with kids," George said. "Who are these friends? Do I know them?"

"You don't know all my friends," she yelled. "What is this? Fascism? I'm going out on Thursday. Kendra can babysit."

"She's too young," he said, his eyes still in the newspaper.

"Too young?" she yelled. "I was letting myself in the house and babysitting for my sister when I was ten. I think Kendra can handle it."

"I won't be home till late," he said. "She's a child. I'll admit. She's a strong child, but she's so young and innocent. She went through a divorce. She couldn't handle the security issues."

Carla laughed. "Kendra is going to be fine with it. She has no anxiety. She hates me and has no anxiety about telling me. She likes her mother and you. Kim is having problems, but you don't do anything about that. Don't you see how clingy she is?"

"There's nothing I can do. She has to get used to it." He threw the newspaper down and straightened his tie. "Kendra wants you to earn her respect, and you're not doing it."

Carla grabbed the newspaper and harrumphed at George. "Earn her respect. When has she shown me respect? When you and I were dating, she'd swear at me." As she held the paper, her eyes zeroed in on a half-page advertisement for the go-go rama. "Someone has to show me some respect," she yelled too late for George had left the room.

The man with the crew cut sat in an old pickup truck behind a mall on Route 9 and flipped through the *Erotic Dancer Gallery* magazine. The sound of trucks making deliveries kept him on edge. He didn't want anyone to see him, but there was no place to hide. The advertisement for the Go-Go-Rama was in his hands.

She might be at this, he thought. *If she's not, I'll bet I can find someone who knows her.* The truck gauge showed that it was low on gas. *Shit. How am I going to get around?* he wondered. He pulled a wad of money from his back pocket and counted twenty dollars in singles.

Well, Abby, you better be at this thing, or I'm a dead man with no money and no gas.

Abby stood outside Nora Daniels Clothing Store, waiting for the security gate to open for work. She was dressed in a conservative black business skirt that went down to her knees, plain white blouse, flat shoes and black stockings. It felt strange to wear so little makeup for work, but she could get used to it. Her thumb toyed with her ring. She never tired of moving the ring around her finger. She did it without noticing it now.

The gate opened, and an African-American woman with a manager name badge walked to her. The woman had short hair and one earring in each earlobe.

"Hello, I'm Nona, and you must be Abby. We've been waiting for you to start today. There are a few forms to complete, and then we'll get you on the sales floor right away."

Nona's back was straight, and her big calves looked firm, probably from walking on her small-heeled black shoes all day. Her clothes were tight at the waist but loose everywhere else. Abby tried to imitate Nona's arm swing when she walked.

The man with the crew cut walked through the mall looking for a place to hide for the day. The mall had a lot of bathrooms that he could go to. There was the possibility that someone would leave something behind at the food court. He passed Nora Daniels, but paid it no mind, until he saw a brunette with shoulder-length hair, deep brown eyes, and a tanned face. He was sure it was Abby, even though she looked thinner than he remembered. He walked in and hid behind a rack of clothes.

"Abby," said a voice behind her. She straightened a clothes rack, thinking she had imagined it. "Abby," the whisper got closer, and she felt bumps on her neck. "Abby." She turned around and looked into his dead dark eyes.

"Penn," she screamed.

"Be quiet," he hissed in a loud whisper.

Nona ran onto the sales floor and saw Abby, crouched over, screaming, and holding her head. The only other person was a guy, backing away from her with his hands up. "What's wrong?" Nona demanded.

Tears streamed down Abby's cheeks as she screamed. "Penn. Penn."

"You get out," Nona said to him. Her voice had a bass tone that gave it authority. "Get out. Security!" she hollered out into the mall.

Penn ran out of the store but turned back to Abby and said, "I'll be around. I've been looking for you."

"Breathe," Nona told Abby. "He's gone." Abby was still crouched over crying. "Those dirtbag people scare me, too, but he's gone," Nona said. She patted Abby's shoulder and helped her stand.

"He's back. Oh, God, why?" Abby cried.

"Who is he?"

Abby couldn't breathe. Her eyes filled with tears. Her back hurt, even though he hadn't touched her. "It can't be. It can't," Abby repeated. Nona held her arm and led her past the cash registers. Abby resisted and grabbed the desk. "I was free," she told Nona. Customers began to gather outside the store to watch them. Nona blocked their view, but they could hear the crying. Abby let go of the counter and went to the back storage room. She collapsed on a stack of boxes and continued to cry.

Abby sat in the back of the store crying for about half an hour. Nona handled customers and found time to bring Abby a cup of water. Abby calmed down, but her face was red, and her eyes bloodshot. Nona had to let Abby leave for the day and told her to come back the next day for work. Abby went to the food court and got a soda and a pizza slice. She didn't really want it, but she thought maybe it would calm her stomach.

"Don't move," she heard Penn say from behind her. His smell made her cringe. She puckered her lips and tried not to breathe.

"Please don't do anything," she pleaded.

"Sit," he growled.

"What are you doing here?" Her hands trembled. He was behind her, but she didn't want to see him. "I left you in Vegas."

"I came for you. You broke my heart when you left me."

"Bullshit," Abby said. The word slipped out before she could stop it. She rubbed her arms, trying to stop shaking. "What do you want? How did you get here?"

"It wasn't easy," he said. "I stole your friend Tiffany's car and drove it as far as her gas and money took me. Then I met this girl in Ohio and stole her money. I did the same in Pennsylvania. They weren't smart enough to cancel their credit cards before I maxed them out. I switched plates on Tiffany's car and kept going. By the time the cops got word, I was long gone."

"How did you find me?"

"I knew you were in New Jersey from Tiffany's purse. She wrote your plane number and destination on a note. There's a lot of go-go bars on the Jersey Shore, but it was a matter of time."

"I should call the cops," she said. She grabbed her paper cup filled with soda. Her shaking made it fizz on the way to a seat. "Can't you just go away?"

"You have to come back to Vegas with me. You also have to buy me something to eat. I haven't eaten in two days." The food court was full of people coming and going. He stood behind her to watch the customers and security pass by.

"I can't go back to Vegas. My big, truck-driving husband wouldn't like that idea."

"You're married," he scoffed. "Who's going to marry you? You're a slut."

"I met someone who realized I'm more than just a dancer." Her back straightened. Anytime she talked back to Penn he slapped her, but she felt stronger now. If she came home beaten, Mark would go after Penn. "You never cared about me. You just liked my money."

"You give a great blow-job, too," he said, loud enough so a woman with a toddler sitting behind them could hear. When the woman glared at him, he gestured with his finger in his mouth.

"I have some money in my wallet," Abby said, as she dug in her purse. "Just take this and leave me alone." She reached behind with the money, still afraid to look at him.

He took her fifty dollars and put it in his pocket. "It's not that easy," he told her. "You are coming back with me and see Hippie Mike."

"He's *your* drug dealer. I never bought anything from him. He don't know me." She stopped shaking so she turned to face him and said, "Don't bother me no more." She was alone. He had disappeared.

🍁 🍁 🍁

Babes Go-Go was packed to capacity Thursday night. Every seat was filled. There was no room for bar backs to bring beer to the bar without pushing someone out of the way. The line at the door was twenty deep. Four dancers twirled, shimmied, and strutted around the stage. "Go-Go Rama" was printed in soap across the mirrors on the walls. The parking lot was so full that some customers parked across the street at a doughnut shop. The security company brought in extra men. The guards complained that they were doing the job of the bouncers, but they were stuck.

Carla parked her car behind the bar and walked in the back door without seeing how crowded it was. When she got to the locker room, she learned that her first set was at eight-thirty, a full hour and a half later.

George walked in the bar with five business associates. Each wore a suit, even though they had loosened their ties and unfastened the top button of their shirts.

"This place wasn't this packed last week," one guy said. "The old man loves this place. He'll be here in a few minutes. You'd think a seventy-year-old fart who owns a million-dollar-a-year company would have a harem, instead of coming here."

"He gets a kick out of these young dancers shaking for him," another guy said. "There's always some slut who lets him rub his shriveled old hands on her. He gets comfortable, and we can talk business. He'll be so distracted that we could slip anything past him."

"I hope so. I don't want to do this all night," George said, as Stacy Ann danced in front of him.

"How's that young wife of yours?" a partner asked. "She could distract him."

George laughed. "You're probably right. When we went to Finneman's party, she wore this tight dress I picked out for her, and Finneman was ready to give us his company."

"You cradle robber," another associate said.

"I saw her first," George said with a smirk. "She's a good little trophy, and she likes watching the kids."

"Hey boys," Stacy Ann said, strutting up to the group. "Having a fun night?"

"Fine," George said. He didn't pay attention or tip her. Another man pushed him out of the way to tip her.

The old man came in at eight-fifteen. He was hunched over, used a cane, and took small steps. His hands were wrinkled and covered with age spots, and his face was worn and saggy. His three-piece suit hung off his bony frame. "Looks like a good night," he said when he saw Stacy Ann bend over.

George gave up his seat to the old man and ordered ginger ales for both of them. "George, relax," the old man said. "You'll like this. We can talk about sales later."

The deejay called the name "Cookie" over the loudspeakers. One of the associates leaned over to George and told him, "You've got to see this one. She's young, and she wears almost nothing. She's one of those really slutty ones who lets you tip her by stuffing it in her bra. The old man almost pinched her nipple off last week."

"I don't need that," George said. "I already got the young wife. I'm going to the bathroom. Let's talk business when I get back."

"Come on—watch her. She's a babe."

George ignored them and left. The old man put a dollar in his shaky hand and stuffed it in Stacy Ann's bra. She turned and wagged her behind at him before taking another dollar. "You're sexy," she said. She kissed her finger and placed it on the man's worn face.

Carla danced out of the locker room wearing her usual stringy outfit. Her breasts were ready to explode out of her top from her shaking. The businessmen had money ready. She swung her leg on the bar in front of the associates and put her elbows on the bar. "Whew, it's crowded in here," she said.

"I want to fuck you," one guy said, as he tipped her.

"We can't do it here," Carla said, pretending to be sorry. She shimmied to the stage and swung around the brass pole as fog covered the dancing area.

George came out of the bathroom and walked through the crowds toward the bar. He sat down. "Are you talking business yet?"

"You missed her," his associate said. "Look on the stage. That's the one the old man came here for."

George turned. "I see her. She looks like my wife." He realized what he'd said and froze. His eyes bulged and suddenly his tongue felt swollen. The perfume already made it difficult to breathe, but now George was ready to choke.

Carla slid off the stage and went to a group of young men in college shirts. George focused on her but couldn't see her face. She swung her leg onto the bar, so one guy could put a dollar in his mouth and lick her leg to her garter, causing her to laugh. She turned to the stage as a spotlight shone on her.

"That's my wife," George blurted out.

His associates leaned over each other to get a better look at her. George bolted up out of his seat and followed her along the bar to catch up to her. "What is she doing?" he asked a stranger, as she bent over slapping her fleshy behind.

"She's spanking herself. I'd spank her and call her bad," the stranger said.

She swayed her hips in front of a man who tipped her by stuffing a dollar in her bra. She pulled his hand out and kissed it before moving away. "You're a bad boy. I like that," she said. Carla had heard Sunflower say that once, and it seemed to make the customer happy.

She could see the clock—three more hours to go. Three more hours of blank faces, sticky bars, pushy customers, rancid perfume, and meaningless tips before Rita's entrapment ended. Her heels ached after one song.

George appeared from out of the blur in front of her. "What are you doing here?" he yelled.

"Oh, shit. What are you doing here?" she asked, as she backed away.

"I'm listening to my business partners call my wife a slut. They're laughing and telling me how they felt you up last week."

"It was for money. It means nothing."

"Get dressed. We're getting out of here." He reached over the bar to grab her.

"I can't. I have three more sets to go." She backed out of his reach. The men around the bar pushed George away from her and toward the back wall.

"You do not. Put something on. I can see through that thing," he said, pointing at the strings that constituted her outfit. He marched to an opening in the bar and called her. "Get over here now!" he yelled.

The college boys booed and chanted, "Don't go, don't go." She took small steps toward George. He grabbed her arm and flung her into the wall.

"We're getting out of here, even if you don't get dressed." George said, as she cowered in fear. Security grabbed his arms and pushed him away. He yelled that he was married to her.

"I have to leave," Carla said in the locker room. The door was stuck ajar. She could hear one of the security guards shout, "Don't touch the dancers." She changed into jeans and a T-shirt. "My husband is really pissed," she said to the other dancers in the locker room.

"You can't go," Stacy Ann said. She grabbed Carla's already bruised arm. "They said I was in charge tonight."

"I don't care," Carla said. "I really have to leave."

"Oh," Stacy Ann said, with a tear in her eye. "I don't want to get in trouble." The tears smeared the makeup around her eyes. "Why does this happen to me?"

"Stacy, I have a bigger issue. I'm going to get a divorce." Carla wiped sweat off her forehead.

"Doesn't he know you do this?" Stacy Ann asked, sniffling.

"No. He doesn't know anything about me." Carla paused and looked at everyone in the locker room. Every time the door opened wide, they could hear George yelling, "She's my wife."

"You hear how he's yelling out there? He's never respected me, but I've never seen him like this." She closed her locker and stared at the door. "He ignores me most of the time—that's why I'm here."

"You've got his attention," Stacy Ann said.

"I'm afraid of what he'll do now that I have his attention." Carla picked up her bag and listened to the commotion outside the door. George's yells were louder than the music. "Where does he get off talking to me like that? I'm not one of his little girls. He wants to think that I'm his little girl wife, but I'm not."

"You tell him," Sunflower said.

"Yeah, show him by staying for another set," Stacy Ann said, brightening up.

"No. I'm going to show him," Carla said. She burst through the back door to the parking lot where George was now waiting in his car. He yelled for her to get in his car, but she pointed to her own car.

"Get in the fucking car," he said through gritted teeth.

"You going to open the door?" she asked, with her hands on her hips.

He unlocked the doors with the remote power lock and sat waiting for her to get in. The security guard watching went back inside. Once Carla got in the car, George locked the doors. "How can you embarrass me like that?" he yelled. He backhanded her cheek.

"Don't you ever hit me again," she said. She began punching and slapping his arms.

"Don't tell me what to do," he answered. He pushed her fists out of the way and slapped her again. He grabbed her hair and yelled, "What is wrong with you? Do you have any sense? My wife." He sighed.

She pulled her hair back and yelled, "Go to hell. I can do what I want. You don't own me."

"Yes, I do. You're my wife." He started the car.

"I don't care what you think," she yelled. "Don't push me around." She slapped him again to punctuate her anger. "I'm happy, George. I'm so happy that you saw me in there. All those other guys wanted to touch me. You don't touch me."

He grabbed her shirt and shook her. "You better stop hitting me, or I'll hurt you."

"You're going to get tough with me," she said in a mocking tone. "Oh, I'm scared."

"You should be. You're a slut. You're lucky I didn't leave you in there with that scum. You act like a slut all the time. You're always running around the house yelling to fuck you, fuck you. I hope my daughters don't end up like you."

"Our daughters."

"You don't care about them. They are my daughters. They live in my house. You don't even try to be a friend to Kendra. You complain about Kim being clingy. You're no mother."

"Fuck you," she yelled back. She unlocked her door and opened it before George could hit the power lock again. "I love Kim." She got out of the car and stomped to hers. George stayed in his car. Carla started her car and roared out of the parking lot. She cut George off at the driveway and sped down the freeway. He raced behind her and flashed his high beams in her rearview mirror.

At a red light, he crept up on the passenger side. He wanted to reach through the cars and shake her. His arms were tense. His fingers squeezed lines into the steering wheel. All he could do was stare. She tried not to look, but she couldn't help it. The light changed, and she floored the accelerator to race the rest of the way home.

She got home first, and burst out of the car for the front door. George slid out of his car and took his time walking up the front stairs. Carla slammed the front door and leaned against it to keep it shut. George hit the remote car locks while strolling to the house. She didn't lock the front door, which wouldn't have mattered, since George had keys. He rammed the door with his shoulder so hard that it knocked Carla away.

George resumed yelling, "Get out! You can't keep me out of my house. Get away from these girls. I thought you could raise my daughters. You slut!" She backed away as he walked toward her. "Just like those guys were saying," he continued. "I let you live in a mansion. My daughters are here with you, and what do you do? You go strip for a seventy-year-old man and a couple of college boys. Get out and go do it. Go sleep with them, too. Don't ever come back."

George's yelling woke up Kendra and Kim. They went to the stairs to listen.

"I don't want to strip for a seventy-year-old man. I never would've done it if you'd paid attention to me."

"Don't you try to blame me for this," he said. "We have responsibilities. This isn't how a mother takes care of children."

"When was the last time you said you loved me? You don't remember. I sure don't," she yelled.

"I don't love you now," he said. He stared through her, his jaw clenched and his shoulders raised. "You've embarrassed all of us. I thought you were a mature woman. I thought I could trust you with my house, my daughters, my money, my car, but I was wrong."

Carla turned away from him and went to her bedroom. She could hear Kendra and Kim at the top of the stairs as she walked toward them. They ran for their rooms. Carla slammed her bedroom door shut and went to her closet, which was full of clothes.

"The bastard thinks I did this for sex," she mumbled. "Bastard thinks I'm sex-crazed." She pulled out a bunch of things and put them in a suitcase she had in the closet. She didn't even look to see what she had. "I never saw something so un-sexy as that locker room in my life. All he ever had to do was say, 'I love you'—just once."

She dragged her bag off the bed and swung open the door. Kendra stood in the doorway to her room. Carla wanted to tell her to go to bed, but she knew Kendra wouldn't. Just this once, she wanted to tell Kendra that she was a bitch, but there was no point. Carla dragged her bag down the stairs where George sat on the couch with an empty shot glass in his hands.

"I'm leaving, but only for the night," she said. "This isn't over."

"It's over. It's all over. I'm calling my lawyer tomorrow."

"I need time to get the rest of my things," Carla said.

"You never had things," he laughed. "I bought you everything. You can leave the wedding and engagement rings by the door on the way out."

Carla twisted the ring on her finger. "No," she replied. Her back straightened and she turned her head causing her hair to sway full. She dragged her bag out the door into the heavy-humid fresh air. She took a deep breath of the open night. The bag was a struggle to lift to her shoulder as she stumbled down the driveway to her car.

George went upstairs and saw Kendra. "Get in your room."

"When is she coming back?"

"She's not."

"That's two families," Kendra said. She turned into her room and looked back over her shoulder. "Next time buy a better woman to boss around."

Chapter 16

Penn took Abby's money to an outlet mall several miles from where Abby worked. He bought some new clothes, and took the rest of the money to a gas station to buy a few gallons of gasoline. He used the dark, smelly bathroom to wash for the first time in a few days. He held the door open with his foot while he splashed water on his face and wiped off with the last of the toilet paper from the stall. This was very unfamiliar to him. He was accustomed to flashy clothes and the best of everything. He always had a place to stay. Plenty of girls were willing to put him up for the night.

His heroin addiction seemed to be getting the best of him. He had accumulated debt he couldn't handle. The treatment worked for the addiction, but it never ends. His body was a wreck. His bloodshot eyes had black rings under them.

He knew Abby wasn't going to just leave with him. He needed to make her want to leave. The advertisement for the "Go-Go-Rama" was still with him. He was sure she would be at the big event. No stripper—or "erotic entertainer," as she called it—would turn down that much money. There was no way he could grab her at the bar, so he had to stake out the parking lot looking for her.

The cops patrolled the parking lot every few hours, after Carla left. Nothing criminal happened. Penn never saw Abby show up. As much as he hated to spend more of his money, he paid the cover charge and went inside to look for her. There was an empty seat in the corner. He sat down to watch Sunflower dance. She looked very skinny and very beautiful, yet older than most of the dancers. She wouldn't make it in Vegas, he thought. Her blue, one-piece outfit had a space at her navel that showed a little flab. He put the last of his money on the bar.

"Yeah," Eli, the bartender, said.

"Gimme a beer and all the rest of this in singles. I'm gonna stay awhile."

Sunflower spun around the brass pole and winked at Penn when she saw the money. She grabbed her breasts and shook. He smirked at her and folded a bill between his fingers.

"Hi," she said, walking over to him. "Just get off work?"

"No," he answered. He looked her over. "You know a dancer named Baby Breath or Doll or something like that?"

Her head shot back. "You looking for her. You a cop?"

Penn laughed. "I'm not a cop. I used to date her. She works here now? I just wanted to see what she's doing."

She put her hand on his folded dollar. "You're a little late. She retired a week or so ago. You're a cop aren't you? Our regular customers aren't so scruffy. You're trying too hard to be an outsider."

"Honest. I'm not a cop."

"She retired." She snapped her fingers and pointed at him. "You're investigating it, aren't you? You know, those murders."

Penn's brow furrowed. "What murders? I told you that I'm not a cop. I want to see Baby dance."

She grabbed Penn's folded money and stuffed it in her bra. "She's retired. I'm here now." Penn didn't react, so she walked away.

"Hey, what's all this about a murder here?" Penn asked Eli.

"You a cop? There's no prostitution here."

"I'm not a cop."

"You're too dirty to be a regular," Eli said. "This has to be a disguise."

"That's it. I've had it with this place. I don't like cops." Penn went outside, pushing past the security guards. He got in his truck and waited for the bar to close. Cars left one at a time starting around eleven o'clock. The bar emptied out at two o'clock. Penn crouched on his seat and watched what was left of the crowd leave. A small woman left through a side door with a guard. Ten minutes later, another accompanied dancer left. A guard accompanied Sunflower, too. They walked to her car, where he waited until she opened her car door. She hugged him and got in. The guard left when she started the car. When she got to the driveway, Penn ran to the driver's side of her car. The windows were dark, and he didn't see the pepper spray she held.

"What murders are you talking about?" he asked, when she lowered the window.

"Are you crazy bothering me?" she asked. "If one of those bouncers comes out, he'll beat the hell out of you."

"Then you have to let me in the car." He went to the passenger side. "I have some coke, if you let me in."

She sat there, still unsure of what to do. He plucked the door handle, waiting for it to unlock. He was certain he would get what he wanted. There was a long pause. Then he heard the door unlock.

"I have protection," she said, when he sat down.

"Let's go somewhere, and you can tell me all about my girl and all this murder stuff."

"Don't you want to drive your car and follow me?" she asked.

"Naw, it's stolen." She turned, and he smiled. "It's fine. I still have my stash."

She smiled. "You're a real comedian." She put the car in gear. "I live really far from here."

"I'll steal another car to get back."

"You're so funny."

Penn woke up next to Sunflower in her queen-sized bed at ten o'clock in the morning. He lifted the blankets and saw that they were naked. His body was so numb from the drugs that he wasn't sure how he'd ended up here. He remembered hearing about Abby and some new bitch named Carla. There was something about murder, but he didn't remember much.

He got out of bed and found his clothes spread out along the hallway leading to the bedroom. Empty cups lay scattered on the rug of her living room. Candles were burned down to stubs. The coffee table was covered in garbage and razors. The room smelled like sweat and perfume.

Her purse was on the couch. The apartment was silent. She wasn't awake. He opened the purse and grabbed a handful of dollars without looking at the denominations. He dropped the purse on a table and knocked over a picture of her holding a baby. It looked old. He opened the front door until he heard it creak. He paused. The door opened more until another creak. There was enough space to slip through so he squeezed out. It didn't wake her.

Mark was awake for work at two thirty in the morning. He got out of bed, dressed, and kissed Abby on the cheek without waking her. She woke up six hours later and went out to get a newspaper. She thought she saw Penn at the convenience store, but it was just a woman with short hair. She thought she saw him in a car that drove by, but the car didn't stop.

Abby went to work and promised Nona that nothing would happen, but she kept looking and waiting for him to sneak up. She went to the food court, eyeing everyone there. Who was the person behind the direction sign? Who was the person in line at the music store? It wasn't him. She scrambled through the parking lot after work so no one could follow her. She parked her car next to Mark's and kept looking over her shoulder as she went to the house.

"What is she looking for?" Penn wondered, sitting in his newly stolen Toyota. The price tag dangled from the binoculars he stole. He could see the front door she went to from where he parked across the parking lot.

Mark was asleep on the couch with the television playing when Abby opened the door. He woke up when she slammed it. "Darling, I was just waiting for you to get home," he said, springing off the couch.

"I can see that. You were just resting your eyes for a minute, I guess." She kissed him and wrapped her arms around him. They walked to the kitchen in step with each other.

"They laid off a district sales manager and two warehouse managers today," Mark said. "All during the merger talk, they said there would be no layoffs. I don't know … It's like everyday we're walking on eggshells around there. If they're going to close the company, I wish they'd let me know so I could buy some different stuff—or at least sell off what I've got."

"I'm sure things will get better," she said. She unhooked her arms from his. "Do we have enough money to get by in case something happens?"

"For awhile," he answered. He looked out the window. "There's that old couple sitting on their front step. The Dumonts. I rarely see them together. She's always running around gossiping about the neighbors."

"I met her. She seems fine," Abby said. She pulled a twenty-ounce bottle of soda from the refrigerator.

"I'm happy you met the neighbors," Mark said. "We aren't moving to a new house anytime soon. They'll all like you once they meet you."

"I hope we do stay awhile." She leaned into his arms. "I don't want to run anymore. Did you ever live here with anyone else?"

"Nope. I had roommates when I first moved away from home and rented. This place is all mine. I bought it myself. I pay the mortgage myself."

"Ever been married before?" she asked.

"We never talked about that?" Mark asked, surprised.

She shook her head. "I was never married," she told him. "There's so much we don't know about each other. What do we really know about each other's past and its effects on today?"

"I was never married either," Mark said. "I haven't had a lot of girlfriends since I bought that truck route three years ago."

"So you went to the go-go bar a lot?"

"Sometimes."

Penn watched the door for hours, but nothing happened. He pulled out a local newspaper and found a cheap hotel near the shore. He started the car and left.

❦   ❦   ❦

Abby woke up alone the next morning. Mark was already at work. She put on her blue spandex jogging shorts and a tight T-shirt. She walked out the front door and started her stretching routine.

A ten-year-old boy rode his bike through the traffic as Abby jogged. He waved at her, and she smiled. A woman pushing a baby carriage waved to her. Another woman, about Abby's age and dressed in business attire, got into her minivan and waved to Abby as she drove by.

Mrs. Dumont was on the corner talking to Mrs. Vesquez, who also lived in the development. "See that girl running? I heard from Kate and Shellie that she's a stripper. She works at that club Babes Go-Go."

"You don't say," Mrs. Vesquez said. "I can't believe it. What kinds of people are living here? I thought the town tried to close that place down."

"I just hope she doesn't have all-night parties with a bunch of druggies and stuff," Mrs. Dumont said. "You never know what kind of prostitutes she'll have in that place."

Abby ran passed them and waved. They didn't wave back. Mrs. Vesquez raised her arm to wave but stopped when she saw that Mrs. Dumont didn't move.

"Do you really think she'll invite those kinds of people?" Mrs. Vesquez asked.

"You can't be fooled by her smile. She's probably planning something."

Abby got back to her front door and stretched her legs. She could feel eyes on her, but didn't see anyone. She stretched her right leg until she heard a voice that startled her so much that she jumped. Abby bit her lip and stood straight. There was no reflection in the windows, and no one near. She felt a chill, but it could be the mid-September air. She felt like someone was watching and coming closer. She spun around, ready to attack.

"Hi." It was just two boys on bicycles getting a kick out of watching a woman stretch. She was normally flattered by that kind of cute attention, but now they annoyed her.

🍁 🍁 🍁

Jake Hersh drove to the convenience store across the street from Babes Go-Go for coffee before the bar opened. His company had called him early in the morning to tell him they had no complaints about the bar's event. He wanted to see Eli when he opened the bar.

"You have a big night?" the Chinese store owner asked him across the counter. "The whole parking lot is still a mess. Cars park here. Cars park there. All a mess."

"I know. The Go-Go-Rama was two nights ago, and we still haven't cleaned out all the garbage. There's an old pickup truck still behind the bar."

"There's a car left behind here, too," the owner said. "Flies all around it. They go from the Dumpster to the car and back. I'm not going back there. Calling a tow truck."

"I think you should." Jake paid for his coffee. As he left, he saw the car the store owner told him about. He'd seen that car before. Jake went to it and looked inside. There was a person slouched over and covered in blood.

"Shit," he yelled. He dropped the coffee and grabbed the door handle. The door opened easily, and the body fell over and hung out the door. The seat belt stopped the person from falling all the way. Jake reached in to pick up the person and saw that the victim had tattoos on her arms. It was Rita. Her business cards were spread all over the seat.

Jake called the cops from his cell phone. He described the scene and realized that he had moved the body. The scene was contaminated because of him.

🍁 🍁 🍁

A woman with a baby stroller walked into Nora Daniels to look for a blouse, just as Abby walked in. She told Abby she wanted something new. "I can finally buy something that doesn't come from the maternity store," the woman said. "I want something nice."

Abby showed her to a rack, keeping one eye on the baby. "How old?" she asked.

"Four months. Do you have children?"

"No." She stepped back from the woman and went to another rack where she pulled out a cotton casual wear top. "I have to find you a blouse," she said.

"I saw the ring on your hand and the way you're looking in the stroller," the woman said. "Do you and your husband want children?"

Abby sighed. "I think we do." Abby knew it was a lie, but she had to make this sale. "It's not a good time." She looked over her shoulder at the empty mall.

"You never know," the woman told her.

Mrs. Vesquez walked in the store next. Abby was available to help her also. Neither one recognized the other at first, until Abby realized they were neighbors. She mentioned that they lived in the same complex, but Mrs. Vesquez still didn't recognize her.

"I was jogging this morning while you were talking to Mrs. Dumont. My name is Abby. Nice to meet you." Mrs. Vesquez smiled. "This is an interesting way to meet the neighbors," Abby said.

Mrs. Vesquez barely heard what Abby said because she kept trying to picture Abby as a stripper and a druggie. Abby wore a black knee-length skirt with a white blouse. Her hair was blown dried and hung straight. Her arms swung straight at her sides. Her back was always straight when she walked. Abby pointed to things using two fingers instead of one.

"We should have coffee sometime," Abby said, when Mrs. Vesquez went to pay for her purchases.

"Maybe," Mrs. Vesquez answered, with a touch of fear in her voice.

Mark was on the couch with his arm over his head when Abby got home. His hair was flat from wearing a cap to protect his face each day that the Indian summer continued through the end of September. She kissed her fingers and brushed his face. Then she glanced out the front window and noticed a car driving out of the parking lot. The car moved slow enough that she could see the driver. It looked like Penn driving. She crouched down and looked at Mark. *Penn could've followed me all day,* she thought. *He knows where I live.* Mark rolled over on the couch and snored.

Abby squeezed Mark's arm, which woke him up. He looked startled to see her until Abby told him she had just walked through the door.

"I was awake waiting for you." He looked at his watch. "I must have lost track of time."

She went to the kitchen. "You're asleep every day when I come home. Can't you stay awake one day?"

He jumped off the couch and followed her. "I have to work early mornings. It's tiring out there in that sun at six in the morning. I have a business that might be closed down, and I'm trying to make sales." He stood in the doorway and watched her stare out the windows. "I have news for you. I always work shitty hours, and I sleep through much of the day. What's the next holiday? Thanksgiving? You can forget about me staying up all night then, too. The supermarkets are open on holidays now, and some pricks in some headquarter office in wherever decided that I have to work that holiday. Of course, he'll be home, but I work shitty hours every day—and holidays. I also get to work on my supposed days off if I really want commissions. Don't give me shit about this," he yelled. Then he turned and walked out of the kitchen.

She opened the refrigerator and slammed it back shut. Penn was out there, and Mark didn't even know, and she couldn't tell him.

Jake walked into Babes West near closing time with his notebook in hand. He bought a beer but didn't drink it. Eli was covering for a bartender who was out sick.

"You work both bars?" Jake asked.

"Yeah, what the hell? Same company owns both, so they let me make money at both bars when I can," Eli explained. "I heard about Rita. I'll miss her."

Jake told him about finding Rita and how he messed up the crime scene. The security company was happy about not having any incidents at the Go-Go-Rama but so angry with him now. "I can't believe I messed it up so bad. I thought the whole thing was over. There has to be a break soon. Rita was a house mom for the dancers. Someone had to know something—even a rumor. I should've known something was wrong when Rita wasn't there for the Rama. All those other guards thought I was in charge, but I was watching dancers. I even left early. I hate to say that I didn't know what was going on. My company will lose the contract, and I'll lose my job."

Eli rinsed out glasses in the sink under the bar. "I don't know what to tell you. I'm too busy watching out for me. I don't want to be a victim."

"I've been working security for twenty years," Jake said. "This is my big chance at a promotion. I catch this guy—I'll be huge."

Sunflower walked out of the locker room dressed in tight pants that hung down on her hips. Her shirt was short to show her navel piercing. "You count up my tip reports?" she asked Eli.

"Why not ask her?' Eli asked Jake. "Everyone goes to her for advice. She's been dancing for years. She knows everything around here."

"Ask me what?" she said, grinning but skeptical.

"I just want to talk to someone from the bar about the murders. He's right. You've been working here awhile at both bars. I want to know what you know."

"I don't know anything," she said. "I'm outta here."

He followed her to her car. "I don't want to follow you around. I'm not on duty now—but I'm lost here. Can you help me?"

"I probably can," she said. She threw her bag in the trunk of her car. "I don't know who's around here. Where is a good place to talk? If that's all you want to do."

He told her to meet him at the National Diner in an hour. She arrived and saw Jake sitting in a booth near the window facing the street. She took a deep breath and walked to him.

Chapter 17

Sunflower watched Jake sip soda through a straw poking from his mouth under his raven mustache. His large hands wrapped around the whole cup. The blower in the ceiling vent blew down on him, messing his thick black hair with hints of gray.

"You sure you don't want a drink?" Jake asked Sunflower, as he tapped on his glass.

"I don't know what I can tell you, Mister Security Guard," she said. The sounds of his straw sucking air detracted from his toughness. "I'm just an entertainer."

Their waitress came to the table and added water to their empty glasses. Jake took a notebook out from his back pocket.

"You can call me Jake," he said. "You're in there. I just want a lead. Give me some kind of lead, so no one else gets hurt."

"I don't know how to catch a murderer," she said. "The cops don't know who it is."

"If you had to guess, who do you think did it?" he asked. His fingernails turned white squeezing the end of his pen. "I'm going to investigate everyone sooner or later. Feel free to talk. I'll be investigating you at some point, so you might as well talk to me now."

"I don't know," she said. "I could name a few people, but I don't even know who you are. What are you doing here, instead of an office or something?"

"Fair enough," he said. "I work for Safeguard Incorporated. The owners of your bar contacted my company. I've been with the company twenty years. For twenty years, I've watched empty parking lots and old buildings. Now I have an important duty, and I want to impress people." He saw this didn't impress her. "Did you know the same company that owns the modern rock radio station in town also owns those bars you dance at?"

"So, why are we here? Shouldn't you be with the cops?"

"Guards don't work with cops. We're not equals at all in their eyes," he said. "The police can't get inside this place the way I can. They can't investigate dancer's files without a warrant. Not that I can either. The owners want to show me something, I'm closer than the police are." He sipped on water. "Don't get me wrong; the police will catch this person, but I want to help. I don't have a forensics team or anything like that. I'm going to the police when I find something. I'll get fired if I withhold evidence. My plans and goals would backfire."

"I'd like to tell you about the murders, but I don't know anything. I'm just as scared as anyone else. It could be a regular customer or another dancer. I just don't know."

He watched her twitch and toy with sugar packets as they talked. Her slender fingers tapped on the table. Her long blue nails looked sharp enough to cut through the wood.

The waitress came back and asked if they wanted anything else. "No," Sunflower said, annoyed that the waitress had interrupted. The waitress handed Jake the tab.

"Well, thanks for your time. I liked meeting you," he said, pulling his wallet from his back pocket. His eyes locked on hers. She didn't seem as nervous as she claimed. He picked up the check. "You leaving?" he asked.

He held out a hand. She put her fingers in his palm and slid out of the booth. "Are we going to talk again?" she asked him.

"I have to do some investigating first."

"Do you think you and I can talk for the fun of it?" she asked. They were less than an inch apart.

"I can contact you." He looked down at her chest, which was now touching his. He could feel her breath on his face. "I'll see you at the club. There's always time after closing."

"I'd like that. You make me feel safe—even though you sip your soda through a straw like a kid. It's not something I would expect from a big, tough rent-a-cop."

Even though she insulted his job, she was still charming. Her three-inch platform sandals clopped on the tile floor with each step, and she wiggled as she walked out of the diner. As he watched her, he bit his lip so much that he caught part of his mustache in his mouth. "Phew," he said, spitting out hairs.

❦   ❦   ❦

The next morning, Carla watched the girls' private-school bus pull away from the front of the house. She walked up the long driveway and opened the front door. She could hear George yelling in the kitchen. Kim sat at the table crying.

Carla's eyes burned with anger. "What are you yelling at her for?" Carla shouted, squaring off at George. They stopped and looked at Kim. She jumped up and ran to Carla, wrapping her arms around Carla's waist with all the muscle she had.

"Why aren't you in school?" Carla asked Kim.

"Because she's traumatized," George said, sneering at her. "She's lost another mother—because of you and your slutty behavior."

Carla tried to loosen Kim's grip, but the girl clenched tighter. "Kim, I have to talk to your dad."

"Don't leave me," Kim cried into Carla's stomach.

"I'm not going anywhere," she assured Kim. "Don't cry," she said wiping away Kim's tears. "Go to your room for a few minutes."

"You're going," George said, after Kim walked out of the room. "You're not welcome here. Do you know what kind of hell I get at work? Can you imagine what Kendra is going to hear at school? People talk. How could you be so stupid?"

"Just as stupid as you are," she said. "You're calling me a slut in front of your impressionable daughter. I asked you for months to say you love me. You never would. All I wanted was a little attention. I didn't want anything to blow up like this."

He slammed down his coffee mug and yelled, "You didn't think! Kim stayed home, because she can't come out of her room without crying. Even Kendra felt bad this morning."

"I can talk to Kim," Carla said. "They need me. They may not want me, but they need me. We can patch this up."

He walked to the doorway. "I don't know," he said. He grabbed his briefcase and left. Carla heard the door slam. She looked around the empty kitchen.

"Is everything normal again," Kim asked, from out of nowhere.

"You weren't in your room." Carla could see there was no point lying to Kim. "I don't know if it'll be normal again."

George went to his office and closed the door. He sat at his desk trying to see through the darkened windows by his door. He knew they were looking at him. He saw people turn away as he entered the building. A guy with an identification badge from Accounting smiled at him. He had to know about Carla. They all knew. George knew they knew.

"Hey there, Georgie-Boy, Richard from sales said, as he barged into the office. "Pete Webster wants to know when your wife is dancing again. Don Harry wants to know if your wife does bachelor parties. Sam Fuji wants to know if she'll do a private dance. It sounds like you had an interesting time with them."

"Get out," he snarled, without looking up.

There was a picture of Carla with his arms around her on the corner of his desk. He grabbed the top of it and pushed it face down. He could feel the people milling around outside. They were looking at him.

"Did you know that the manager here slept with a lot of the dancers?" Jake Hersh asked Eli, as they talked before Babes Go-Go opened for the day.

"It's a rumor," Eli said. "It's more of a badly kept secret."

"Couldn't he be fired for that?" Jake asked. He walked to the back of the bar before he got an answer. Eli was busy rinsing glasses. No one was near the back. Jake took one last look and snuck into the manager's office.

The office was a mess. Files were scattered on the desk and floor. The windows were muddy on the outside. Flies fluttered around the desk light. He went to the filing cabinet and found the file on Carla, the newest dancer. Rita had started the file with small notes: "Rich husband." "Looking for a thrill." "Big tits." "Friend of Baby Doll." "Trained with Baby Doll." There was also a newspaper clipping about the billion-dollar merger of two computer companies. The top of the paper had creases, like it had been clipped to something. Someone else had looked at the file before him. While Jake was reading, the police showed up to talk with Eli. Jake shoved the file back in the drawer and snuck back out the door. He walked around the pool tables to the bar so it looked like he was walking around the entire time.

"You guys are here a lot," Jake said. "Come to check out the place again? We've had new dancers if you're investigating that."

"Can we come in? It's the Police. We have a search warrant."

"Si," answered George's maid, Rosita. She hid behind the door, opening it only as far as the chain lock permitted. She could feel perspiration start on her legs. She wore street clothes, rather than a uniform, and her shoes were in the kitchen. "No one home," she said. "Everyone left for the day."

"You're home."

She undid the chain and opened the door for the three policemen. They identified themselves and showed her the warrant, which she didn't understand. One of the officers asked her to call George while they waited. She called George at his office and then she put on her shoes and went to the den.

George rushed home to find the police waiting. They told George that they had a search warrant. There were witnesses to his fight with his wife at the Go-Go-Rama. It took them a few days to get witnesses with proof to get a search warrant. George laughed and said that he had nothing to hide. He even opened up doors for the police to search. One officer went in Kendra's room, where he found a pocketknife and a bag of marijuana in Kendra's closet. Another officer watched him bag it as evidence. The third officer picked up a glass tube with a rounded bottom off Kendra's night table.

"Did you know your daughter had that?" the officer asked George.

"It's a candleholder. My daughter bought it at a record store."

"It's called a bong," the officer said. "It's used to smoke what we found in that little bag there." He pointed at the marijuana.

"That's ridiculous," George said. "You don't have a warrant for that. What do you have a warrant for anyway? I'm not opening anymore doors. I'm calling my lawyers."

The maid snuck out to her car and drove away while the police were still there.

Meanwhile, Carla took Kim to the mall to feel better. They bought milkshakes and tried on clothes. They threw pennies into the water fountain and made wishes. Kim smiled for the first time that day, which had been Carla's wish. They loaded the trunk of Carla's Lexus with clothes by the time they left.

The front door was unlocked when they got home. The den was a mess. Drawers were open. Pictures were taken from the walls. Carla told Kim to go back to the car while she pulled out her cell phone. She called George's office and was told that George had left earlier in the day.

"What's this?" Kim asked, holding a copy of the search warrant. "It was by the sink."

"I said go to the car," Carla yelled. Kim's eyes teared up again. Carla apologized and took the paper. "Come on, we have to go to the lawyer's offices. When we get there, you stay in the car."

"What's wrong?"

"I don't know."

Carla parked and told Kim to lock the doors and stay in the car. She went into the office and asked how to find their lawyer. An older man in a pinstriped blue suit walked up behind her. She recognized him from Babes Go-Go, the night George had seen her there. She cringed when he said he was George's lawyer.

"The police found a file on you at the go-go club and they were told about the parking lot yelling," the lawyer told her. "You were at that club every time someone turned up missing or dead. The police went to your house with a search warrant to get information on you. When they got there, they found Kendra had drugs and drug paraphernalia in her room. I was called to calm things down. Your husband is in another office explaining this for the records."

"They think I killed people at the club?"

"It's hard to say," the lawyer said. "There were no notes about how long you worked at the club. It looks like a couple of times, but you were good," he smirked. The police confiscated all the knives in the house. Those victims were all stabbed the police told me."

"I didn't kill anyone."

"I don't think so either. The drugs were confiscated illegally, so we'll get that thrown out. There's going to be rumors about this at the office."

Mark drove his car into his parking space after work and saw Sue, still in her work clothes. She had grown her hair out and curled it. This was the first time he noticed. She stood at her mailbox going through envelopes. When she saw him, she walked over to his car.

"What's this about your wife's troubled past?" she asked. "The whole complex is talking about your wife the stripper."

"I can't believe this place," he said. "I never told anyone she was a stripper except Eddie."

"Well the whole place is talking about it," Sue informed him. "I didn't say anything. I like the two of you. I'm not getting involved. I think you rushed into things, but you seem happy. Didn't you notice how everyone watches her when she comes home?"

"She's beautiful. I figured people would notice her. Why are people talking about her? She waves and smiles to everyone here. She is the friendliest person around," he said. He spotted the Dumonts' place. "It's that old bitch up the street, isn't it? That Dumont bitch is gossiping again, isn't she? I'll get her to stop."

"What are you gonna do?"

"I don't know," he said. "Punching her would make things worse." He calmed down. "I knew what Abby did when I married her. What can I do to Mrs. Dumont? I can't curse her for telling the truth."

He turned back to his house and walked away, shrugging his shoulders. Sue stood there watching her friend—deflated. Penn, sitting across the street, watched them, too.

🍁   🍁   🍁

Jake Hersh talked to Sunflower at the Go-Go, but she brushed him away. She gave him her address the previous night and said she would only talk to him outside of work. He drove his dirty black sedan to Sunflower's apartment. She lived thirty miles from Babes in an old neighborhood. One-car driveways ran next to small, fenced-in front yards. She lived in a brick apartment building off the main road. The parking lot was filled with mostly old cars. Each apartment had two windows facing out, and one of those had a Fedders air conditioner sticking out.

"Jake," she said, sounding surprised when she opened the door in faded sweat pants and a T-shirt.

"I told you that I wanted to keep up with you. Can we talk?" He wasn't dressed in his guard uniform. He was out of style, but casual in his sweater vest and khaki pants.

She welcomed him in and pushed empty boxes off the couch in an attempt to clear a spot where they could sit down.

"The police investigated Carla's husband," Jake said. He sat across from a thirteen-inch television with a dusty cable box on top. There was a stack of old, torn magazines on a scratched coffee table in front of him. "I can see how he would be angry about the situation. The guy was worth a lot of money and his wife was …" He stopped.

"Showing her tits to everyone," she finished for him. "I know what people say. This isn't what I told my high school guidance counselor I wanted to do when I grew up. This is easy money, and I need money really bad."

"Why?"

She sat next to him. The couch was worn, and she sunk lower than Jake. Her long hair was stringy and unbrushed. Without the heavy makeup that she wore while dancing, she had a light, artificial tan that made her skin look like old newspaper. She pointed to a picture on a shelf by the door. "That's my son. He turned nine last month. He's with foster parents. I know who they are." She stopped and picked at her airbrushed nails. "I want to get him back, but that takes more money than I have. There are lawyers and all that."

"Why is he with foster parents?"

"I made a mistake. I did a few drugs in my past. I dated some real losers and spent all my money. You probably hear this all day at the club." She crossed her leg under herself. "The neighbors talked. People saw the drugs, and reported me to Child Protection. They took him away. I was so stoned that I didn't notice. I was stoned through the hearings. I cleaned myself up. But sometimes I slip. When I slip, I really fall. The other night, I slipped and … well, never mind. If I ever see that guy again, I'll … never mind."

Jake squirmed.

"I can be a good mother," she continued. "I take care of things. That kid will have it so good when he comes home. I will try my best. That's a lot more than his father could say. He didn't even stick around for the whole pregnancy." She stopped picking at her nails and put her hand on Jake's leg. "They took him away, but if I can get one more chance.… I see him from time to time. I have to hide in a bush to get a peek at him."

"So you're doing this purely to get your son?"

"Who doesn't? Do you think any of those girls really like being groped like that?"

"I figured it was usually for drug money," he said. "I guess you almost have to be on drugs to do this."

She exhaled a deep breath. "Can I get you a drink?"

"Sure, Mona," he said, watching to see her reaction.

She relaxed. "No one ever calls me by the right name. I spend all night being called 'honey' or 'Sunflower.' You may call me Mona."

Chapter 18

Abby parked her car in the empty spot next to Mark's after work. She was perspiring, even though the weather was cool. Her hair was frizzy, and her feet hurt from standing all day. She was tired of Muzak. Her nerves were tense from ducking in the back storage room every time a man walked in the store till she was certain it wasn't Penn. She knew Nona didn't want him to come in the store and create a scene like last time. Business had been slow that day. Toward the end of her shift, a crowd of young people had come in and handled a bunch of merchandise but didn't buy anything. The down time gave Abby moments to think and worry. Now, as she got out of the car, she looked over her shoulder for Penn. No sign of him.

The sun was no longer visible in the dark blue sky. The moon was a faint shadow over the trees across the complex. The only noise was the sound of her jangling keys as she walked to her door. She didn't see any new cars in the parking lot, which was a good sign that Penn wasn't around.

She opened the front door and saw Mark asleep on the couch. The television was on a news channel, and the remote control was on the floor. She slammed the door, which woke Mark up. He jumped off the couch. "You're home late," he said.

"It isn't even really night yet. It's dusk," she said. "You fell asleep again," she said as she walked to the kitchen, annoyed that he couldn't stay awake to wait for her.

"Well, you won't have to complain about it next week," he replied. "It's all over."

She walked back into the living room holding a twenty-ounce Coke in her hand. "What do you mean?"

"The merger went through. The new company is shutting down the Dewey's brand. There'll be no more Dewey's Donuts on the shelves after next week."

"That's sad."

"I am an independent contractor," he continued. "I didn't pay unemployment tax, so I can't collect unemployment while I look for another job." She sat down next to him. He reached out and patted her shoulder and said, "You're the big bread winner after next week."

"I could work extra hours at the mall. Can we live on that?"

"I doubt it," he said. "But it should be easy for me to get another job. I own my own equipment, and there are a lot of delivery jobs out there." His hands made circular motions on her back. He hoped she would get the hint and lean against him, but she didn't get it.

"I haven't had a real vacation in years," he said. "I could use the time to regroup. You know, get my strength up again." He gave up on her back and gripped her hand with both of his as he sighed, without looking at her. "This is such bullshit. I worked so many hours, so many holidays. Two fuckers on the West Coast merge companies, and now I'm fucked with no unemployment."

"You have me."

"Yeah," he chuckled. Besides his job, she was *all* he had. "Thank God I can trust you with all of this. I can just imagine what my parents are going to say. They're going to have a field day telling me how my brother still has a job. Everyone around here has jobs."

"It's funny you should mention your parents," Abby said. "While I was watching TV this morning, your mother called. We had a nice talk. You never told her we were married, did you?"

"I was going to. I just didn't know how to say it," he said. "You have to believe that."

"Why didn't you tell her? This is big. You can't hide this. Do you want to hide this?"

"No." He tried to laugh, but he was so nervous it came out as a hiccup. "It's just that no one knows. I don't know any of your friends at all."

"I don't have any. I only moved here three months ago." She wiggled her fingers and freed her hand from his. "Why doesn't the whole world know about us? I've seen those wedding pictures of couples in the papers. We didn't do that."

"I don't know a lot of people. The whole complex knows we're married." He paused to take a breath. "Did you tell my parents about us?"

"No. I'm more …" She paused and waved her hands to pull the right word from the air. "I'm more bothered … no … upset … no … fucking pissed that you didn't rush out and tell everyone you know."

"I promise I'm going to tell them. I'm going to tell everyone."

"Good, they're coming over tomorrow night."

"What?"

"I invited them."

"I just lost my company," Mark reminded her. "I really don't think I can deal with them. Oh, God, I didn't invite them to the wedding. They'll complain about that. We didn't even have a big wedding. They'll complain about that, too."

Abby got off the couch and walked to the window while Mark blabbered to himself.

"The house needs work, too," he muttered.

She watched teenage boys ride circles around the cars in the parking lot. "What's with the boys around here?" she asked. "They're always standing around when I get home. They never seem to have anything to do."

"I can't believe you invited them," Mark still blabbered.

Abby turned to face the night. There was still a lot of darkness, even with the streetlights close to the houses and the cars. Penn was out there. She knew it. She heard Mark talk, but she felt alone with the darkness.

Abby got home at six o'clock the next night and found Mark dusting the coffee table, dressed in ironed trousers, dress shoes, and a button-down shirt.

"Wow, you're awake today—and dressed up," Abby said, when she opened the front door. "You're cooking too," she added, walking to the kitchen. "Mini-pizzas. You're dusting and making appetizers for your parents?" She laughed watching him shove things around in the closet to put away the dusting wax. "They're your parents. What are you so worried about?" Abby headed toward the bedroom.

"You've heard me talk about them," Mark answered. "If they see dust, they'll criticize."

The doorbell rang. Mark sprinted to the door, took a deep breath, and opened it. There stood his parents dressed in matching blue jogging suits.

Abby came out from the bedroom, still wearing the black business skirt, black stockings, and sweater she wore at work. She walked behind Mark to kick her shoes out of the way of the door.

"Mark, are you going to invite them in?" she asked.

His parents walked to the couch past Mark, who seemed frozen in place. His father pressed down on a cushion before he sat. His mother picked lint off. They stared at Abby as she got a chair from the kitchen.

"So, have you always lived in New Jersey?" Abby asked his parents. "I just got here. I'm from Las Vegas. This is a very different place." She watched Mark's mother move the magazines around on the coffee table.

"Have you known Mark a long time?" she asked Abby.

"No," Abby replied. "We've only known each other maybe eight weeks."

"And you're living together?" his mother asked. "You hardly know each other."

Mark sat down next to Abby in another chair from the kitchen, but he didn't say anything.

"Well, how did you two meet?" his mother asked.

Mark looked at Abby for an answer. She looked at him to see what he would say. He took a deep breath and said, "There are a few things you should know. I didn't tell you about her and me. Well, I didn't tell you anything. I should have told you a while ago."

"Spit it out," his father said. "We're not going to live forever."

"We're married—Abby and me. We got married about a month ago."

Mark's mother gasped. "You never said anything."

"It was all quick," Mark said. He reached to put his hand on Abby's thigh and felt her twitch. "We met in a club not too far from here. She was dancing, and we started talking. Things happened."

"Oh, you like to dance. It's called 'clubbing,' right?" his mother asked.

"No," Abby answered.

"In shows? We used to go see the musicals on Broadway. I like musicals from the 1930s. You don't see many musicals anymore."

"Yeah," Abby said.

"No." Mark held on to both of Abby's hands. "Dad, maybe you should grab a pillow for Mom. She's going to faint in a minute." His father leaned forward. His mother looked around the room. "Abby was a go-go dancer at Babes."

"Erotic entertainer," she corrected him.

"We met and started talking."

Mark's father's jaw dropped. "So you dance naked?"

"No," Mark answered for her. "Not quite. She wears things like bikinis or lingerie."

"So you're almost naked on a stage, and guys pay you to prance around," Mark's mother said. She ignored Mark and looked straight at Abby, who squirmed in her seat.

"Yeah, that's kinda it."

"And you," his mother said to Mark, pointing at him. "You went to those places—those biker bars—and saw her do that?"

"Yeah, but it wasn't a biker bar."

"And you met her there?"

"Yeah."

"And you paid her to prance around naked?"

"She wasn't naked. Hey, look, there's more to her than a naked body. She's funny, intelligent, and far more interesting than anyone I've ever met before. I married her because I really think she is the most spectacular person in the world."

All of them stared at each other. The clocks in the room were digital, so there wasn't even the tick of a clock to break the cold silence. Mark's father moved his mouth, as if words were caught in his teeth. Mark's mother's eyes rolled up toward the ceiling. Abby's eyes darted around the room, but she didn't move her head. Mark let go of Abby's hands and cracked his knuckles.

"Well," Mark's father said, "proves he's not gay. We wondered."

Abby coughed out a shocked laugh.

"He shouldn't have said that," Mark's mother said. "It's just that his brother was married when he was twenty-two. Mark was never very good with the girls in high school. His brother had all the girls. I thought Mark would at least try to date one of the girls his brother broke up with, but he didn't."

"But when Mark hit thirty and wasn't married, I wondered," his father continued.

"You thought I was gay!" Mark shouted.

"Don't yell like that," his father said.

His mother cut him off. "This is why you don't have company over. Look how you treat people. You're yelling like a lunatic. I figured maybe his brother could teach him about girls."

Abby kept turning her head to follow the conversation, and Mark kept asking why they thought he was gay.

"How is Las Vegas?" Mark's father asked, finally changing the subject. "We were thinking of taking a trip out there. Those people know how to treat a guest," he said, looking at Mark.

"Well, sorry." Mark stood up and started pacing. "I didn't date a lot, so you automatically thought I was gay. I can't believe this. I drive a truck, for Christ's sakes."

"What happened to that fiancée of yours?" his father asked.

"I was working this job, and I didn't have time for her."

"Well, see … that's what we mean," his father said. "You gave her up instead of trying to change your job. I bet you haven't been laid since then."

"Don't say that," his mother said, slapping her husband's leg. "We don't know her. We can't say things like that in front of her."

"Oh, stop it," his father continued. "I asked your brother to level with me. He didn't know if you were going to just work and be a hermit or what. What else could we think? I would've been OK with the gay thing. I see it on television."

Mark's mother turned to Abby. "If you danced in a chorus line, you'd probably be good. Busby Berkley was a great director. He used to have these dancers line up in all different ways and make all kinds of designs with the chorus lines."

"I liked Ginger Rogers. She was really pretty and feisty," Abby answered. "I don't usually watch musicals. My favorite all time movie is *The Gold Rush*."

Everyone stopped talking. They stared at each other for another long, silent stretch.

"You know a lot about movies?" Mark's mother asked Abby. "Why weren't we invited to the wedding?"

"The wedding happened really quick, at Town Hall. It was very small," Abby said. "My walk down the aisle was three steps, but it was wonderful."

"His brother's wedding was huge," Mark's mother said. "The wedding party had twenty people. There were at least two hundred guests in the church. The reception lasted almost all night. I should show you the pictures. We've got two picture books. Mark never saw the pictures or the videotape. We just had it transferred to DVD. We keep asking Mark if he wants to look at it."

"I was there."

"He brought his last fiancée," his mother whispered.

"I've got mini-pizzas in the kitchen," Mark said. He got up and went to the kitchen, groaning.

"Straight people don't make appetizers," his father yelled.

Mark slammed down a plate from the cabinet.

Abby looked at his parents. "I retired from dancing," she told them. "I have a job at the mall."

Mark slid pizzas onto the plate, still groaning. He heard Abby talk, but he couldn't hear what was being said. He hoped they wouldn't be too rough on Abby. They were always rough on him. His mother could spend a lot of time on morals and the decline of the country because of immorality. When he got back to the room, Abby was sitting on the couch between his parents.

"See, I want to paint that wall," she said, pointing across the room.

"They have a big paint section at the hardware place on Route Thirty-Six," his mother said. "What do you want to do with that kitchen? I told Mark it's too dark."

Abby laughed. "I like it. It needs a paper towel holder, though."

"It's a bachelor place," his mother whispered. "Mark isn't gay. He can't decorate. You have to add a woman's touch to this place."

Abby laughed. "I'm not much of a decorator. I can design costumes and sew, but I don't know what to do about a room."

"You can sew?" his mother asked, surprised. "His last fiancée couldn't sew. She could shop for new things."

Mark sat down and exhaled. They liked her.

The next night, Abby came home from work tired and sore. She found Mark slouched over on the couch watching television, with his shirt open and pants undone. His shoes were off, and his feet were on the coffee table. It didn't look like he'd shaved or combed his hair all day.

"Anything on television?" she asked.

He didn't answer, even as she walked past him going to the bedroom.

"A woman came into the store and wanted white slacks," she said. "It's past Labor Day, so I don't know what she was thinking." Abby came back and walked to the window wearing a pair of stained sweat pants with an oversized T-shirt.

"Why do you always stare out that window?" he asked, without looking at her.

"Just to see everyone."

"Someone bothering you?"

"No."

"Neighbors say anything to you?"

"I saw a few at the mall," Abby replied. "I sold Mrs. Vesquez another blouse and invited her over. A lot of neighbors come to the store to look around, but they really don't buy much."

"So why are you at that window?"

"No reason." She spun around and walked in front of the television. "I'm away from the window. What's your problem?"

"I got a deal on my truck. I'm going to sell it. I was thinking that I'm tired of the holidays. I'm married. I should be home. I didn't ask a lot for it, but it's something. I had second thoughts after I put the check in the bank."

Her shoulders drooped, and she relaxed her defensive stance. "Had that truck a while?"

He cracked his knuckles. "I rebuilt the engine myself, and I don't know crap about engines. I had to read from a manual while I did it. I spent a lot of money on that truck. I bought new seats and new racks in the back. I climbed up top and put sheet metal on the roof when there was a hole."

She walked over, sat next to him, and put her hand on his shoulder.

"I lived in it for twelve hours a day … every day … snow storms, heavy rain, freezing cold. There were times when it was so cold and rainy that the inside of the truck would turn into one big sheet of ice." He forced a smile and laughed. "One time behind Food City, I slipped from the front of the truck, right out the back door. I landed on a cat. It was four in the morning and pitch black. It scared the shit out of me. He ran away, and I slipped on the bumper trying to get back in the truck." He stopped laughing and sighed. "I remember Christmas Day last year. I went to bed early Christmas night—like nine o'clock—so I could get up and get in my truck to deliver doughnuts."

She rubbed his back and felt him lean toward her. She leaned with him until she lost balance. "It's tough letting go," she said. She sat up and put her hands on her knees.

"I went to junkyards from Newark to Cape May trying to get parts for the truck," Mark continued. "Do you know what a flywheel is? I didn't, but I replaced one in the engine. I held engine belts in one hand and a manual in the other. I got it done."

He leaned over and let his head drop onto her lap. Abby sat stunned looking at him. *What was he doing?* His stubbly face scratched her legs.

"I got maybe four or five days a year for vacation," he said. "I spent them painting my truck. I spent days off going for tire rotations. I didn't have enough jacks for that."

Abby stopped squirming and put her hands on him. There was something in the way he said "that." His voice cracked. His deep voice that was usually so easy to hear became soft. He hadn't actually said "that." He only got out "th," then he turned his head to bury his face in her thighs. She felt moisture seeping through her pants to her leg. His arm wrapped around her waist, and she could feel it trembling. His other hand wrapped around her ankle with his fingers kneading her calf.

"That driver's seat is more comfortable than this couch," he said. "That's the way it feels to my butt."

"I understand," she whispered. Her fingers raked through his messy, knotted hair. She tried to nudge his head around to face her.

"I bought my last drop of gas for it at the gas station on Route Thirty-Four yesterday."

"It'll be all right. We ..." She paused as it sunk in. "We'll be all right." Mark rambled on about his truck, his voice breaking up as he tried to talk. *He needs me*, Abby thought. *He's holding me for support.*

"I'm losing it," he said. His voice was faded and weak. "I just realized it." His face burrowed into her thigh, and his fingers gripped her waist and leg.

"We're not losing anything," she said. "We." She used that word again. She realized she finally had a lover who loved and needed her. A family. "We will get by."

Abby got to work at nine thirty the next morning. Penn was outside the store's entrance waiting for her. His beard was long and dirty, but he was wearing a long-sleeve shirt and jeans that appeared to be new. He told her he had to talk to her. She tried to walk around him.

"We have to go," Penn insisted. "I saw some guys following me yesterday. I don't know if it's Hippie Mike or Vegas cops or Jersey cops. I have to get out of here. You're coming, too."

"No, my husband needs me," Abby said. "He has his own company. He needs me. You don't need me. His business is in trouble, but that's none of your business."

"So, mail him some money from the dance club," he said. "I can't play around. Tell your husband, your in-laws, and the neighborhood boys who stare at you when you come home that you're leaving. Your husband can go to the bar and find another slut. It's the hot gossip. He used to go there a lot. I spent some time listening to the gossip about you. They filled me in."

"Get away from me," she said, pushing past him. He turned and watched her walk to the counter. She could see him from the mirrors in the fitting areas. She couldn't face him, and she knew Nona would find a reason to kick him out. He punched his hand and stormed off down the mall. She watched him leave and exhaled till she crouched over.

That evening when Abby got home, she parked her car next to Mark's and looked around for Penn. She didn't see him, so she walked in the house. Mark sat on the couch staring at the television. She hiked up her ankle-length skirt to the top of her thighs and sat on his lap.

"I didn't have to wear stockings with the long skirt today." She saw that he didn't respond. "Rough day, honey?" she asked, kissing his neck and leaving smears of her dark red lipstick.

He put his hand on her soft white silk blouse and hugged her. "I hate selling nothing all day. They don't give out stock anymore. I have to get rid of what I have left. And I've got a lot of accounting records I need to clean up."

"I can help."

He pulled back from her. "You can?"

"Yeah," she said. "Dancers are independent contractors, too. My trips to the lingerie store were tax write-offs. What a job. Anyway, I can do a 1099 form in my sleep."

"No kidding. I learn something new about you every day." He paused to look at her firm stomach and solid breasts. "Thank you for how you dealt with my parents. God, last night, I just lost it. I was being so whiny."

She put her finger on his lips. "Shhh. It's OK. I'm here for you."

"You were there for what could've been a nightmare. Thank you." He kissed her, breathing her in until his lips tired. He broke the kiss but saw her lips puckered and her eyes closed. She didn't want the kiss to end. She leaned into him and kissed him. Then the doorbell rang.

"Gotta get that," Mark said. She slid off his legs and sat on the couch with her legs open. "Stay like that," he said.

When he opened the door, a fist holding a palm-sized revolver punched him on the side of the head. Mark fell to the floor with blood all over his temple. Abby stood and screamed.

"Shut up," Penn yelled. He rushed into the room pointing the gun at Mark and closed the door. "Did you pack yet?"

She ran to Mark and held his head in her lap.

"Pack your fucking bags, or I'll kill him. I don't fucking care."

Tears ran down her cheeks as she wiped the blood off Mark's head with her hand. She told him not to move, but he put his hand up to his face.

"What the hell?" Mark asked. Then he heard a metallic click.

"Don't fucking move," Penn said through gritted teeth. "Abby, get the fuck up and get packed. Bring your car keys. I had to ditch my car when it ran out of gas. Get money, too."

Abby lowered Mark's head to the floor and stood up. His blood was on her skirt and thighs. Tears ran down her cheeks. She saw the cold intensity in Penn's eyes.

"Don't hurt him," she pleaded.

"Shut up," Penn answered. He pointed the gun at her. "Get your shit."

She ran to her bedroom. Mark sat up and stared at the gun pointed at his face.

"This isn't a robbery, is it?"

"You …" Penn paused. "Stole from me. I'm taking it back." Penn looked around the room. "Nice place you have. What the fuck were you thinking marrying a stripper? Didn't you realize they're trouble?"

"Who are you?"

"An old boyfriend," Penn answered. "We're getting back together."

"So you're Penn?" Mark asked. "You're the reason for the scar on her forehead and the one on her back. You're the guy that talked her into being a stripper. You're the big drug user she's afraid of."

"You should be afraid, too," he said, waving the gun.

"I've been shot at. Try delivering doughnuts at four in the morning. You see all kinds of shit." He watched Penn's movements as he talked. Penn bumped into the television stand. He stretched his neck looking for Abby. He kept switching the pistol from one hand to the other and rubbing his palms on his pants.

"So was this all bullshit?" Mark asked. "Did you two have this planned so the two of you could rob me?"

Penn sighed. "No, she loves you, but that doesn't matter now. I need her in Las Vegas. If I have to kill you and beat the shit out of her to get her there, I will."

"Why?"

"I made a deal with a drug dealer, and she was collateral. He wants her now, and I have to get back. I think they're following me."

Abby threw her rolled up clothes into a suitcase. Her eyes fell on her wedding ring as she zipped the bag. *He loves me.* She saw the telephone on the dresser.

"Don't do anything, and I won't have to shoot you," Penn said to Mark, who was now sitting up.

"I'm not going anywhere," Abby said, walking into the room. "If you have to shoot someone, shoot me." She pointed to her heart.

Penn turned from Mark and squared his stance in front of Abby. "I need you alive in Las Vegas," he said, as he aimed the gun at Mark, without looking at him. "I'll shoot him. Move your ass."

She said, "No."

He slapped her across the face. Blood trickled from her nose. Mark spun around and hit Penn behind the knees, sweeping his legs out from under him. Penn fell back and hit his head on the floor. The gun slipped out of his sweaty palm and flew across the room. Mark jumped on Penn's stomach and punched him in the face for slapping Abby. He punched him again for hitting him with the gun, for breaking in, for threatening them. Penn raised his arms to block the punches, but Mark punched his arms and through his arms. He didn't bother to aim—he swung and hammered down on Penn, shattering his nose. Mark punched him because the company was folding. He punched him for the lost money, for the time he invested, for the years of hard work. He saw Iggy's in his mind and punched Penn for the robbery he couldn't stop, for Jennifer.

"Mark, stop!" Abby screamed, but he ignored her. She jumped on him to hold him back, but he pushed her off, sending her to the floor. He pounded Penn's shoulders and chest. He punched him for Abby, for trying to take her away, for threatening her. He punched till he was tired of raising his arm. He used all the muscle in his shoulder and arms to punch one more time—for the truck he'd never use again.

He slid off Penn to catch his breath. There was blood on his hands, clothes, and the floor. "Did you call the cops?" Mark asked, without looking at Abby.

"Of course. There's a phone in the bedroom, and I called from there. Did he hurt you?" she asked, staring at the blood on his hands. "Did you kill him?" Penn coughed. "Damn."

Penn rolled over and coughed again. He looked at the blood on the floor. He tried to talk, holding his split lip together with his hand.

"Shut up," Mark said. He got up and went to the windows. Three of his neighbors in the parking lot seemed to be staring at him. Abby walked to him and hugged him.

"My hero," she whispered into his neck, as she put her head on his shoulder. "You could've been killed because of me."

"No," Mark said. "I could tell he was scared of me. He kept waving the gun around and looking for you. He couldn't wait to leave. I wouldn't be surprised if the gun wasn't loaded."

"The gun?" Abby and Mark asked in unison.

Penn grabbed the gun and pointed it at Abby. He pulled back on the trigger, but it didn't move. "Damn safety." He couldn't see how to get the safety off because of the blood in his eyes. He ran for the door, and Mark ran after him. Mark punched him in the back of the head, sending him sprawling on the front lawn.

Two police cars stopped in front of the house. Penn stood up, threw the gun that he didn't know how to use at the police, and ran. One car chased after him while another stayed behind. A policeman got out of the car and went to Mark's door.

They took a report from Mark. Abby refused to talk to the officer. The police were there for three hours, examining the scene and asking questions. Mark pressured Abby to tell them about Penn, but Abby said she couldn't. The car that chased Penn drove back and said they lost him going through some backyards. It was midnight before things settled down and Mark and Abby were alone. She sat on the couch, while he paced and cracked his knuckles.

"Why did you go in the bedroom?" he asked.

"When?"

"When what's-his-name was here. He said to pack, and you went in the bedroom."

"I didn't want him to hurt you. He barged in. I was afraid if I didn't go with him, he'd kill you. He's crazy."

"Would you have left?"

"I didn't want him to hurt you."

He paced, and she fidgeted in her seat. He wasn't sure what to believe, and he didn't understand why she didn't want to talk to the police. "I have to go for a walk."

"Where are you going?"

"I don't know." He walked out of the house, leaving Abby on the couch.

She crossed her legs and sat there shaking. She stood and walked to the door. The street was empty and dark. "I have to find him." She grabbed her keys and walked out.

Mark got back at two in the morning and found Abby asleep on the couch. She wore the same clothes as when he'd left her. Streaks of blood smeared her thighs and stained her knees. Blood was splattered on her blouse, and the cuffs were bloody, as well. He picked her up and carried her to bed. Abby woke when he cradled her, but she didn't move. He put her down on the covers of the bed on her side. Her eyes were open, but she didn't speak. He went to a mirror and rubbed the long scab from where Penn had hit him. His hair was sticky and drenched with blood. *I must've really bled when I got hit*, he thought.

Early the next afternoon, Jake Hersh arrived at Babes and saw two cop cars and an ambulance outside the bar. Police told him to stay back, but Jake was able to see a male body leaning against the side of the Dumpster. The police put up a sheet to shield the victim, but Jake walked around and saw the body. The victim had been stabbed in the neck. His nose was bloody like it was broken and his lip was cut. It wasn't a robbery, because his wallet was hanging out of his pants.

"He had a Nevada ID," said the officer who had found him to another officer.

No one offered any more information about the body. "It fits the MO of the past victims," Jake thought. "Sounds like the serial killer. It's not just dancers anymore."

Chapter 19

George walked in the front door of his house looking like he'd survived a tornado. His suit was wrinkled. Notes and papers stuck out the sides of his briefcase. He passed Carla sitting in the living room reading a newspaper. She wasn't allowed back in the house. He backed up to snarl at her. "Get out."

"What's going to happen?" she asked.

George didn't answer. She followed him to the kitchen. He stayed on the opposite side of the room from her.

"I came for the girls," she told him. "I got worried. I know Kendra doesn't care that I want to help. I'm waiting for them to get home from school."

He dropped his briefcase and punched the wall. "They are away," he told Carla. "My ex-wife took my girls. Everyone's whispering. Because of you and your whoring around, I'm going to lose my house, my money, and my family."

"Me. Me. Me. Everything is my fault. Kendra had a bong. But it was my fault."

"Probably. I don't know what you brought into this house."

She picked up a saltshaker from the table and threw it, hitting the wall inches from George. He faced her and yelled at her to watch what she was doing.

"Well, you finally looked at me."

"I don't want to," he said. "I just don't want you throwing my stuff."

"Everything is your stuff," Carla shouted. "This house and your daughters are your stuff. Am I your stuff?"

"I don't want you near me. You aren't anything to me," he yelled.

"That's all anything is to you—your stuff. Thank God we're getting divorced," she said as she turned and walked to the front door.

"You bet we're getting a divorce. You won't get a dime of my money either."

"Your money really doesn't mean anything to me. It never did." She grabbed the door handle. "All you had to do was love me, and none of this would've happened." She paused, waiting for George to say something, but he didn't. "If you'd paid attention to me instead of collecting me, this wouldn't have happened." She heard no response.

Carla left the house and drove to Babes Go-Go. Sunflower walked in from the back entrance at the same time Carla went in. They made eye contact but didn't talk. Carla sat down at the bar and watched a dancer who looked like a skeleton with skin and tattoos sway to a slow song. She could hear Jake Hersh talking with Eli, as he rinsed mugs. Stacy Ann was crying in the deejay booth, and the deejay sat watching her.

"What's going on in there?" Jake asked Eli.

"The club needs a new house mom. Stacy Ann went to the new manager and asked for the job, since she was in charge of the dancers at the Go-Go-Rama."

"What happened?"

"Do you really have to ask?" Eli said. "She didn't do such a great job that night. She scheduled herself on stage ten or twelve times, leaving other dancers sitting in the back for at least an hour at a time." He leaned close to Jake facing Carla and said loud enough for her to hear, "One dancer got into a fight and was dragged out by her husband."

Jake looked at Carla. "She just walked in."

Eli nodded. He grabbed another mug and rinsed it out. "It was a big mistake trusting Stacy Ann with anything. I heard the manager tell her she couldn't have the job. Now she's crying to the deejay. I see all the dancers trust him. I'm just a bartender taking their tips. You're not part of our little family here."

"I'm fine with that," Jake said. "The police said Rita had been dead for a day before I found her. I overheard them say it doesn't look like she was murdered there. There was blood from the Dumpster to the site. That was a terrible night for a lot of us." Jake sighed.

Carla heard enough of the gossip that didn't make sense to her. If it was so dangerous, the bar would be closed. "Hey, where can I find the manager?" Carla asked Eli, as he put away a mug.

"Why?"

"I want to apologize about the other night." She got off her seat and leaned into the bar.

"He's in the back room where we keep the beer cases."

"Thanks." She tapped the bar and walked liked she was a long time employee straight to the back. There was a skinny, bald, five-foot-five man with big glasses counting boxes of beer.

"Do you know where the new manager is?" she asked.

"That's, um, me. I'm getting acquainted with the place. I heard a lot about it. What can I do for you?"

"My name is Carla. Well, they used to call me Cookie, but I hate that name."

"Oh, I heard about you."

Her toes curled up in her tennis shoes. The floor was sticky, so her shoes squeaked on the wood floor. "I need a lot of money quick. I have to hire an attorney," she told him.

"Why?" asked Sunflower, who was leaning against the door dressed in her street clothes. "Do you need an attorney for your husband's investigation? Do you think you'll be welcomed back here with open arms after what you pulled at the Go-Go-Rama?"

"Fuck off," Carla yelled. She bit her lip. She had never talked like that to another person in her life.

"OK, let's calm down," the manager said.

"Don't hire her," Sunflower said.

"I'm not scared of you," Carla said.

"Yeah," Sunflower laughed. "You should be."

"I'm not." She walked to Sunflower and stood inches from her. "I'm not scared."

Sunflower pushed her and said, "Yeah, you are."

Carla pushed back. Sunflower grabbed her hair and yanked. Shoes squeaked on the floor as they circled around tugging and slapping at each other. Carla swung her open hands at Sunflower's arms. Sunflower yanked her down. The manager got between them and got hit on the head. He wrapped his arms around Sunflower and led her out of the room. He closed the door.

"Maybe because of what I just saw, you shouldn't work here." he said.

Carla ran her hand through her hair. The sleeve of her shirt was stretched out from Sunflower. She sighed and straightened. "Fine. I'll find something else." There was no sign of Sunflower when Carla opened the door out. She took out her cell phone and held it to her ear as she rushed out of the bar. It wasn't turned on, but it gave the appearance that she had somewhere to go.

Carla drove out on Route 36 by the shore. She sat in the sand in at the beach in Sea Bright and watched the waves crash down on the empty shore. There was one last option. She pulled her cell phone out of her bag and dialed Abby.

"Can you call me?" she said to Abby's voice mail. "I'll give you my cell phone number. I don't have a home phone anymore." As she put the phone back in her purse, her eyes fell on a picture of Kim, taken at a mall camera stand. A tear ran down her face, as she ran her finger over the picture of Kim's face.

Mrs. Dumont was at Sue's mailbox with her hands in her windbreaker, which was zipped up to her neck. She still shivered from the breeze, when Sue came home. Sue was still dressed for work in her business pantsuit. Sue tried to brush past her, but Mrs. Dumont blocked her at the mailbox.

"All the neighbors are talking about that woman," Mrs. Dumont said. "You need to know what's going on. You know about her past." Mrs. Dumont could see that Sue was more interested in getting her mail than listening to her. "Did you know she's been to that porno movie place on Route 9?"

"Did you follow her there?" Sue asked. She motioned for Mrs. Dumont to get away from the mailbox. There was a stack of envelopes in there. Sue looked at her mail with the hope that Mrs. Dumont would get the hint and leave.

"No, I don't follow her," Mrs. Dumont laughed.

"Then how do you know that Abby went to the porno place?"

"It's a busy highway."

Sue sighed. "I don't care what she does. Why don't you go gossip to someone else?"

Mark went inside Iggy's holding his last bill for the store. Jennifer stood behind the deli counter cutting lettuce on the backup meat slicer. Her black hair was tied into a ponytail. Her bony fingers wrapped in plastic gloves guided the slicer. Mark saw her pale cheeks when she looked up.

He knew this was the last time he'd see her. This part of his life was over. Did she know that? Did she care? Did she know that he had pined for her for so long? Did she care that it had bothered him when she became engaged?

"What's this?" the manager asked, interrupting his thoughts.

"I'm settling all my accounts. Dewey's is going out of business, so I'm collecting the last of the bills."

"Hold on," the manager said. "I'll see what I have for records in the back."

Mark watched Jennifer put the lettuce away without looking toward him.

The manager walked back out. "We have a company account. We send in our payments to the accounting office. You should've known that."

"Yeah," Mark answered as he flipped through papers on his clipboard, pretending to be confused. "I must have mis-filed you."

"Is there anything else you want?"

Mark heard Jennifer drop a ham into the refrigerator and grunt. "Nope, I guess not," Mark said, as he turned and headed out the door.

On his way home, he stopped by Babes Go-Go for a beer. Under the stage lights, there was a scrawny, flat-chested, black-haired dancer with pale skin that made her look like walking pneumonia. She wiggled her hips and massaged her stomach as she stared at a mirror. Three drunks played pool, ignoring her.

"I'll have a beer," Mark said, rubbing his forehead.

As Eli brought Mark change, the dancer bounded off the stage toward him. "Hon," she said, like she was truly happy to see him.

"Hi," he said, without looking up. "What's your name?"

"Jennifer."

Jennifer, he thought. *She looks like Jennifer from Iggy's. I should get a lap dance with her and pretend. Jennifer. Of all the names to have.*

"Why are you smiling?"

"Nothing," Mark said, offering her a tip.

Stacy Ann walked out of the locker room and waved at Mark. The stage was all Stacy Ann's. She did a spin around the brass pole and went to him for a tip. "Hi, sweetie."

"Hi, I've seen you before," Mark said. "We did a lap dance together at West."

"Yeah, I remember," she said, even though her face showed that she didn't. "Came by for more?"

"I don't know if I should. I'm married now."

Stacy Ann turned, but didn't move. She looked back at him as he sipped his beer. There was something familiar, but she didn't know why.

At seven o'clock, Abby got marinara sauce out of the cabinet for the ziti she'd cooked. Mark opened the door, grumbling as he came in. She knew he was closing out accounts and was probably going to be moody. She put the ziti in the oven to keep warm. He was tipsy but not drunk as he scurried down the hallway to the bedroom, sliding along the wall. The odor of beer and perfume lingered long enough for Abby to smell it.

"Mark, I have dinner almost done," she said, walking to the bedroom. "Are you sick? You practically ran in here."

"I just want to be alone right now."

She leaned against the closed door and said, "This was your last official workday. I want to know how you are."

"I don't want to talk about it. Just leave me alone for awhile," he yelled. "I just want to think about what to do next."

"We'll talk about it. This is about both of us," she said.

"I just want to be alone."

"Then why did you go to a bar?"

"I don't know what you're saying."

"I worked in them long enough to know the smell." She heard a crash and threw open the door. "What are you doing?" she asked. Mark stood over a broken cologne bottle.

"You have to know everything, don't you?"

"Don't talk to me like I'm nobody," she said. "We're a team."

"Then why didn't you tell me about Penn?" he asked. His chest was expanding and his shoulders were heaving up and down like he just had carried something heavy. "You told me about Las Vegas. You didn't say he followed you here. You didn't say he would come barging into the house. He knew who I was, so I know you talked to him." He stood two inches away, panting on her face. "Why didn't we talk about that? We're in this together, aren't we?"

Images of Penn taunting and yelling at her flashed before her eyes. She could see the time he grabbed her hair and pulled her into the kitchen to cook for him. She saw him go through her purse. Now, the man who beat Penn to the floor was in front of her, angry. She turned away.

He put his arm in front of her to block her. "Tell me all about Penn. What else didn't you tell me about him?"

The images of Penn were so real that she thought it was Penn for a moment. "Don't hit me," she screamed, swinging her arms in every direction. She ran out of the room as he backed away. Her purse was by the television, and she grabbed it on the way out of the house.

❦ ❦ ❦

Carla sat at the water fountain at the center of the mall watching a toddler struggle to get near the water as his mother held him back.

"I wanna see," he whined.

The young mother, dressed in neatly ironed clothes with everything just so, seemed to be trying hard to remain calm. Her outfit contrasted with her frizzed hair and worried face. She picked the boy up and held him against her while they leaned over to see the water. "See all the pennies? Those are wishes. You throw a penny in, and your wish comes true. Want to try it?"

He nodded and yelled "yes" so loud that people stopped to watch. The mother let him down at the side of the fountain as she searched her purse for a penny. "Don't move," she said. "Stay right there." He held on to her pant leg but looked around, ready to investigate something new. She gave him a penny and put the purse on her shoulder. "Do you know what you want to wish? You can't tell anyone your wish."

He shook his head. His father, who looked like a living perfect plastic doll, said, "Wish that your mother would stop shopping."

"Very funny," the mother said, grinning at him. She picked her son up as he flailed his arms to throw the penny. It splashed down with such force that it moved other pennies to make a space for itself at the bottom of the fountain. "Now your wish will come true," she said. "Let's go to Nora Daniels and shop."

"Yeah, your wish will come true. You have money to throw away," Carla sneered. "All that money down there doesn't make dreams come true."

Abby still had perspiration on her red forehead as she sat next to Carla.

"I read in the papers about your husband," Abby said.

"The stockholders voted him off the board. He was let go from work."

"So why are you here?"

"He kicked me out," Carla said. Her arms shook and she tried to hide her emotions with a laugh. But her laughter turned to tears. "The girls are with their mother somewhere. I'll never get to see them again. I miss that little one. She was a lot older than her years. George and I are getting divorced."

Abby put her arms around Carla. "I know you'll see them again," she said. "Maybe you'll have a daughter of your own someday. You're young."

"I know. Things don't look so good right now, though," Carla said. "I can't even get a job as a dancer. I got into a fight with Sunflower in front of the manager. He said it would be better if I just went away. So now I'm broke, unemployed, and have nowhere to go." She looked at Abby's face. "What happened to your face? You're all red."

"I was crying," Abby said. "I jumped to conclusions about my husband, and we had a big fight." She laughed, and then her eyes welled with tears. Carla put her arm around Abby so she could cry, but Abby wouldn't let herself.

Abby reached into her purse and took out money. "Look, here's a few dollars. I'd invite you home with me, but my husband's business is closing, and he's miserable. Maybe you can move in after a few days. Can you make it for a few days?"

Carla nodded, as Abby gave her the money.

Abby left the mall and drove to Babes Go-Go where Sunflower was on stage slithering around and flirting with a businessman who had his shirt out and tie undone. She blew him a kiss and rolled over to stand up and take a tip.

Abby went to the manager's office and entered without knocking. The bald guy was sitting at his desk, and Stacy Ann, wearing her pink bikini, sat across from him. He asked Stacy to leave when Abby entered.

"Maybe some other time ... I just started seeing this new guy," Stacy said as she rose to leave.

"Baby Doll, coming back to work?" the manager asked, as he walked toward her.

Her nose hairs curled when she smelled how he had slathered himself in cologne to combat the smell of the bar. "How did you know me?" she asked.

"Pictures. Cops are investigating everyone. I saw your picture a dozen times. I'm just finding out about this place. I read a file on everyone."

Abby put her purse on the chair and closed the door. "I want to ask you about my friend, Carla. Why doesn't anyone want her to dance?"

"Who knows?" he scoffed. "I'm new here, and I hate it already. I spent my night listening to stupid catfights. This one shows too much tit. This one looked in my bag. You would think with a murderer running around that everyone would watch out for each other. No. Cops are snooping around trying to crack that case." He stopped. "Do you want to dance again?"

"In spite of the murders, fighting, and drunks, do I want to dance again? Hmm. Are you crazy?" she asked.

"Remember the money?" he asked, with an accounting book in his hands. "You see the parking lot. Who owns the sports cars? From what I hear, these dancers make a lot of money that they squander on cars, tattoos or drugs." He put down the accounting book. "It's a small bar, so maybe it's not the best money. They tell me that you can actually dance. Stacy Ann can shake her hips and lick her own tits. That's fun to watch and all, but it gets stale after five hours a night."

Abby pointed at the door and asked, "How old is she anyway? She looks young."

"She's twenty. It's messed up. She's not old enough to drink here, but we can let her dance. I'd let your friend dance, if you dance also. You can dance, and you've done this a while. I can use an unofficial house mom to take care of the petty things that I can't do." He sat behind the desk and pulled out a cigarette. He held the pack out to Abby, who refused. "Most of the girls here are just little girls. Sure, some of them are mothers, some are married, some of them are actually going to college, but when you get down to it, they're little girls, and they act that way. I could use a level of maturity around here. Let's face it, your friend Carla is a little girl."

Eli stood by the door. "Why would Carla give up a family to do this?" he asked.

The manager shot a look at Eli. "You have a bar to go to." Eli walked out, and the manager turned back to Abby. "I know what you're thinking. You want to come back."

Her mind raced. *We need the money. It would be helping Carla.* "I need to think about it. I'll let you know." She passed Stacy Ann walking to the lockers.

"Don't I know you?" Stacy asked.

"I used to dance here a while ago."

"You're that Baby Doll everyone talks about. They say you married a customer here."

Abby smiled. "Yeah, I got lucky. We met here."

"Oh, I know that guy. I remember him now. He talked to me. He asked if I recognized him. He still comes here."

Abby froze. Her suspicions about Mark being in a bar were right—but she hadn't thought it was Babes.

"It's so cool that you don't mind him coming here," Stacy said. "He tips good."

"He's crying about saving money, and he tipped you," she muttered.

"Where were you?" Mark asked when Abby walked in the door. "I'm sorry," he said. She ignored him. "I should've come home to be with you. I'm really sorry about that. I know you thought I was going to hit you, but I would never do that." He followed her to the bedroom.

"I had to go to Babes today to see an old friend. I saw Stacy Ann," she said. She pointed her finger at him. "She told me about you. You couldn't come home to me, but you could go to her. Do you know how it made me feel?"

"That bitch didn't have to say anything," Mark said, through gritted teeth. "I wasn't thinking."

"Don't talk to me."

He went back to the couch and sat for a moment. He couldn't believe Abby had found out about his one trip to Babes. *I have to get out of here*, he thought.

Abby came out to the living room and saw that Mark was gone. She went to the kitchen and found his bowl of noodles in the microwave. She got a fork and ate it herself.

Mark came home an hour later while Abby was sprawled on the bed sleeping. He grabbed a pillow she wasn't using and slept on the couch.

She continued to ignore him the next morning and left for work at noon. Mark was on the couch with empty soda bottles surrounding him when she got home at seven. He hadn't changed his ketchup-stained shirt and his faded jeans since the previous night.

She walked around the house in silence and finally sat on the couch next to him. "He hit me, you know," she said, while playing with her wedding ring. "Back in Las Vegas. All my life has been one disaster after another. I finally thought I got out of it. I thought …" She paused when she felt his hand on her hand. "I thought this was the one right thing I did. I don't know what to say about Penn or what happened or why I ran out yesterday. I don't want to fight anymore."

"I don't want to fight," he said.

Jake Hersh found Stacy Ann's driver's license on the ground outside the bar. He put it in his pocket and planned to keep it until he saw her, but by midafternoon, she hadn't come back for the license. He called her apartment and left a message on the machine. The bar was slow, so he left to go home. On the way out, he saw Stacy's sports car across the street in front of an empty music store.

He walked to the car, wondering why her car was there instead of in the bar's parking lot. Stacy was inside. "Hey, Stacy," he hollered through the rolled-up window. "Why are you way over here?" She didn't react, so he tapped on the window. She still didn't react. He ran around to the passenger side of the car and looked in. From her rib cage to her waist was covered in blood. Jake backed up trembling.

"Fuck, no," he yelled, running around the car. "Stacy." He banged on the roof, "Stacy, open up."

He ran back to his car and threw his files around looking for his cell phone. He couldn't punch the buttons, because his fingers shook. Jake had to take a deep breath and start again. "Come on, answer." The phone rang three times before he got someone. "I need help. I just found a dead body."

The police got the location and told him to wait. He dropped the phone in the car and walked back to Stacy.

"You're so young," he said, staring through the window at her. "You could've gotten a better job." His hands shook. She was sitting straight up in her seat with her eyes closed and mouth open. The sound of the siren shocked him. "There! There!" he screamed to the police. "You have to get her out."

Mark and Abby spent their two-month wedding anniversary apart. She worked while he stayed home and drank beer. Abby knew he drank, and he had stopped caring that she knew. Most nights he passed out on the couch while Abby slept in the bed. Abby started working longer hours at the mall, and Mark used the last of his savings ordering out lunch every day.

Chapter 20

Jake Hersh sat in his parked car outside Babes Go-Go watching the crowds of customers. Detective mystery books were on his dashboard, papers were scattered in the backseat, and a newspaper was on the passenger seat.

"What brings you by?" Sunflower asked, as she strolled to his car.

She startled him, and he jumped in his seat. "I was looking for clues," he said. "How have you been?" He tossed the papers he had on his lap into the backseat.

"Too many things to talk about."

"Have a seat," he said. "It's only seven o'clock. Customers don't really come in for a few hours."

She went to the passenger side and got in. Her knees were up against the dashboard, and her head hit the roof of the compact car. Jake tried to adjust the seat with her in it, but it didn't move.

"I don't know about life," she began. "I leave here, and it's lonely. I went out with this guy last week. He found out what I did for a living and was gone. I told you about the son I gave up, right?"

"Yeah." He reached between her legs to find the seat handles. His hand grazed her soft skin. He sat back up and crossed his arms to look innocent.

"I don't know if he remembers me," she continued. "He was real young. I wonder if he thinks that the people he lives with are his real family."

"Do you want to take off from work and go out for a while?" he asked. He didn't wait for an answer before he got out of the car. She protested but didn't move to stop him. He went into Babes to tell someone that she wouldn't be working. Eli was in the back room talking to Carla and counting cases of beer.

"So you're single again?" Eli asked her, as Jake walked in. She sat on a case of beer dressed in street clothes. Jake looked her over, but tried not to imagine her in her skimpy dance outfits.

"Sunflower isn't feeling well. Tell the managers that I'm taking her home."

"You tell them," Eli said. He motioned at Carla. "I have something going on here."

Jake looked at Carla, who seemed more interested in her shoes than in their conversation. "Tell the managers, Romeo," Jake said, and he walked out.

Jake took Sunflower to the beach in Spring Lake. It was October and dark already at eight o'clock. No one else was on the beach. The strong wind carried the salt air to the boardwalk. Sunflower paused to breathe it in. She smiled and went to a gazebo at the end of a pier.

"The managers let me see the files upstairs. There's nothing new in those personnel files that help me with the case," he told her. "It's dangerous there. Doesn't it bother you?"

"I'll be just fine," she said. "This open air is incredible. It's a little cold, but I need to feel this ocean breeze. How come you don't guard at the doors like a bouncer?"

"That isn't my job. I'm security. I walk perimeters. No one's been killed in the bar during working hours," he said, looking up at a seagull flying overhead.

"These murders don't sit well with the community. They always wanted us closed. The town council never changed the zoning. That's why we are still open. The town has a good reason to shut us down now." She looked down at gum on the boardwalk. "I wonder if the murderer is a local. Babes got a lot of bad press out of this."

"I don't know," Jake said. "I can't believe they're keeping the place open after what happened to Stacy Ann. She was so young."

"All the dancers are young. That's something you don't realize. They're all young. Guys don't like older women. They keep me around out of loyalty. I really didn't know Stacy Ann," she said. She watched moths flitter around the lights. "Did anyone come to claim her from the morgue?"

"Her mother," Jake said. He looked at an older couple walking. The man was slower than the woman, but they held hands. "Her mother had no idea Stacy Ann was a dancer. She's so embarrassed that she doesn't want anyone from the club to go to the funeral or even send flowers. We were probably the last friends she had, too."

❦   ❦   ❦

The next day Sunflower showed up late at Babes in her sweats and no makeup. She rushed to the lockers as Carla walked to the stage dressed in a bikini with her hair teased out.

"Hey, wait," Carla yelled to Sunflower. "We really shouldn't hate each other. We're going through the same thing. Maybe we should talk."

"What kind of thing are we going through?" Sunflower sighed.

"Well, they told me about your son," Carla said.

"You don't know a thing about my son," Sunflower growled at her. "Even if you did, it's none of your business. Go hang around with that slut friend that got you this job. I don't need you."

"I was just trying to help," Carla whined, as Sunflower walked away from her. "Bitch." Carla went to the deejay's booth. "I heard you got some new music."

The deejay perked up and pointed at a shoebox full of compact discs. "You know the deal about the money," he said. "Can I welcome you back to the club? I saw you yesterday come back to get a schedule."

She turned to him and sighed with her hands at her hips. It felt like there was no choice if she wanted to keep this job. She extended her arms to hug the overweight deejay. He wrapped his arms around her and slid his hands on her oiled back down to her thong while he smelled her perfumed hair. She pulled back and went to the shoebox.

"It's good to have you back," he said. She didn't look at him. She rolled her eyes and shook her shoulders to get the goose bumps off.

Abby watched Carla and turned away. She just wanted to do her set and go home. It seemed like Carla really liked the atmosphere.

Sunflower got dressed in a black camisole with thigh-high leather boots and panties. She saw Jake. He was dressed in jeans, apparently trying to mix in with the crowd at the pool tables.

"Jake Hersh, why are you telling people my business?" she yelled, walking over to him. "I thought we were friends. You went and told everyone about my son."

He put his hands up, motioning her to calm down, but she didn't. "I told Eli. He told everyone. I only told him. I didn't tell everyone."

"Well, everyone knows. Don't talk to me anymore."

She stomped to the stage and tapped her heels till her music began. Her mind drifted away as she spun around to the music. Jake Hersh walked to the bar and watched her hips sway as her legs propelled her movements. Her hands ran over her body teasing a lone drunk at the other end of the bar.

Jake had seen many of the dancers while he was there. Some danced while some just stood and shook. It all got boring after the second day. Jake saw something different in Sunflower. She danced with fury as she spun around. She was dancing out her emotions.

"I'm sorry," he said, when she got off the stage. She brushed past him. He waited for her to come out from the locker room to talk, but she ignored him again.

The next day, Abby went for her morning jog wearing her new jogging suit and a wool hat. She wasn't used to fall weather after all the years in Las Vegas. Mr. Dumont waved to her from his mailbox while his wife just stood there. She saw Mrs. Vesquez wave, but the woman next to her didn't. On her return lap, Mr. Dumont was still by the mailbox smiling at her, but his wife was gone. Abby stretched on her front lawn when she finished. Mrs. Dumont watched from the windows as Abby bent over to touch her toes. "Terrible," she muttered. Mr. Dumont had no complaint.

Carla had called Abby before her jog. They had arranged to meet at the National Diner later in the afternoon. Abby went in the house and showered. She met Carla at the diner, and they took a seat by the windows and stared at the road in silence for five minutes before Abby spoke.

"I think the neighbors talk about me. Some people are really nice, and others just stare. I'm sure some of them are wondering why the police were at my place the other night. If they knew what Penn was like, they would love Mark for beating him senseless. It seems like there's so much tension at the development, now."

"Maybe it's because of your husband and not you," Carla said. "He's lived there a lot longer than you. Maybe they're scared of him. Look what happened to your old boyfriend. It was in the newspaper."

Abby's eyes bulged. "It was in the newspaper? I had no idea."

"It was in the same article as his murder." Carla saw the fear in Abby's face. "What's wrong," Carla asked.

Abby played with a napkin as thoughts whirled through her mind. "Penn told me he was afraid some people were following him from Vegas. What if those people found him?"

"What if it was someone from here?" Carla asked."Maybe someone else here didn't want to put up with him."

Jake Hersh was in the manager's office with a stack of files in front of him. He read about each dancer. The stories of desperation and arrests looked the same on file after file. The security company had called to ask why there was still trouble, and he didn't have an answer. The corporate owners also called for answers that he didn't have. The manager had thought his job would be easy, but he found out he was wrong. Tough-guy customers left after hearing about the murders. After each murder, more dancers quit. Dancer tips were down.

Jake couldn't find a breakthrough. He wasn't supposed to be in the files, but he convinced the new manager that it was part of his job. Jake didn't have to hide when he went into the manager's office. There were so many naïve people there. The only people Jake really cared about in this drugged out hell-hole were his cousin Eli and Sunflower, and he wasn't sure he could trust her. The manager threw a new file on his desk: Abby Broughton.

"Who's this?" Jake asked, without looking up. He saw no point remembering this manager. He'd be gone soon.

"A dancer who moved from Las Vegas. She's a rehire."

"Las Vegas? Why does that sound familiar? When did she dance here before?"

"I think during the summer. Just before you came around."

"I don't remember the name. I want to take a look at this."

"Go 'head."

Sunflower got to the locker room that night, ready to dance. She had a bouquet of roses waiting for her on the bench in front of her locker. Dancers asked whom they were from. Some asked what she'd done to get them. She ignored them and went out to find Jake. "What's this for?" she asked him.

"I shouldn't have said anything to anyone about you," he said. "I went to the florist and bought them for you, hoping you'll forgive me."

"It's all right," she cooed. "I'll see you when my night's over?"

"Sure."

She leaned in and kissed him on the lips. Jake felt tongue. He couldn't believe it.

"You sleeping with the dancers?" Eli asked, carrying a case of beer.

"Don't say that. Nothing's happening."

"She's a bad influence on the kids here," Mrs. Dumont said to a woman in her twenties pushing a stroller around the parking lot.

"I don't even know the Winstons," the woman said. "I can't condemn someone. I just moved in here last week. I know some people weren't happy about my moving truck blocking parking spaces."

"You bought your place to have nice surroundings for your kids. Right? That woman has had the cops here. She jogs around in the mornings half-naked." Seeing that the woman wasn't concerned, she added, "Flashing the boys. She goes to porno places. Her husband used to be a good neighbor. Now he just sits home all day. I heard that he mugged a guy while working and lost his job. She ruined him."

"So what do you want from me?"

"We're going to have a meeting at the condo complex recreation center to draw up an official petition. We want them to sell their place and move away."

"I'll go to the meeting," the young woman said.

Mrs. Dumont smiled, ready to move on to the next neighbor. Sue got out of her car. Her clothes were wrinkled, and she sneezed when she slammed the car door. Mrs. Dumont didn't like Sue, but she needed her signature on the petition. She walked over and explained the meeting to her.

"Why would I turn my back on my friend like that?" Sue asked. "He helped me shovel out my car last year when it snowed. He never messes up the place. He never did anything wrong. Why would I want him to move out?"

"Because of that wife of his," Mrs. Dumont answered. "You saw the cop cars that one night. You have no idea what kind of transients she's bringing into this place."

"Neither do you."

"I don't want to know what kind of people she associates with."

"Leave them alone," Sue said. "I don't know her that well, but I know there's a good reason for all of that. I have to go home. I have a cold." She brushed past Mrs. Dumont without looking back.

"All your neighbors are joining this. It's a matter of time before that woman is out of this place," Mrs. Dumont yelled. Sue closed her front door.

The phone rang while Mark was watching television. It was his mother. He held the receiver away from his ear while she talked, because he just wasn't in the mood.

"I just don't know how I feel about your wife calling me 'Mom.' I'm sure she's a nice girl. She must be an angel to marry you. I just don't think I'm comfortable with that."

"Is this why you called?" Mark asked, rubbing his forehead.

"I've been thinking about this. I don't think your father wants to be called 'Dad' either. Your sister-in-law doesn't call us 'Mom' and 'Dad.' Your wife asked me if she could call me that. I didn't know what to say. Why don't you answer the phone? Why does she always answer the phone?"

Mark opened his mouth to answer, but she kept talking.

"What about your nephew? What are we going to do at Easter or Christmas when the whole family is there? We can't tell him that his aunt is a nude dancer. What will he think? You really should've thought of your family when you decided to just run out and get married."

"I don't know what I was doing," he said, rolling his eyes. "I must've been thinking about my own happiness instead of yours. I don't know how I could do that to you."

"Now you're being sarcastic," his mother said. "I'm just trying to talk to you. You didn't think about this. You've made mistakes before, but you didn't have to rush into this one."

Mark put the phone on the coffee table while his mother talked and went back to watching television. He picked up the phone every few minutes to say he agreed with her and put the phone back down while his mother lectured him. The door bell rang after ten minutes, so he told her he had to go.

Sue was at the door, looking around. "Is Abby here?" she asked.

"No. You need her?"

"No, I need to tell you something." She walked into the room and told him about her conversation with Mrs. Dumont.

"What did Abby do to cause a petition?" he asked.

"I think it's because she jogs in spandex, and she's a go-go dancer," Sue answered. "I don't like Mrs. Dumont. I never did. I didn't like Abby at first, but

I think she's OK. Mrs. Dumont talks behind your back to everyone, and no one wants to be on Mrs. Dumont's bad side."

"She's a piece of shit," Mark said, clenching his fingers into a fist. "Abby has been so good to the neighbors here. Fuck that old bitch. She's jealous that people pay attention to Abby and not her. Abby's not even a dancer anymore."

"Calm down," Sue said. "Don't let her get to you like that."

"I can't help it. Everything is a mess." He dropped on the couch as Sue leaned against the wall. "I've been reading the newspapers every day. It's filled with all these stories about millionaires and their stocks. The stock market is making these rich people richer. And I'm broke and can't get a job. You don't know what it's like going for interviews. I ran my own business, but I'm not qualified for a supervisor job. I did all the work to run that business, but I didn't actually supervise anyone. I did all the accounting and inventory for my business, and yet I'm told I have to start at entry-level bookkeeping. I can't live on entry level. Have you seen what they pay entry-level people? I would do it, but I can't live on that. We're living off what my wife makes at the mall, which isn't much. We're paying for a lot out of the savings account. I should get another truck and never see Abby because of work."

He pointed at the phone as Sue walked to the couch. "I just got a call from my mother. She doesn't want Abby to call her 'Mom.' She says I should've thought about my brother's family when I married Abby. Like I'll say, 'This is Abby, my stripper wife.'" He leaned back on the couch and exhaled. "She didn't even strip when she danced. She wore this bikini thing with a cape. I don't need Mrs. Dumont's shit on top of everything else."

Sue put her hand on Mark's leg and told him everything would be fine. They had known each other for years and never even shook hands; now she had her hand on his leg.

"Why don't you relax for awhile," she said, taking her hand back. She went to the door. "Things will pick up. I'm sure Abby will be fine."

Abby came home later and found Mark on the floor reading a newspaper. Scattered around him were classified ads, torn from the newspaper. She took off her flat shoes and walked on her toes so she wouldn't mess up the slips of paper when she kissed him. He reeked of cologne and sweat. He held her hand in both of his hands and squeezed it gently.

"We're in a good mood today," she said.

"I just want you to be with me."

She smiled. "Since you're in a good mood, I have something to show you." She ran to the closet near the front door and pulled out a box covered in brown paper. "My friend is in this." It was a DVD. "Her name is Tiffany, and she's the star. I didn't think she'd really do it. She said it would help her career."

She put the DVD in the player and snuggled next to Mark. He picked up the box and studied Tiffany's face. Her mouth was wide open with a white dot next to it. Mark figured a large penis was behind the white dot.

"We used to dance together at the clubs in Las Vegas. She said she'd get better places to work and more money after the movie came out. I sent her a postcard a few weeks ago, but I haven't heard anything back yet." Abby faced the screen and watched her friend take off her clothes by a pool. "She's so thin. She's almost bony. I hope her career really took off. I don't know if she made another movie or if she even wants to. She's having sex with three guys at one time now," she said, putting her hands over her eyes. "There are some things you don't need to see your friends do."

Mark grabbed the remote control to fast forward past the scene. She lowered her hands when the scene was over.

"Before I left, she told me that she didn't even get the chance to meet these guys. She had to go to a studio apartment and wait for the director to say, 'Have sex with these people.' Can you imagine?"

"I can't," he answered, only hearing part of what she was saying, because he'd lost feeling in the arm Abby was squeezing.

"I can't move like her during sex, can I?" Abby asked.

Mark panicked, unsure how to answer that. "I'm not sure. Maybe we could give it a try," he said. He leaned on her and kissed her.

"Wait," she said, moving away. "I'll be right back." She went to the kitchen while Mark shut off the television.

"Did you ever make a porno?" he asked her.

"Me?" she laughed. "I'd be too embarrassed."

"Where did you get the dancer name Baby from?"

She walked back to the room and sat next to him. "Abby and Baby are anagrams. Abby has A, B, and Y. Baby has B, A, and Y. They're the same word almost. Why do you ask?"

"I'm just wondering," Mark said. "There's still a lot I don't know about you."

"I wonder things about you, too," Abby said. "What were you doing at Babe's when we met?"

"It's embarrassing to admit, but I used to go to that club a lot. It's close to home, and I used to work a lot of hard hours on that truck."

"There's nothing wrong with that," she said. "When I first met you, you got a lap dance from Stacy Ann. Did you talk to her the way we talked?"

He toyed with the DVD box trying to think of an answer. "Before you, I don't really remember names. Don't get mad, but every dancer was just tits and ass. I really didn't know any of them." He knew that everything he just said was a lie, but he hoped she wouldn't find out that he tried to date a dancer named Buffy. "Did you ever work for that owner that was murdered?"

"I think so. He might have been there. Why are you asking about that now?"

He hesitated. "I was just thinking about how much danger you were in while you danced. Good thing you got out of it."

She smiled. "I know. It's a good thing I'm out. Anyone could be the killer. It could be a dancer or someone who stalks dancers or maybe an ex-boyfriend of a dancer."

"Or a dancer?" he asked.

"I wouldn't say for sure, but I don't think so. Dancing's a lot of work. It's not just prancing around," Abby said. "I had to handle my finances, sew up my costumes, and keep receipts for taxes. I had to stay on top of things. Who has that kind of energy?"

He took a deep breath. "When I beat Penn to the floor, he said he was a dead man. It had something to do with drug dealers. What was he talking about?"

Abby turned away. "Penn was mixed up in some kind of drug thing. He was a real junkie. My dancing supported his drug habit for a long time. I tried some grass and a couple of pills back when I was with him, but I was never a junkie. I never met the drug dealer. I wasn't directly involved with the stuff Penn was involved in." She grabbed Mark's chin and turned his face to meet hers. "You have to believe me—I never had a part in that whole thing. He followed me, because he was a sick, crazy person."

Even though she was holding his face, he kept moving his eyes so as not to look at her. "You never did any of that stuff?"

"I didn't. I won't."

He hugged her, but it didn't feel right. He knew other dancers had drug problems. It's possible to get addicted to prescription drugs.

Mark left the house the next day dressed in a blue suit with polished shoes and a new tie. He brought the newspaper and copies of his resume that he had prepared on the computer. Abby was still asleep when he left.

After a long day, he drove home and parked his car in an empty parking space near his house. He undid his tie as he walked and shrugged his shoulders. "Another wasted interview," he muttered.

"How's things?" Eddie asked.

"Not looking so good," Mark sighed. "I've been to companies that sell potato chips, companies that sell cookies and then ice cream companies. I don't think I want to drive a cab in some parts of town, but I'll take it if they call back."

"So that's why the wife is dancing again?" Eddie asked. Mark stopped mid-step. "Did I say something wrong?" Eddie asked.

"My wife stopped dancing," Mark replied

"I saw your wife at Babes Go-Go two nights ago. I was with a few of the guys after the ball game. We played touch football. You should've come with us. I ran half the field for a touchdown. I'm still sore from it."

"You didn't see her dance at any club. She's been doing extra hours at the mall," Mark stammered.

"Then it was someone who looks a lot like her," Eddie said.

"Forget it, I'm going inside." Mark walked in the house and slammed the door.

Abby wasn't home by seven o'clock. Mark paced, replaying the conversation with Eddie in his mind. Abby wasn't home by eight o'clock. Mark watched television till nine o'clock, and Abby wasn't home. Still no Abby at nine thirty, ten, and ten thirty. Midnight came, and Abby wasn't home. Mark knew the mall was closed. He grabbed his keys and stomped out to the car.

He drove around the mall parking lot twice looking for Abby's car. It wasn't there. He drove to Babes Go-Go.

It was a foggy night on Route 35. He wondered if it could be true. Sue had said the neighbors were talking about Abby. They said she flashed people on the streets. They said she's lewd. Eddie claimed to have seen her dance. Why would she dance again? Angry, guitar-driven rock music blared from his radio. He gripped his steering wheel with such force that his arms were tense from fingers to shoulders. *Is it my fault?* He asked himself. *Am I a failure because I can't get a job? Is Abby not satisfied with me?*

He cut off a minivan making a left-hand turn into Babes Go-Go parking lot, which was a sea of sports cars and pickup trucks. He found a space, got out of the car, and slammed the door. Maybe Abby's car was there, maybe it wasn't; he didn't stop to look. He walked to the door, trying to talk himself out of this. *Abby wouldn't dance again without telling him*, he thought.

The dancer on stage was a blur of platform shoes, skin, and brown hair. She shimmied to thunderous hip-hop dance music with bass that shook the seats of the customers. The flashing lights blinded him to the dancer's features. He pushed his way through the small crowd and went to the woman bartender getting a beer from the tap.

"It's Dani right?" he asked her. "You know a dancer named Baby Doll?"

She put her hand to her ear and yelled, "What?" but Mark couldn't hear her.

Mark told himself that she wasn't here. *I don't know what I'm doing*, he thought. *She would talk this over with me.*

He turned to see the dancer one last time and glimpsed a dancer with a cape at the back of the stage fixing her platform sandal. She bounced up the stairs onto the stage and spun around.

"Nice ass," one guy yelled.

"Here's Baby Doll," the deep-voiced deejay said. "She looks like a naughty baby tonight. Tip her good, guys. Let's not forget her friend Cookie coming out also."

Abby spun around and undid her cape. Men threw dollar bills at her while she did a handstand leaning against the brass pole. Her legs wrapped around it, holding her in place till she spun down to the floor, where she rolled over and winked at a crowd of guys in college sweatshirts. They whistled at her. She slid off the stage and went around for tips. One guy held a dollar to her chest.

Mark's chest tightened. A guy with a dollar groped the woman he loved. Men whistled at her. He heard someone say she had nice tits. Someone else said he'd "fuck her." The man could've meant one of the other dancers, but Mark didn't care. Abby was one of those dancers.

"I'd slap that ass."

"I'd fuck her ass."

They talked about his wife. Abby smiled at them. She laughed and took their folded money. One guy held her fingers in his hand as he eyed the rest of her. She went back to the stage and smiled at those people who'd said they'd "fuck her."

Mark made a fist. He'd fight them all. Punch 'em in the balls—that'd show 'em. A tipsy guy wobbling around to a seat knocked into Mark. The bump made Mark tenser. He was ready to unload at this drunk, until he saw Abby smile at someone from the stage. *What's the point?* he thought. *She likes this.*

He shrugged his shoulders and walked out. The radio was off on the way home. He could still hear the voices in his head: "I'd fuck her." "Show your tits." "I'd slap that ass." When he got home, he sat on the bed with the lights off.

Abby came home at three AM and snuck through the house to the bedroom, where Mark surprised her by turning on the lights. She jumped back and gasped, holding her chest.

"What are you doing up? You're asleep by nine o'clock every night." she said. "How come you're dressed?"

"Why are you doing it?" Mark asked.

"Doing what?" she replied, as she slipped off her coat.

"You know what. Why are you dancing again?"

She let her coat fall to the floor and stood with her arms at her sides. She knew she was caught. "I'm helping." She could tell he was in shock from the look on his face. "How do you know?"

"People told me," he said. He rubbed his knuckles, trying to get his hands to stop shaking. Then he cracked his knuckles, which made the pain in his hands worse.

"We needed the money. Is it really so bad?"

"Yes. A bunch of drunks are drooling over you," Mark said. "Don't you see a problem?"

"I know you don't like it. You said that once about the married entertainers," she said. He moaned, but it sounded like he wanted to howl with rage. "You used to like it. You were turned on when you first saw me. You were one of those drooling drunks." She rubbed her nose like she did when she was nervous. "This is a lot of quick money. There is no other easy way. Think about what we could do with the money."

"You have a job at the mall. You told me you could handle your money. You're smarter than just being a slut dancer."

"What did you call me?" She made a fist, and her chest tightened. "I am not a slut. I'm doing this because we need it. I hate this. I don't want to do this."

"I'm tired of this. First there was Penn, and now this." He watched Abby pace in front of him. "Why don't you dance for me?" he asked.

"No," she answered. They stared at each other without saying anything. "I can't."

"You can dance and show your tits to a total stranger, but you can't do it for me. You danced when I met you. What's the difference?"

"It's different now. We have something special."

"What about the drunk at the bar who gets to touch you and talk about you? I love you, but you can't dance for me."

"Fuck you," she yelled. "You didn't save me from a terrible life. I had plans. This is money. It means nothing to me. I don't care if they think I'm a slut. I care if you do. You mean something to me. I was doing this to help out you and Carla."

"I mean something," he grumbled. "If what we have is so special, why do you lie to me all the time? Where is this Carla? You always talk about her. I never see her. What makes her so special that you would lie to me?"

"I knew you wouldn't understand. She's living at the efficiency motel on Route 33. She's alone. I'm trying to help."

"What did I do wrong?" he asked. Before she could answer, he said, "I can't provide for us. I can't run a business. I can't get a job. I can't do it sexually. Why did you do this? Give me a reason."

"It was the only way I could help."

He stood up. "I didn't ask for your help. I don't want your help," he yelled.

She stomped her foot in frustration. "I'll quit again. I'm trying to help us." She waited for him to say something. "I'm going to sleep on the couch." She waited for him to respond, but he didn't. She walked to the bed and grabbed a pillow and walked out of the room.

Three hours later, Mark was back on the bed asking himself why? He walked to the living room and saw Abby on the couch with her eyes open.

"Why don't you go to bed? You're not comfortable here."

"I didn't think you wanted to be in the same room with me."

"Yeah, but …" he stammered. "Well."

"Are we all right?"

"No, but what can I do?"

"No," she yelled, sitting up. "We have to be all right," she pleaded. She rolled off the couch and crawled to him. "I should've told you everything. We should've talked this out. We should've done something." She held on to his pants pockets crying.

"But we didn't." He twisted away from her and walked to the kitchen.

She picked up her pillow and went to the bedroom. Mark came back from the kitchen and sat on the couch.

The next morning the phone rang and woke up Mark. He was twisted trying to fit on the couch and fell on the floor trying to answer the phone. It was his mother. Mark sighed. She asked to speak to Abby.

"She's not here," Mark lied. "She left early this morning. Why are you asking for her?"

"Well, I don't really like that she used to be a stripper. She did marry you. She is part of the family, and she talks to me when I call. You just sit there and say yes, with the phone away from your ear."

Mark pulled the phone close to his ear. "You talk to her?"

"She's a nice girl," his mother said. "You could've done worse. I can't change someone's past, but she seems like a decent girl."

"Says you," Mark said, without realizing it.

"What's that mean?"

"Nothing."

"There's a woman's expo at the arts center. Maybe she wants to go. So where is she? Is she working?"

"She might be," he answered.

"Did you sleep late?" his mother asked. "You can't stay in bed all day and think a job is coming to you."

"No, I didn't sleep late," he fired back. "I just don't know where she is."

"When you see her, tell her about the expo."

Abby met Carla at the National Diner during brunch time. She told Carla about getting caught and said she didn't know what to do. Carla thanked her for helping but didn't offer any advice.

"It's exactly what cost me my marriage," Carla pointed out to her.

Abby walked in the door at home at four o'clock. She found Mark sitting on the floor in sweats and an old Dewey's T-shirt. A newspaper was in front of him with classified ads circled. Abby tiptoed past him, even though he was awake. As she glanced out the window, she noticed crowds heading toward the recreation center.

"What's going on at the rec room?" she asked.

"I don't know."

"All the neighbors are walking over there. Are they having a meeting?"

"I don't know."

Abby rolled her eyes. "Do you think maybe we should go? We could meet more of the neighbors."

"You don't want to," Mark said.

"Yes I do. Let's go."

"Abby, they don't like us. Why should we go?"

"They need to meet us." She walked to Mark and grabbed his hand. "Come on."

Mark sighed and got off the couch. They locked the front door and walked behind a group of older couples they didn't know. Every seat in the rec room was full. There was a coffee urn with Styrofoam cups and powdered creamer on a table near the door. Mark saw Maggie, Eddie's wife, sitting at the back of the room. Mrs. Dumont was seated on a stage at the front, dressed up. She smiled and chatted with another older woman whom Mark didn't recognize.

"What's going on?" Mark asked Maggie.

She didn't turn before she spoke. "Shhh, it's a petition."

Mark's eyes widened. He'd forgotten that Sue had warned him. "Abby, we need to leave."

"No, I wanna see."

Mrs. Dumont stood up at the lectern and held up a piece of paper. "This meeting is to see if we can get enough residents to object to our new neighbor and her lifestyle. The gunfights, the lewd jogging, and all the visitors are disrupting this quiet development. This used to be a nice, quiet complex, but now it's not safe for our children."

Abby gasped. "That's terrible. Who is she talking about?"

Mrs. Dumont scanned the room and saw Abby in the back. Their eyes locked. "You," Mrs. Dumont yelled, pointing at her. "You weren't invited here. You and he are a menace."

"Why? What did we do?" Abby yelled. People turned. Abby scanned the room and recognized some of the faces. The nice men who waved to her when she jogged were there. The women who came in to browse and touch everything in Nora Daniel but would never buy anything were there.

Maggie turned around and saw Abby and Mark standing together. "You're the person doing all that stuff," Maggie said to Abby.

Abby wanted to scream, but she stepped behind Mark to hide from all the people turning to look at her.

"Mark, I don't know how you could marry a woman like that," Maggie said. "Eddie told me you were such a good person."

"Maggie, why?" he stuttered.

"Mark, I have to think about my child. We can't have kids living here with someone in porn."

"What?" he yelled. "She never did porn. She's never done anything lewd. She doesn't take her clothes off in bars, and it's none of your business if she did."

"Eddie told me she still does it. She was at that bar the other night. Eddie told me how he hates that club, but was forced to go there with the guys, and he saw her. She's disgusting."

"Maggie, stop."

Abby shook. *That's it. Defend me, Mark,* she thought. *Don't let them talk like that about me.*

"Maggie, I ..." Mark stuttered.

"Mark, face it. We have to worry about our houses and our kids. If you want to live with a porn star, do it somewhere else and don't tell Ed where."

"She's not a porn star."

"They saw her go to those places on Route 9."

"She knows a porn star. She's not one of them."

"This is no place for someone like her," Mrs. Dumont said. She told the room how quiet and peaceful the complex was. Children played together. Everyone looked out for each other. A parent could trust that their child was safe even after dark. "We've had police here, now that she's here."

"Yeah, move out," someone yelled from the middle of the room. This stirred up more people.

"No one wants that stuff here," another woman yelled out.

"Go back to the dive bars with the other tramps."

"Slut."

"Whore."

"Yeah, it's tough enough being a parent. We don't need that type of trash living with us," another woman yelled out. Most people sat in silence, but the one's that said something got louder. They pointed at Abby. Mrs. Dumont waved her arms to get more people to stand and yell. She waved the petition and asked for signatures.

Mark was silent. He didn't act disgusted or tense. Abby stood frozen and thought that Mark leaned away from her.

"Yeah, she's trash," someone shouted.

"Maggie, I don't know what to say," Mark said, while the yelling continued. "It's not that bad."

"That's it? It's not that bad?" Abby said, before running out of the room crying.

"You didn't have to do that," Mark said to Maggie. Women were still yelling, and people lined up at the front of the room to sign the petition.

Abby grabbed her stomach while she ran. The pain was worse than the time Penn gave her heroin. It was worse than the time Penn slapped her for forgetting his cigarettes. Her face turned red as she ran, trying to breathe and not cry.

She grabbed the door handle and crouched over unable to breathe. Tears rolled down her face. She closed her eyes, but more tears came, making it more difficult to work her key in the lock. It took a lot of fumbling, but she got the door open and fell to the floor inside.

"He doesn't love me," she wailed.

She crawled to the bedroom coughing and gasping for air. *Why did I go back there*? She thought. *Why did I dance again*? The carpet was like sandpaper on her knees. She'd left a scattered trail of blood from her knees as she crawled to the bedroom. Coughs came from her stomach, causing her whole body to curl up. She shook, trying to catch her breath.

She curled up at the side of the bed and cried. Penn had slapped her face dozens of times, but this stung more. Her rubbery legs collapsed when she tried to stand, but she held onto the bed.

"He hates me," she cried out. "It's true. I am garbage." She could hear her neighbors' voices taunting her: "Whore." "Slut." "We don't like you." "Go away."

Her legs gave out, and she fell to the floor again. She once fell off a stage dancing and twisted her knee. The pain in her legs was worse now. She coughed and rubbed her eyes, but the tears stung and made her cry more.

I love him. I finally had a family. Why didn't he say something?

She crawled to the closet and pulled out her suitcase.

"Abby," Mark yelled, running into the house. "Abby, where are you?" He heard coughing in the bedroom and followed the blood stains in the carpet. "I'm sorry about them. They talk about everyone."

She looked down at her bag full of clothes. It was still tough to breathe. Her hands shook. She tightened her arms to keep steady.

"People gossip," Mark said, leaning against the door.

"I don't care about them," she yelled. She put her hand to her stomach to control her breathing. Her face was strawberry red, and her eyes were drained from crying. "I only care what you didn't say. You didn't stop them. You said that it wasn't so bad. You really think I'm a slut. All those years, I thought it was Penn's fault. I was better than a slut. I thought you thought more of me. I'm a slut in your eyes." She grabbed her bag and pushed him to get out of the room.

Carla went to work at Babes Go-Go that night. She hadn't met the new scheduler, but she was scheduled to dance for five hours. She didn't have enough outfits. Perspiration had stained her silk outfit after one set. Her black leather go-go boots scraped her knees while sitting on the edge of the stage after her third set. Her feet hurt. Another dancer trotted around the bar waving to the patrons. Carla took advantage of the break to tap Eli on the shoulder and ask for a bottle of water. Eli smiled and got her the bottle.

"You start your overtime?"

"Yeah, I'm covering for the dancer who quit today. I guess she got scared about those murders and the guy still not being caught. It works for me because they didn't want me without Baby Doll before."

"I'm here till closing," Eli said. "A bunch of us sometimes go out to the diner after work. You want to go?"

She smiled and shrugged. "Maybe I shouldn't. I don't think everyone here likes me." She saw Sunflower walk into the bar as she spoke.

"So, we'll go together. Everyone can go somewhere else," Eli said, glancing at her chest.

"I'm still married," Carla said. "I don't think I should get involved with anyone yet."

"Yeah, whatever," Eli said, turning away.

She knew it bothered him, but she wasn't concerned. She'd seen other dancers go out with him. There was music to select. She went to the deejay's booth and found a box of new compact discs sitting out.

"All the new stuff," the deejay said. "You could be the first to dance to the newest music."

"Great, but I'm going to stick to what I know."

"Well, you gotta keep the customers coming back." He turned with his arms out to her. "It's not that hard for you to do."

She shrugged and leaned into his hug, but kept her arms straight down, not hugging him back.

"Oh, but you make it hard," he said, squeezing her and smelling her hair. He smiled as he lowered his hand to her ass. She pushed at his arm, but he didn't move away. He even laughed when she wiggled around.

Eli walked past the booth and rolled his eyes at them. He heard the deejay say, "You're so bad. I like that."

"Married and can't get involved," Eli muttered, while picking up a case of beer from the back room. "Can't get involved with me."

❦   ❦   ❦

Abby drove to the motel where Carla was staying. She got there at two AM. Carla's Lexus wasn't there. Abby parked where she could see Carla's room and waited. She thought about Penn and dancing in Las Vegas. She left Las Vegas and it followed her here. *I can't believe I'm so stupid. Why did I go back to Babes? Why did I marry him?*

The cold night air blew through the closed windows in her car. She wrapped her coat around her. *I should've gotten Carla a job at the mall.* Abby fell asleep after an hour. When she awoke, Carla's Lexus was parked in front of her. Abby took a deep breath and went to Carla's room.

As she walked to the door, she practiced saying, "I'm quitting dancing again. You're on your own." When she got to the door, she heard Carla moaning and the bedsprings bouncing. Abby tried to see through the window, but it was dark in the room, and the curtain was drawn.

She's just like the rest of them, Abby thought. *Her marriage is over.*

Abby turned and went back to her car. *Her ruined marriage is my fault, too. I mess up everything for everyone.* She sat in her car and waited for someone to leave Carla's room.

Chapter 21

Jake Hersh knocked on Mark's front door in the middle of the afternoon the next day. Mark looked through the peephole in the door to see a guy with a wrinkled brown suit. When he heard Mark on the other side of the door, Jake introduced himself.

"I'd like to talk to your wife," Jake said.

"I don't know a Jake Hersh, and I don't need more neighbors bothering me." Mark waited for the man to say something. Instead, the man rummaged through his pockets. "I've never seen you before," Mark shouted through the still-closed door.

"I work at Babes," Jake replied. "I have a security badge in my pocket, but I also have a lot of notes stuffed in there. A lot of things are going on. I wanted to talk to your wife. May I come in?"

Mark didn't open the door. "You have some nerve."

"I don't actually work for the bar. I work for the security company they hired to watch the entertainers. Now there's a new situation. There was a murder recently of someone you might know—Patrick Pennington. You might have called him Penn."

"I didn't know him," Mark said, finally opening the door.

"Your wife did," Jake said. "You don't have to tell me about him. There's a lot of information on the Internet. The Las Vegas Police Department knew him. I made some calls to check on his background. Penn was arrested four times in Las Vegas—drunkenness, vagrancy, and drugs. His last known address was with your wife."

Mark cut him off. "My wife doesn't dance anymore," he said. "You would know that if you worked for the bar. I don't know you, but I'll tell you this, that Penn guy had an obsessive thing for her. He followed her here. He wanted to take her back to Las Vegas. She said 'no.' He must have been desperate, and now he's dead. That's all I know."

Jake couldn't tell if what Mark said was true or not. He didn't look like the most reliable source: he was dirty and unshaven and wore pants with holes in the knees and a stained Dewey's T-shirt. He was definitely down on his luck. "Doesn't it bother you?" Jake asked. "Her old boyfriend is dead, along with a bar owner and house mom where she worked, as well as two dancers found just outside the bar. According to her driver's license, your wife hasn't lived here long, but she knew all those people. Then she quit."

Mark never realized how many murders there had been. *Could Abby kill someone*? he wondered. "You better leave," Mark said. "You're talking crazy, and I'm just too busy for it. I don't even know where she is." Mark was shaking, and he knew that Jake saw it. "We had a fight, and she walked out last night."

"Did she walk out angry?" Jake asked.

"I don't know. I think she was. She may have been hurt, too."

"Her friend Carla was found murdered this morning," Jake said, straightening his tie so it looked like he wasn't watching Mark's confused reaction. "She lived in a motel. The maid service found her stabbed in bed. She fought her attacker. Whoever it was sat on her on the bed and stabbed her. The night desk person saw your wife's car in the parking lot last night. The cops are looking for her."

"My God," Mark gasped, stepping back. "It could be my fault. I thought she was making this Carla person up. I yelled at her about Carla."

"Tell me how I can find her," Jake asked in a mild whisper.

"I don't know," Mark paused. "Why should I help you?"

"If she's innocent, I'll help her."

"Well, she isn't going to talk to me anytime soon." Mark thought for a moment. "What do you mean 'if'?"

Carla was buried on a clear Monday morning after a rainstorm that made the grass look like shiny shards of plastic. Her parents couldn't afford much for her, and George didn't care. His business associates didn't send flowers at his demand.

The manager of Babes told the dancers about Carla. She didn't have many friends, but a few of the girls felt bad. Six of them arranged to attend the funeral together. Jake parked beyond the group and watched.

George stood by the coffin with his hands on Kendra's and Kim's shoulders. Kendra yawned as the priest said a final prayer. Kim looked down at the grass she mashed into the mud with the toe of her shoe. She tried to fight the tears that still welled in her eyes by biting her lip until she left marks. Kendra tossed a rose overhanded onto the coffin and walked to the funeral cars. Kim clutched her rose, even though her father told her to throw it. She dragged her feet as she was led to the casket.

"She was my friend," Kim said. "She felt like a Mom." George squeezed her shoulder. She placed the rose on the casket, lingering a moment with her hand on the casket. "You didn't have to leave us, Carla. Remember when we danced around the room? Remember when we talked about horses?"

"Let's go," George said, turning her around by the shoulder.

"No, I want to stay."

George tossed his rose sidearm at the coffin and pulled Kim. People headed down the hill to the cemetery road. Carla's parents walked to the front car. Her father was an older man, but still fit; he looked like he could've been an athlete in his younger years. Her mother stayed behind her husband, covering her face with a tissue. Kendra leaned against a car and lit a cigarette. A group of beautiful, skinny, big-chested and small-hipped women left behind the relatives.

Jake pulled out a notebook and noted that he didn't see Abby. He was surprised to see Sunflower leaning at his window.

"What brings you here?" she asked. "Have a thing for checking out the entertainers?"

"It's another murder involving someone who worked at Babes. I'm just searching for clues."

"Do you have any ideas?" she asked, as she ran her finger along the window frame of the door. "It's getting a little scary at the bar."

"It's not a nice office job. There are some unsavory customers giving you tips to make your living," Jake said. "You don't surround yourself with the best and brightest the world has to offer."

"I surround myself with big businessmen, college grads, and professional athletes," she responded. "Some of the girls go on to big things. I'm saving up. I won't be doing this dancing thing forever."

"Sorry," Jake said. "I feel bad for those two girls, losing a parent."

"I never liked her," Sunflower said. "I think she had things most of the girls dancing only dream about. She traded it in to flash drunks."

"That's a bit harsh," Jake said.

She stood up and took a step before turning back to him. "You want to go for a coffee?"

"Get in with me," he said and let her into his car.

Eli watched them from the top of the hill. "She's trouble," he mumbled.

Kim looked out the window of the funeral car at the gravesite thinking about their shopping trips. Carla talked to her as they went from store to store. Carla bought her things. Carla asked her questions about her day.

"Stop smoking," George yelled at Kendra.

"Make me," Kendra snarled.

"I don't want my daughter smoking," George said. "Besides, that's all we need. You get busted for underage smoking, and I'll get busted. Put that out."

"You. You. You. I want to smoke," she said, reaching into her purse. She pulled out a lighter and taunted George with it. "I'll light up all the cigarettes I want."

A man knelt down to pull weeds from the lawn of the apartment building where he lived in the Eastside of Providence, Rhode Island. He took off his Minor League baseball cap to wipe sweat off his forehead. The strong winds blew through the last strands of his hair. His Boston sweatshirt rode up his back exposing boxer shorts under his dirty jeans. The warm sun beat down on his scalp, so he put the cap back on.

He felt around for garden shears with one hand while he focused on fighting with a thick root in front of him. Someone came up behind him and took the shears.

"Do you remember your daughter, Mr. Broughton," said the voice.

He let go of the root and turned to face the person. He stared in shock and curiosity at the person in front of him.

Chapter 22

Jake went to George's home two days after Carla's funeral. He was interested in Carla's lifestyle—the things she liked doing; the type clothes she wore; why did she want to work at Babes Go-Go; something she owned that might give a clue as to what happened to her. George answered the door to see a rumpled and unshaven Jake. He didn't look much better. The sleeves on his button down shirt were too short. He wore dress slacks and sneakers.

Jake explained who he was and why he was interested in Carla, but George closed the door on him. Jake didn't go there to give up. He pulled out his cell phone and called the house phone number he found from the records at Babes. Carla had listed it when she worked at the bar.

"I don't know who you are," George said. "I've never seen a security guard as sloppy as you. This is ridiculous." He hung up.

Jake rang the doorbell until George finally answered. He explained that he was trying to help, not to harass George.

"The police asked me questions already," George said. "Why should I help a rent-a-cop? I should call the police on you for disturbing me."

"Those murders happened at the place I'm guarding. I couldn't go to the motel where Carla was killed, because it was cordoned off as a crime scene. I don't have access to all that fingerprint and hair DNA stuff like the police do, but I want to know about Carla." He waited for George to say something. Instead, George walked into the living room, maneuvering around some boxes. Jake followed.

Folded clothes hung out of one box. Stacked shoes were in another open box. It looked like about twenty boxes of Carla's stuff. Jake pulled a plastic bag from his coat in case he found something he could use. One box was loaded with an array of makeup and perfume.

George picked up a pair of tennis shoes and threw them into a box. "I sent most of her stuff to charity. This is just crap that I'm going to throw in one of those bins at the store parking lots."

"Was she buried with her wedding ring?" Jake asked George. "Your marriage didn't end too well, did it?" Jake persisted, when George didn't answer.

"She almost ruined me," George said. "My business partners wanted dances from her. I was embarrassed in front of a bar full of people. She disrupted my home. My oldest daughter talks back. She never did that. I have to go to court to keep custody of my children. I'm not sure I even want them anymore after what she did to them."

He picked up a box of clothes so big and unmanageable that he had to brace it against his hips to carry it out of the house. He threw it into the back of his Hummer and slammed the door, crushing the box. "I don't want to talk about her. She messed up my life, my house, and my things." He carried more boxes, while Jake asked questions. George stuck to his mantra: "She almost ruined me."

George crammed on last box in the vehicle. "Is there anything else you want here?" he asked Jake.

"No, I guess there's nothing I could use here."

🍁   🍁   🍁

"I … I … I … nevah thought I'd see you again," Mr. Broughton said to the hands holding the shears.

Abby turned the shears so the handles faced her father. He took them and stood up to look at the daughter he hadn't seen in eight years. She was now a tall brunette. Her hair was hair tied up, and she wore silver sneakers, blue jeans, and a flannel shirt over a New Jersey tee shirt.

"I missed you," he said. He reached out to hug her. She stood with her arms at her sides afraid to touch him. She leaned toward him to be hugged, but the anger toward her parents rose in her. She didn't want to be angry, but it was there. He stopped trying when she didn't move. "It's not the time for a hug." He used his cap brim to wipe perspiration off his forehead without taking the cap off. "You can come in."

They walked into the apartment building keeping distance between them. Her father had a one-room studio on the first floor. His sofa bed was in the center of the room surrounded by white walls, a bureau, and cardboard boxes filled with pieces of his past.

"Aftah all that happened with that football guy, I wish we hadn't push you out like that," he said, toying with his cap. "I see you turned out well without us. You're here, and you're healthy. I see a wedding ring on your hand."

She twirled it around her finger. "Dad, you don't know what I've done the past few years. I'm not sure you want to know."

"It doesn't mattah," he said. The Providence accent, which she once had, made her relax. "You came back to see me after all these years. I didn't know if you were still alive. I hoped the Lord would bring you home. You …" he said, stepping back from her. "You look great."

She went to the sofa, and he followed to sit next to her. She clutched the arm of the sofa when he sat down. There was less than one cushion worth of space between them. She slid off the sofa to the floor.

"I've done so many things wrong," she said.

He reached down and stroked her hair. "Your past doesn't matter. The Lord watches over his sheep. I'm the one that has to make up for my past with you."

"Oh, quit it with the Lord stuff," Abby said. "You guys never followed that stuff except when it was on TV."

He slouched and exhaled. "Fine. Can you stay here a little while? We could make up for lost time. Your husband might like it here. Where is he? I want to meet him."

"He's not here," Abby said. "I wanted to work this out myself. I need to do a lot of things for myself."

"What do you mean?"

"Why did you kick me out?" she yelled. She couldn't face him, but just being near brought back the feelings from her teen years. "I was only sixteen. I know I got pregnant, but two people were involved. Why was I automatically the slut?"

"We overreacted," her father said. He leaned away from her and couldn't face her. "Bring the child to see me. I'll make it up to you."

"There isn't a baby." She quieted. "I lost it. I told Mom, but she didn't care."

"Maybe you and your husband will have one."

"No." She shrugged. "I can't. I'll never have a baby. If you hadn't kicked me out, things would've been different."

"Of course they would be different. Is this why you came back? Are you here to blame me for every mistake you made? I made mistakes, too. Your mother, God rest her soul, made mistakes, too. I can't change that." He stood up and paced around the room. "I don't want to argue with you after not seeing you for so long."

She sighed. "I had to get that out." She crouched over and inhaled a long, slow breath. "I want to try to fix this." They stared at each other for a moment. The room was so silent that they heard cars outside drive down the street. "I got a GED," she said into her hands. "I traveled around the country. Want to hear about it?"

Mark drove his car to the old stops he used to make on his delivery route. He stopped at Iggy's at eight in the morning for a coffee like he used to do and saw Smitty's truck. Smitty came out from the back of the truck with empty carrying trays.

"Long time, no see," Mark said.

"Happy to see you," Smitty yelled. "I heard about you guys losing your jobs. The stops aren't the same without ya." He grabbed Mark's hand and shook it till Mark's arm hurt.

"Yeah," Mark said, staring at the ground. "I just wanted to see what happened to the space I used to fill. I ... uh ... just wanted to know how the stores are doing."

"Hard to walk away," Smitty smirked. "I always say I can't wait to retire or win the lottery, but I would miss this. How's married life treating you?"

"Good," Mark said. "Yeah, good. It's good."

"Hey, I'm racing the clock, so I gotta go. Keep in touch." Smitty pulled a card from his clipboard. "They say the dispatcher is retiring soon. It might mean job openings. If you want to give up the truck and go into office work, keep this in mind." Smitty went to the driver's seat of his truck and started it up. The engine was loud and creaky. The truck bucked when Smitty slammed it into gear and drove away.

Mark saw Jennifer walk through the store carrying mustard to the deli section.

Her eyes lit up when she saw him. "How are you?" she asked. "I haven't seen you in so long."

"I'm all right. They sold Dewey's so I don't come here anymore."

"I know," she said. "You never said good-bye. You used to come by every morning."

"Well," Mark said. He didn't know what else to say. She used to ignore him. "Are you married yet?"

"Oh," she giggled. "I'm engaged. We're not really ready yet. You can't rush into these things. I don't want to get married and then find out there's still guys I want to date. Guys here ... wherever," she said, laughing.

"You would date guys here?" he asked, cracking his knuckles.

"Maybe, depends on the guy. I have to get back to work." She shifted her weight when the mustard jars got too heavy. "I'll see you again, right?"

Mark agreed and walked out of the store. After he got in his car, he realized he never got a coffee or looked at the doughnut stand. He drove away rather than go back.

"Why do you live here?" Abby asked her father. "I went to our old home on Thayer Street. When you weren't there, I had to look you up in the phone book." She cut a radish in the closet-sized kitchen.

"Aftah your mother died and your brother moved out, I didn't need all that space. I'm sorry. Your mother threw out a lot of your stuff," he said, reaching around her to set the temperature on the oven. "I have a few small things." He left the kitchen and got a cardboard box from a closet. It was too heavy for him, and he let it drop to the floor in front of the couch. There was a dirty fifteen-inch plastic doll with a pink gown, pink heels, and faded, shiny blonde hair, which was missing in places. "She was your favorite toy when you were little," he said, looking at it. "I pulled it out of the garbage after you moved away. Here, take it," he said, holding it out to her. She didn't go near it. He put it on the couch and reached into the box for a videotape. Abby walked over and looked at the tape box.

"A Charlie Chaplin movie?" She picked up the box and read the title. *The Gold Rush*.

"It used to be your favorite movie. I don't understand what you see in the movie, but you loved it."

Rain poured so hard on the windshield of George's Hummer that even with his wipers going as fast as they could, the road was not visible. Thunder crashed in the distance and shook the ground beneath him. George drove to a clothes donation bin at an empty strip-mall parking lot. He pulled his coat over his neck and went to the back of the vehicle to pull out Carla's clothes.

Rather than take out the clothes and put them in the bin, he left the opened cardboard boxes on the ground. The cardboard soaked through and fell apart within seconds. Her rain-soaked clothes fell out of the boxes onto the concrete and dirt of the parking lot. George sped away.

🍁 🍁 🍁

The night was cool and dark in Providence. Abby felt like she'd said what she had to say and wanted to go back home. "I'm going back to New Jersey," she told her father. "My husband might be wondering about me. It's been a few days already. I went to Boston and stopped here on my way back. I'll come visit you again," she promised, as she walked to her car. "I don't want to be apart."

"I wish your mother was alive to see you again. She had no idea what she was doing," he said.

"Yeah, but like you said, there's nothing we can do about it now. I have a lot of other things I need to fix first."

"When will I meet your husband?"

She looked down. "I don't know. That's one of those things I need to work on."

"Be careful."

"I will," she hugged him with her eyes closed and took a deep breath before she broke the hug and got in the car. She flashed back to the time when she was six years old and fell off her bicycle. Her father ran to help her up and told her that he wouldn't let her get hurt.

"I really have to go," she said. She felt her father's hand press the sore on her back. Her eyes bulged open, but he didn't say anything so she kept quiet. "A lot happened over the years," she told him.

"I remember that you used to rub your nose when you were nervous. I see that you stopped that because your eyes look nervous."

"It's a long trip," Abby said. She saw her doll in the passenger seat ready for the ride. "I'm going to stop along the way and sightsee. I need time to think." She put the car into gear.

Her father stepped away from the car to watch her. He turned and picked twigs off the bush in the front yard of the apartment building before he went inside.

"Not even his house, and he takes care of the lawn," Abby muttered to herself.

Jake tried to see George again, but there was no answer at the front door. He walked around the house and looked through a window at George's home office. George yelled into a cordless phone. Even with the windows closed, Jake could make out most of the conversation.

"Kim, listen to me. You need to answer your teachers when they talk to you. Don't you understand that? You were such a good student when you lived here. Can't you be a good student at your new school?" He squeezed the phone like he wanted to crack it. "Answer me, God damn it!"

Jake swallowed a lump of nerves in his throat while watching George.

"What is the problem?" George yelled and rubbed his eyes. He lowered the phone to his chest and took a deep breath before raising it back up. "You don't understand. We went over this. She did something that was very bad, and I can't explain it to you."

Jake lowered his head and went to another window. It seemed like there was no one in the house but George. There were three cars in the driveway. Could they all be George's? Jake went back to the window.

"I didn't get rid of you," George yelled. "Your mother thinks you should live with her now." He fixed his tie in the wall mirror by his desk. Light reflected from the desk light off his shoes. "Kim," he yelled. "Don't you hang up on me." He pushed the end button of the cordless phone like he wanted to ram it through the handle before he hit the redial again and again.

Jake went back to his car. "At least he had time to look at himself in the mirror," Jake chuckled.

Abby drove to Babes early the next night. The dip at the front of the driveway was fixed. The front door had a real handle, attached with more than one screw. She walked inside and focused on the tattoo that covered the entire back of the dancer on the stage. The dancer spun around, and Abby saw that her belly button was pierced, as was her nose. Her long legs were bony thin. She looked like a stick figure with breasts so heavy it appeared she might topple over at any minute.

When Abby got to the locker room, Sunflower was sitting on a bench, rubbing her feet. Abby said hello as she went to a locker. "I have to get the last of my stuff out."

"Sorry to hear about your friend," Sunflower said, as she grabbed the door to leave.

"What do you mean sorry?" Abby asked.

"You didn't hear? Your friend Carla was killed about a week ago. It was all over the papers. Everyone was surprised you weren't at the funeral. I guess it was tougher on you. I figured the two of you out," she said, winking at Abby.

Abby dropped to the wooden bench behind her and stared at the empty locker in front of her. "Figured what out?"

Sunflower paused. "It's OK. Half the dancers here are gay. I knew you two were." She walked out before Abby could deny it. The stage outside the lockers was now empty and Sunflower ran to it with a blast of fury. Two guys played pool in the back. The pounding and rapping of the next song blasted through the bar. Her hair swung and swept across the brass pole. She dropped to her knees and ran her hands all over her body.

The men from the pool table stopped to watch her. The music got more powerful as the rapper wailed to a sonic guitar riff.

She did a split and stretched to touch her toes. As she curled her legs inward, she watched the eyes of a man at the bar. He didn't stop looking at her, even as he took a drink.

Jake Hersh walked to the bar as she went for a tip from the guy. She walked to him. Her hips swayed and her hands roamed up her body to her hair. The drums of the music were in time with her heartbeat. She grabbed Jake's hand and put it to her waist as she leaned in and kissed him on the lips. She stepped back and mouthed, "See you after the set?"

"I met Carla's husband," Jake yelled over the rap song. "He's not the least bit concerned that she's dead."

"It's sad," she said. Her nail had chipped, and she seemed more focused on that than on what Jake had said. She turned around and went back to the stage. Jake walked away from the bar and went to the deejay.

"Are you any closer to finding out what happened to Carla?" asked the deejay.

"Not really. You really liked her, didn't you? I noticed you two were always hugging and talking."

The deejay's hands shook. "I really wanted to fuck her. She was hot. Her tits were real." He leaned into Jake like he was telling a secret. "I grabbed that ass all the time. She tipped me really good. So I guess I really did like her."

"What kind of tip?"

"She just tipped me better for the music than most dancers."

"I thought dancers just gave you a couple dollars. You're on salary, aren't you?"

The deejay ignored the question. "She was very nice."

"She was very gullible," Jake countered. "How much money did Stacy Ann and Buffy give you?"

The deejay squared off at Jake. "Don't try it," he said. "Don't try to point all that bullshit at me. Carla and I had a deal. Don't try to make me into some kind of suspect. You aren't even a real cop. You're some rent-a-cop trying to make a name for yourself. You're not going to do it by fucking with me. I don't care who you are."

"Calm down, I'm just asking questions."

Abby walked out of the bar without Jake noticing her. She went to the car, thinking about the night Mark found her dancing again. He was angry. He knew those other dancers. He beat up Penn.

Mark went to Eddie's house when he saw that Maggie was out. They went into the kitchenette to sit with Eddie's baby.

"I'm sorry about all that petition stuff," Eddie said. "I didn't know Maggie was part of it. We had a big fight about it, because it was none of Maggie's business. She's going to apologize to you. I mean, come on—all you did for us when we needed help moving in. We can't turn our backs on you. If anything, we really should get to know your wife."

"I don't know about that," Mark said, cracking his knuckles. "I went back to my old stops on my route. I saw Jennifer. She's not getting married anytime soon. I doubt if she ever will, with her attitude about it. I had a thing for her for the longest time—much longer than I've felt anything for Abby."

"Are you thinking about cheating on her?" Eddie asked.

Mark shook his head. "No, I was thinking about getting rid of Abby."

"That's crazy," Eddie stammered. "You're going to dump a hot dancer for a girl that has ignored you for years. You'd have to be crazy to divorce her, just to maybe get a shot at a girl from some convenience store."

"I'm not serious," Mark said. "But things aren't working out with Abby. I don't even know where she is right now. I went through her things at the house trying to figure out where she went. She claims to know a porno star named Tiffany. There are postcards in her drawers that she never mailed addressed to Tiffany. She has no pictures of friends. No pictures of family. She has no things that a person just gets in the course of living. There are no souvenirs. I don't know her."

"You've only been married for a couple of months. How bad can things be? She just moved here. She's probably bringing all that stuff back with her from wherever she's gone. She'll come back."

Mark lowered his voice and leaned into Eddie. "I don't know if I want her back. I talked to a security guard at the bar. Abby might be insane. I just don't know if I can handle her."

"You're married. You have to give it a chance," Eddie urged.

"I don't know … if she could just go away."

Chapter 23

Abby opened the door to her house thinking no one was home. As she walked to the bedroom, she noticed that the bloodstains from her knees had been cleaned off the rug. She opened the door and jumped back against the wall behind her. Mark lay on the bed, dressed in sweatpants and a T-shirt. He had a few days worth of stubble on his cheeks. His hair was a mess and his eyes looked tired and bloodshot.

"Abby, where have you been?" he asked, eyes wide and mouth agape. "I didn't know how to find you."

"I went to Rhode Island to see my Dad," she said. "It was like seeing my childhood. He has that Providence accent I used to have."

Mark nodded like he understood. He moved slow and talked down to her. "Did you have a good time?" She had said in the past that she was disowned. "So how was Providence?" he asked. "Before you answer, I'll go to the kitchen and get us some wine to celebrate your return." He slid off the bed and went toward the door.

She was against the wall and couldn't move. He walked within an inch of her. She wanted to melt into the wall to get some space. "Wait," she said. "Why don't you stay with me for awhile? How about you get back on the bed? I might have something for you."

So you can pin me down? he wondered. "Well," he said, "if you don't want wine, I'll go to the living room while you get unpacked, and then we can catch up on lost time."

"OK, you go wait for me, and I'll be right out," she said. "I don't have much to unpack really. I just got a few things to get me through the time in Providence."

Mark left the room and ran to the phone in the living room. She picked up the phone in the bedroom and heard Mark's voice, but she didn't listen to the conversation. She hung it up, with her hand covering the transmitter part of the receiver as she pushed the "end" button. She wondered who he was calling. As she looked around the bedroom, she noticed her bureau drawers were open. The postcard she had written to Tiffany and forgotten to mail was sitting out. Her clothes in her drawers were messed up.

Penn used to go through her things looking for money. Doubts rose in her mind. She knew Stacy Ann had danced for Mark. He hung out at Babes a lot. She'd seen him almost beat Penn to death. Carla's questions about Mark also came back to her. The other dancers asked her what she knew about him. Abby recalled that she couldn't even remember his name when he was at the hospital. She paced the room, wondering what Mark was doing.

Penn seemed nice at first, she recalled, then she talked back to him, and he showed what he was really like. He got high, locked her in the bathroom for five hours, and ripped her clothes to shreds. The sore on her back still hurt sometimes.

She had to get out.

"Jake, she came home," Mark whispered into the phone. "You made me think. I don't know anything about her. She has no past. I can't find a picture or anything in her stuff. You better come now and question her." Mark paced. Jake said he needed to get help before he came over. Mark sighed. "Hurry," he said. "You know she was friends with Carla. Just when Carla disappeared, Abby went missing for a week. She claims she was in Providence with her father, but her parents kicked her out when she was a teenager and have wanted nothing to do with her since then. This is the time to catch your killer."

Abby rubbed a scar on her leg from Penn when he had burned her leg throwing lit cigarettes at her. She heard cars outside. If she could get to a car, she could get to safety. There were heavy footsteps down the hall. She locked the bedroom door. Then she heard metal clanking down the hallway. It went quiet again. She heard whispers and plodding footsteps.

She panicked and stuck her head out the bedroom window. The ground was far below, but she knew she had to get away. It had sounded like Mark was carrying something heavy and painful. She wiggled out of the window. She got her hips through the small frame and was hanging by her legs, but she was still four feet off the ground. Someone knocked at the door. She let go of the window frame, landed in a handstand, and rolled over to her feet. Her dance moves came in handy.

She hid behind a bush under her window to hear what was going on in the room.

"She got away," said a voice she didn't recognize.

"It's eight feet from the window to the ground. She couldn't have jumped," Mark said. "I didn't know she heard me call."

"Well she did," the other voice said. "When you trap a killer, you don't leave a getaway window wide open!" From the sound of his voice, Abby could tell he was running down the hallway.

He called the cops on me, Abby thought. *He thinks I'm the killer! Then he can't be. I feel so bad. What was I thinking? How could he suspect me*? Just then a police cruiser roared around the building. She ran from behind the bush into an alley.

Jake Hersh arrived at Babes before opening and saw Sunflower at the bar nursing a beer. It wasn't approved policy that an entertainer sit at the bar dressed to dance drinking. He sat next to her and said it was nice to see her early for work. When she lifted her head off the bar, he saw mascara running down her red face.

"I went to see a lawyer today," she told him.

"About your son? What happened?"

"The lawyer said he would never take me as a client. 'What person would send a kid home with a stripper?' he said. He made me feel like dirt." She snorted. "Fuck it. Maybe everyone is right. I do this shit, and no one thinks I'm a human anymore."

"Don't say that," he said. He put his arm around her shoulder and pulled her close, but she swatted him away.

"Don't touch me," Sunflower said. "Don't bother with me. I just don't give a fuck anymore."

"Mona, calm down."

She slammed her hands down on the bar. "Fuck you, Jake Hersh. You calm down. This is great for you. You're getting paid to watch tits and ass, just like every other man around here. You're trying to fuck me, too. That's all any of you see." She guzzled her beer and slammed the empty mug on the bar. "Play my music. I'm just a dancing machine. We're all just machines."

Jake grabbed her shoulders. "Go home, Mona. Just take the day and get away. I'll call you later to make sure you're doing OK."

"I said play my music."

"Mona, if you go on that stage, I'll get the owners to get you off of it."

She stared him down, but he stood solid. The three men playing pool stared at her.

"Fine, I'm leaving." She slammed the door to the lockers.

Jake sighed and told everyone that the commotion was over. Sunflower burst back out of the locker room and went to her car without changing into street clothes.

"This time it's really over. Nothing to see," Jake said.

❧   ❧   ❧

At nine o'clock at night Mark went to a convenience store for a magazine. He looked at the doughnut display and was tempted to straighten it up, even though it had never been one of his stores. There were no Dewey's products in the store. He had to walk out. He couldn't take it anymore.

"Hi, Mark," Abby said, stepping out of darkness from the side of the building. "I followed you. We need to talk."

"Where did you go?" he asked.

"I had to run away. You called the police on me. All this craziness around us …" she said. Her voice was deep and scratchy, because she had been crying. "You and your company … my job … the neighbors … the murders … I did go see my father. I found out my mother had died without looking for me. I also hear that someone killed my friend. Married couples should stick together through times like these … if these things happened to normal couples. I thought we would lean on each other during all of these bad things, but we didn't. You called the police." She stared past him, looking for the right words.

"You thought I could kill those people," she continued. "I hated Penn, but I couldn't kill him." She took a deep breath and said, "I want a divorce."

Mark looked at her coming into the light. Her sweatshirt was tattered at the sleeves, her hair was straight and combed, and her eyes were red and swollen. She was very different from the girl he'd watched on stage, twirling and flaunting her body. Abby shifted from leg to leg and rubbed her nose.

"Divorce?" he repeated.

"You thought I would kill you," she said, struggling to get her wedding ring off. "I could never kill anyone." She gulped and took a deep breath. "I asked you to believe me about my past. I was never a bad person. I just knew terrible people. I was naïve," she sighed. "I guess you don't believe me. I'm at fault, too. I was scared." Her voice lowered and cracked. "You told me you always went to those bars. You knew the dancers. I let my imagination run wild. I suspected you, too. We can't stay married if we really thought we could hurt each other."

She knelt down and put her wedding ring and two quarters on the ground. "If you think I did those things, here's enough money to call the police at the pay phone. I'm going to walk to Route 36 and take a cab to the motel on Route 33."

"Keep the ring," he said.

"I can't keep the ring." She rubbed the bare spot on her finger. A tear fell from her cheek to the ground. "All that has happened to me in the past few months ... For the first time, someone loved me. Or I thought you did, until you called the cops on me. Now it seems that the midnight talks in bed, the holding hands, and all the good stuff seem bittersweet." The bones in her ankle cracked as she shifted back and forth. "Maybe we should've gotten to know each other better. Or maybe we should've never gotten to know each other at all. I'll get a lawyer. I'll see you when the divorce case comes up." She turned to walk but stopped. "I have the good memories, at least."

She walked down the parking lot and along the sidewalk. Mark bent to pick up the ring. The gleam of the diamond shone back at him from the lights of the store. He picked up the two quarters and held them in his fingers.

I can't call, he thought. *She's right. I am an asshole.* He threw the quarters down and walked home into the darkness.

Abby scuffed her feet along the ground. Her head was down, but she could sense something around her.

"Hey, dancer," shouted a voice from across the street.

She looked up and sped up her steps. A large man who looked like he could've been a football player at one time walked toward her. She was about to run away, when she heard him say he was the manager of Babes.

"I had your address and was coming to see you. I know you quit, but I need help. I'm used to managing motorcycle stores. I don't know how to handle a bar. And I really don't know how to handle this one. I thought one business was just like another, but I was wrong. I need help."

"I don't think I want anything to do with that place anymore," said Abby. I didn't really help Carla, did I?" She rubbed her arms and looked at the ground.

"You won't have to dance. You can help manage the girls. I thought I could handle them. Those girls are wild; some are sneaky, and some are good con artists."

"You said they were girls."

"I was wrong. They are women. Please help me. Can we talk about this over coffee?"

Abby sighed. "Fine, we'll go to the National Diner."

🍁 🍁 🍁

Jake went to George's house the next morning, but George wasn't home. Jake was welcomed by George's British housekeeper, who was dressed in black spandex shorts with a dirty, ruby-colored pullover shirt. She walked around barefoot. She was only slightly over five-foot with long, stringy brown hair that went down to the small of her back. If she hadn't told him she was the housekeeper, Jake wouldn't have guessed. She said George had left the day before.

"What do you mean he's not here?" Jake asked. "I really need to ask him about his deceased wife."

"He had to go on a business trip," the housekeeper said. "He wanted me to watch his things. I can't let you in. He said his house is no one's business. I have to keep his things in perfect shape."

"His things?" Jake repeated. "He really cares about his things."

"They're his."

"He should've cared about his people as much as his things."

The young woman stood and looked past Jake. "I'm just a student. I don't know these people. I don't know what you're talking about."

"I don't either anymore." Jake turned and went to his car, convinced he would never get help from George.

Jake drove to Sunflower's apartment an hour later. He smelled something burning in the hallway of her apartment building. Faint, white smoke came from under Sunflower's door. He banged on the door and yelled for her.

"Mona, let me in. It's me, Jake." He heard her grumble. "Let me in. Come on."

She was in lingerie when she answered the door. Her skin was pale around the muscle on her arms, and fresh needle marks showed at the elbows. "What do you want?" she asked.

"What are you doing?" he asked, and pushed his way into her place. The apartment was a mess. Newspapers and pictures were scattered around her couch. Rolling paper, a lighter, and a small spoon were on her coffee table. "I thought you gave up the drugs," Jake said.

"Quitting's for quitters, or something like that. I don't remember the phrase."

"What about all you were working for?"

"I told you—no lawyer wants to take my case. It's over. I'm nothing." She dropped on the couch, letting her arms and head flop as she landed. "I just need to feel good again."

"What's good about this? Get cleaned up, and I'll get you help."

"I don't need it."

"Just do it for me," Jake urged. "Come on get up." He reached down and grabbed her bony arm.

"Don't touch me," Mona said. "I don't need help." Her eyes were closed, even when she yelled.

"Mona, I want to help you."

"I don't need help. What do you think? You're saving me? I was crazy to think I could change. This ..." she said, picking up a small spoon. "This never misled me. You ... I don't know what you ever did."

"I want to help you. I care about you."

"Fuck you. I'm not your project. I told you not to care about me. I have my own things to worry about. Get back to your life. Go save someone else."

"Mona, if you don't get help, I will recommend the managers fire you. You don't need this."

She picked up a picture and tossed it like a Frisbee at him. "Fine. Fuck you. Go get me fired. I knew you would stab me in the back, too." She picked up more pictures and flung them at him. "All of these people left. You want to know something? I fucked that guy Penn when he came to the bar. I think it's great that he's dead. Bastard stole my money." She kicked a shoe away. "I wish I could've done it." She relaxed. "You're going to run out on me. That's fine. I don't want any of you. Fuck you for thinking you were my hero or something."

Jake backed out of the apartment dodging whatever Sunflower threw at him. He slammed the door but could still hear her yelling profanities that would make the men at the bar blush. He sighed and punched the wall. The door was unlocked, and he could rush back in, but he stopped in the hall to listen.

"Jake," she whimpered, "I act tough at the bar, but I couldn't hurt anyone. I just wanted to love someone."

He grabbed the door handle but didn't turn it.

"I don't know how to love anyone," she cried out, choking back tears. "I don't want to love anyone."

Jake shook his head and walked away. There was nothing he could do.

Chapter 24

Mark went to Babes Go-Go a week later. There were fewer cars on a cold October night than in summer. The harsh wind whipped the front door wide open when he opened it. He walked in and sat at the side of the U-shaped bar. There were security cameras at the door. He stared into space, not really paying attention to the dancer on stage. Dani, the buxom bartender, was working, but she covered herself more now that the weather was cooler. She had a pepper spray container attached to her hip.

Every time the front door opened, cold wind blew through the bar. Mark's frosty beer lost its foam after a few minutes. The dancer finished her number and came toward him for a tip.

"I haven't seen you in awhile," she said. Her breasts stretched the fluorescent pink bra top she wore. Her hair was in a braid, and she wore heavy black makeup with false eyelashes. Mark didn't recognize her.

"No," he said, looking into his beer. "It's been a very long time. I don't remember if we met. I also grew a beard since I was last here." He leaned back. "I put on some weight too."

"You sure? I can make you remember me," she put her breasts on the bar and licked her lips.

Mark laughed. "Tonight I'm celebrating my new job. I lost my company when this big merger happened, and they closed down Dewey's Donuts."

"Dewey's? I love them."

"Yeah," Mark said. "I had a friend who used to run the same routes as I did. We'd often run into each other at the stores. He sold other products, but we were in the stores at the same time." Mark didn't notice her yawn. "So my friend Smitty tells me about this job as a dispatcher at his company. He loves driving a truck, so he didn't want it. He told me to apply for it, and I got it."

She clapped for him.

"I'm a supervisor now," he said, as he lifted his beer to salute himself before taking a sip. "I know most of the routes and the stops around the state. Ever been to Wanaque? It's up in the mountains. I know the routes there. I was a good choice for a dispatcher."

"Celebrating then?"

"I was hoping that maybe I would see Baby Doll dance. We're still legally married. My attorney said she listed Babes Incorporated as her employer. I figured she'd be here." He guzzled beer and wiped his mouth with his hand.

"I'll go get Baby Doll for you." She stopped and looked at her hands. "What the hell? You didn't tip me yet."

Mark took a folded dollar and put it in her hand. She smiled and went to the locker room. Abby walked out dressed in a big, gray sweatshirt, jeans, and old sneakers. A pencil was stuck behind her ear, a tape measure hung around her neck, and safety pins were fastened to her shirt. Her eyes brightened when she saw Mark, but she bit her lip so she wouldn't smile as she walked toward him.

"I wanted to talk to you," he said.

"Well," she said as calm as when they first met, "it's nice to see you." Mark put his arms out to hug her, but she stayed back at first. Then they made some awkward movements toward hugging each other but couldn't seem to position themselves.

"We haven't touched in awhile," she said.

"I know." He felt her hands shake on his back. "Can we talk later? There's a lot I want to tell you."

"You going to stay all night? It's only ten now," she said, looking at her watch.

"I'll come back in a little while. Like we used to do. I'll see you at closing." He got off his seat. She leaned her head toward him, signaling that she would welcome a good-bye kiss, but he turned away.

Mark went home and took a nap. At two-thirty, he was back at the bar. Jake Hersh came from around the building and yelled to him.

"What are you doing here?" Jake asked him.

"Get away from me," Mark answered. "I want to talk to my wife. Don't you ruin it. What are you doing here?"

"I work here," Jake reminded him. "I was just coming to check on something. The bar's closed."

"I should really break your head," Mark said, tightening his fists. "I listened to all your stupid questions and accused my wife of murder."

"It's not my fault you didn't know much about your wife."

"You know what?" Mark said. "The bar's closed, and I'm going to kick your ass." He ran around the car.

Jake ran behind another car and told him to calm down.

"You cost me my marriage," Mark shouted. "Just because Abby knew those people, I accused her."

"I was investigating," Jake said. "She knew those people, so I wanted to talk to her." Jake stopped dodging behind cars. "I'm not running. You want a piece of me?"

"I do," Mark said, squaring off in front of him. Mark pushed Jake, and Jake pushed back. They tussled, without throwing any real punches, until Jake got Mark in a headlock.

"Your wife worked at the bar," Jake said. "It made sense to consider her as a suspect." He felt Mark squirm. Jake tightened his grip. Mark punched him in the small of the back, which sent Jake sprawling on the loose-gravel parking lot. "I should've been suspicious of you," Jake said from the dirt. "You spent a lot of time here."

Mark backed away from Jake and rubbed his neck. "That hurt. I can't believe I let this happen."

"What are you doing here anyway?" Jake asked.

"I wanted to see Abby," Mark replied. "It looks like she got a job as a seamstress. I want to talk to her again. Maybe we can fix things. She has no one here except me."

Jake stood up and rubbed his knees. "The only person in there is the bartender."

"Abby's in there," Mark said. He pointed at her car behind him. "She wouldn't leave when I said I was coming back. And she's not a killer"

"I know," Jake said. "I got the chance to talk to her when she came back to work here. I figured she knew this place as well as anyone else."

"Then don't bother us any more," Mark said. "Go bother some of the other employees. There are several who've been here a long time and know this place inside and out."

Jake stopped mid-step. There *was* someone always here. And he'd never realized it. "This place was the one thing all the victims had common." Jake quickly replayed the murder scenarios in his head. "You've got wait here," Jake yelled. He pulled out his cell phone. "I'm calling a cop."

❧   ❧   ❧

"Abby, thank you for staying after closing to help clean up," Eli said, wiping down the bar.

"I made a mess making sure that the dancers were dressed and clean before they went on stage." She dragged a plastic bag full of rags, cigarette butts, and discarded makeup to the bar.

"Well, I need to clean everything else up," he said.

"I'll be right back," she said, walking to the back to leave a bag of garbage at the back door. Eli followed her, his shoulders tense. When he got very close to her, she asked, "Make sure someone throws that out." Eli didn't move. "What are you doing?"

He pulled out a small knife.

"Why do you have that?"

"You saw me kill Carla," Eli said.

"What?" she screeched. "I never saw Carla the night she died."

Eli snorted, and his eyes went dark. "At the motel. They told me your car was there all night. You had to know. Then you left town all of a sudden. When you came back to work tonight, I tried to find out what you knew. You played it good—you stayed quiet about it. But I can't trust you."

"Why did you kill Carla?" asked Abby, stalling for time.

"Because she thought she was better than the other entertainers. She got a good schedule right away. She acted like she was entitled," Jake Hersh yelled, bursting through the bar with Mark. Eli turned and lowered the knife.

"The cops are coming, Eli," Jake said. "Just put it down."

"How? Why?" Eli yelled.

"You were the only person who knew everyone involved. I didn't want to believe it," Jake said. "After all, we're cousins … but things just started adding up. I was all set to blame anyone else in the bar, especially the deejay."

"I hate him," Abby said.

"He's next," Eli said, with a smirk.

"No one's next," Jake said.

"You're my cousin," Eli pleaded. "Just let me get a head start out of here."

"The cops will shoot you if you run," Jake said.

"What's going on?" Mark asked.

"I told you to stay outside and wait for the police," Jake yelled at Mark.

"I'm not leaving Abby in the middle of this," Mark answered.

"You don't know anything," Hersh told Mark.

"I don't know anything," Abby said.

"I had a feeling Eli knew something about the murders," Jake sighed. He pushed Mark aside to block the door out. "He killed Penn because Penn slept with Mona, um, Sunflower and took all her money. He wanted to help Sunflower. Hell, I wanted to help her, too. Eli killed that cigar-smoking house mom because she was pimping out dancers. You thought you were protecting everyone. I can understand that."

"So why Fire and Stacy Ann?" Abby asked.

"I don't know," Jake said.

"What? Those women?" Eli answered. He swung the knife at Abby, but missed her. Jake yelled and Eli turned back to him. "Those almost naked girls were around me every night. Total strangers felt them up for a dollar, but they wouldn't give me the time of day. Fire called me names. They laughed at me when I tried to put the moves on them. I'd had enough. If they were going to treat me like garbage, then I was going to dump them in the garbage. Protect them—never! I hate them all. I hate the owners, the customers, the dancers, and their families. Your friend Penn," he said, pointing to Abby. "He was all bloody when he came here looking for Sunflower. She agreed to help him after her shift and told him to wait outside. Can you believe that?"

No one responded.

"That smelly bum who couldn't leave a bartender a tip had her after one night. Why him? I had to get rid of him." He surveyed the room. There was no quick escape. Abby would have to get cut and moved away to get at the back door or Jake had to get cut to run out the front way. Eli sighed. "There were plenty of knives at the bar.... That cigar-smoking bitch actually set up the managers with the same girls I wanted. The managers used those girls. I wanted in. I wanted just one girl. Instead, they laughed at me. They told me to tend the bar and be quiet. Who's quiet now?" he yelled. "I thought you would stick with me." He looked at Jake and sighed again.

Eli lowered the knife and scuffed his sneaker on the sticky floor. "Carla was beautiful. She was naïve and real and didn't belong here. I wanted her. She kept telling me she was married and wouldn't go out with me. Then I'd see her all over the deejay. She did it with him just to rub it in my face. I followed her back to the motel. I wanted her to know how disgusted I was that she had lied to me. She told me the deejay forced himself on her, and she hated him." He chuckled.

"It was you in the motel room?" Abby asked. "She was fighting not having sex. I could've stopped you." She lowered her head in shame.

"The deejay did force himself on her," Jake said. He moved toward Eli.

Mark moved to the side, while Abby moved away from the back door.

"The deejay was fired for it. He felt her up and took her money. You should've known that," Jake said.

"I'm getting tired of everyone treating me like I'm nothing," Eli said.

"Drop it," said a policeman, aiming his revolver at Eli.

Abby's eyes were red with rage. "Did you rape her?"

Eli held up the knife and threw it at Abby. Mark spun and grabbed Abby. Jake blocked the knife and got stabbed in the shoulder. The officer shot at Eli's wrist, sending Eli back against a stack of beer cases piled chest high. Bottles hit the floor and exploded like firecrackers. Two more officers charged into the room. Eli rolled on the shards of glass that had spilled from the boxes.

"I never had any of them," Eli moaned. "I'm not a rapist."

"Get up," the officers said. They grabbed his arms and handcuffed him.

Mark shielded Abby as the police dragged Eli out of the room. Mark didn't realize it, but he squeezed her arms and kept her body against his smelling her hair.

"It's over," she whispered.

"What?"

"The shooting. You can let me go if you want to."

"Oh," Mark said. "Yeah, I, uh, guess the coast is clear."

"I guess they took Jake out to an ambulance," she said, still clutching Mark.

"Are you OK?" Mark asked.

"I'm surviving."

He backed away from her. "I just came to see how you were," Mark said. "I didn't know all this was going to happen." He looked down at the floor. "That's a lot of beer."

"Yeah," she chuckled.

"I, uh, wanted to make sure you were fine."

She swung her arms and smiled. "I'm here. You're here."

"Yeah." He cracked his knuckles. "I'm really bad with saying things. There were things I should've said. There were things I never should've said. I don't know."

"It was a tough year for us." She paused and looked around the room. "I guess it will be over soon. You know ... the lawyers have everything pretty much done."

He shook his head. "I ..." He paused. She waited for him to say something. "I guess so. Lawyers."

Her shoulders drooped. "I guess so, too."

Mark walked out of the bar and saw Jake sitting in an ambulance with his shirt off. Medics worked on Jake's shoulder. Eli sat in a police cruiser, facing forward and showing no emotion.

Mark pulled the door latch to his car and stopped. "I guess it is over."

Chapter 25

"Hi, Mark," Abby said, as she walked into the conference room of the law firm of Ricci and Ricci. Mark was already seated. He had shaved his beard and wore an old, faded suit.

"This is the second time I've seen you in a suit. The brown tie needs work," Abby said, pulling on his dark chocolate-colored tie that had the word "Dewey's" at the bottom. "It's not knotted right, and besides, brown ties don't go with blue suits." She sat down in front of the lawyer's desk and crossed her thin, bare legs. "It's been six weeks since that night at Babes," she said. She clutched the arms of her chair.

He toyed with his tie, as he looked her over. She looked like she'd lost weight. The black skirt and white blouse she used to wear at Nora Daniels hung loose off her shoulders. She'd cut her hair to shoulder length and added some highlights.

"All those people that wanted Babes gone got their wish. There was so much bad press that both Babes were shut down. I went to Providence to stay with my father," she said. "I never could talk to him growing up. He was petrified of saying the wrong thing in front of my mother. Now we can't stop talking. I didn't tell him about my dancing, but I filled him in on other things. I even went to church with him," she said, cracking her knuckles.

Mark nodded. "My brother's marriage is still going strong. My mother calls at least twice a week to tell me."

"I also borrowed money from my father to go back to Las Vegas," she said. "I wanted to see my friend Tiffany. Last I'd heard, she was going to make that porno movie and hoped it would be her big break for fame and money. Now, she's going to a therapist. She met this guy and thought he was wonderful. But he hated the porn and left her. She's all confused."

Abby uncrossed her legs and leaned over to Mark. "It's funny," she said, "I started dancing because Penn and I … because Penn thought it would be our easy way to quick money, and you know what happened to us. Every quick way seems to end up slowing us down. I don't get it.

"I went back to one of the Vegas clubs to see the dancers. I watched all these guys. They were looking for a quick way to see a naked girl. At the end of the night, they left with no money, and the girl doesn't recognize them after she takes the dollar. It seems so empty. I could never bring myself to dance again."

A middle-aged lawyer in a gray silk suit entered the room and sat behind his desk in front of Mark and Abby. He opened his jacket, revealing a gut he seemed proud to have. It was the gut of a man with the money to eat out a lot. He wore his pants just below his gut. "I'm Mr. Ricci," he said in a low, booming voice. "A matter of divorce," he said, opening a folder. "Have you talked about the assets?" He flipped a page. "I see lawyers did work out most of it. I just need to mediate a few things. Then it's off to the judge to finalize."

Abby cracked her knuckles as the lawyer spoke. Mark pulled out her wedding ring from his suit jacket and put it on the desk.

"I want you to have it," he said to Abby.

"No," she argued. "It cost you a lot of money. You should keep it."

Mr. Ricci cut in, "Do you know how much it's worth?"

"Doesn't matter," she said. "I'll have money coming soon."

"Are you sure you want to say that?" Mr. Ricci asked her.

"I'm starting a business," she said. "A couple of dancers saw my handmade outfits and they want them. My capes are popular, too."

"Do you need money to start it?" Mark asked.

"What?" Mr. Ricci yelled. "You don't ask something like that in a divorce proceeding."

"No," Abby said, ignoring the lawyer. "I have a contract with a lingerie store in the mall—that mall out on Route 66. I don't want alimony."

Mr. Ricci's eyes came close to popping out of his head. "Slow down," he yelled. "Are you sure?"

"Yeah, are you sure?" Mark asked her. "I got a bonus, and I can afford to give you a few bucks."

"What?" Mr. Ricci yelled again. "Your lawyers said you were fighting over getting assets, not giving them. No one fights over giving them. Who is getting the house?"

"It was his before we married," Abby said.

"I'm selling it," Mark said. "By the way, when the newspapers reported that we were heroes in catching the killer, Mrs. Dumont came over to apologize for starting the petition against us. She brought us a fruit basket. I wanted to throw the apples at her, but they were really red and looked good. I've started getting back in shape. She'd heard rumors of our divorce, so she asked if I was doing OK. I'm OK, but I don't want to live there alone. I can give you part of the sale money."

Mr. Ricci slapped his forehead. "You two … you're trying to give him back a ring," he said, pointing at Abby. Then he pointed at Mark. "You won't take it, and you want to give her money. Are you sure you want a divorce?"

They looked at each other. Abby's eyes looked as bright as the night he met her in the dark bar.

"You called the cops on me," she said.

"You left, because you thought I would beat you," he answered. He looked down. "I'm sorry about the cops. I'm sorry I walked out of the bar when I last saw you. You know how you said that *The Gold Rush* was your favorite movie and that words would've gotten in the way? Well, sometimes I can't find any words either. I should've said more words to you."

A tear fell from her eye. She was touched that he remembered her favorite movie and why she liked it. "I don't want a divorce," she said. "I know you're not like the other guys in my past. You wouldn't hurt me."

"Want to go outside and talk?" Mark asked.

"You're not seeing a courtroom, are you?" Mr. Ricci asked.

Mark shook his head and picked up the ring off the desk.

"Good," Mr. Ricci said. He folded a piece of paper and packed a folder into his briefcase. "This gives me a free afternoon."

Mark stood up, holding Abby's hand. "I love you," he said. They walked out of the office leaning on one another until they got outside.

"My car is over there," Mark said, walking toward it. "This is yours." He put the wedding ring on Abby's finger. "It's still bright," he said, when the sunlight reflected back at him. "I know this little place we could go to. I call it home. You've been there. It's not far from here."

"I know a quick way there," she answered.

978-0-595-41208-2
0-595-41208-4

Printed in the United States
71947LV00005B/77